THE GREEN CROSSING

A Novel

DIANA LEE

Libri et Scientia

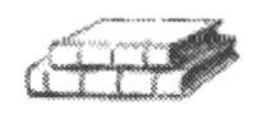

2021

Cover design by *the*BookDesigners
Formatting by Polgarus Studio

for
my amazing daughters

Here's to just being
the girl in the adventure

&

for
dearest K

Chapter One

When we assumed the soldier, we did not lay aside the citizen.
—George Washington

18 Sept., 1945, Fussa Army Airfield, Japan—Momma always says judging a man by his looks ain't Christian-like, but I swear the devil stared back at me from outta those empty blue eyes. Sounds crazy, but for a split second, I thought the man wore a mask.

His face held a blank, unnatural expression, like one of those creepy porcelain dolls sitting on old Miss Ada's couch back home. Heavy, dark eyelashes and a slender frame gave the impression of youth, though I didn't make the mistake of thinking he was just a kid.

He wore a lieutenant's insignia, but no name or unit patch. No one else was in the office, just him and me. The whole setup felt off from the get-go. The war might be over, but my gut told me to be wary.

I snapped to attention and trained my eyes on a spot just over his bent head. He sat at the desk turning the pages of my journal with a slow, deliberate hand. I sensed his scrutiny, even though his eyes were cast downward, reading. Like a praying mantis, he waited, silent and deadly.

I cursed Frank under my breath, though I knew it wasn't really his fault. I lied to him. Told him I'd lost my journal back in Okinawa, but like an idiot left it sticking out of my barracks bag for anyone to see. When Sarge collected them, Frank turned mine in with his, figuring he'd found the damn thing.

I don't really blame him. Frank just thought he was doing me a good turn.

"Corporal Hawkins, what is this?" The lieutenant's high-pitched voice grated on my ears.

He tapped two fingers on the journal. I recognized the entry, and my spine tingled with the same kind of dread as when those Japanese planes screamed down from the sky.

Most of these officer types held your average GI in low esteem, but I hadn't survived the war by being a complete dope. Anyway, he had probably read my journal and figured I wasn't too stupid.

I stuck to the facts, only the few written down. Hell, I usually recorded every detail of every day, sometimes pretending to be a hotshot reporter. Not this time; I couldn't get the incident down on paper without being sick.

I even lacked the courage to think back on what happened. I tried to block the whole thing from my mind, but the look on the girl's face haunted me. I'll never forget her frozen shock, and her brother's sobs near broke my heart. I sure didn't want to bring those kids more sorrow, or worse.

I steadied my breathing and kept my voice calm. I couldn't tell if the lieutenant believed my innocent act. His face remained impassive, and he put the same question to me over and over.

"And that's all?" he asked for the hundredth time.

"Yes, sir, that's all," I lied. "Haven't thought much about the incident since, sir."

"Really?" He regarded me with emotionless, unblinking eyes.

I stood silent and tried to look cool.

"No one else witnessed it?"

"No, sir."

"And the village?"

I swallowed rising bile and cleared my throat. "Musta been the work of holdout Japanese soldiers. I didn't see the action go down, sir. Can't say for sure what happened."

He stared at me for a full minute without talking. My hands, balled into fists at my sides, grew slick with sweat. I tried not to lick my lips or blink too much.

He flipped through the diary and stopped again at the offending entry. He cut out the pages with an X-ACTO knife, folded them into a neat square, and stuck them in his breast pocket.

"Take it." He pushed the book to me from across the desk. I picked up my journal, mindful to keep a steady hand.

"Corporal." His voice dropped to a low and sinister monotone. "You are not to speak of this incident or write it down ever again. If you do, things will go very badly, very quickly for you. Is that understood?"

"Yes, sir. Understood, sir."

"Dismissed."

I was never so glad to get out of anyplace. I hightailed it back to the barracks, my skin twitching like a hunted rabbit.

He'd keep digging. I could tell. He was not the type to let go.

Maybe he'd trace my movements that day. Maybe he already had.

Just in case, I decided to tear this entry out and hide it. Kinda like an insurance policy. I'll smuggle it out under the sweatband of that beat-up bush hat I picked up in New Guinea. Nobody would think to look there.

I'm embarrassed to admit I got the idea from a story in one of my sister Lois's trashy Hollywood magazines. If something happens to me, there's the off chance that busybody sister of mine will find this.

One thing's for certain. I'm not gonna get much sleep until we're stateside again.

Chapter Two

The memory of a great name and the inheritance
of a great example is the legacy of heroes.
—Disraeli

JD Hawkins, famed author of popular westerns, dies at 96

JD Hawkins was the author of over thirty-five literary works, including the internationally bestselling Marshal Clyde Jameson series. In later years, he wrote dense histories of his beloved West Texas. Mr. Hawkins grew up during the Great Depression and described himself as a "good ole country boy." Known for his iconic Americana, he recorded his childhood in an award-winning series of short stories, *Six Minus One*. As a boy, (Cont. pg. 52)

**

"Damn." Meliz jerked her hand out of the battered cardboard box and barely stopped herself from sucking on a grimy fingertip. She squinted at the thin line of blood forming on her skin. A paper cut?

Meliz peered into the box. A small book lay nestled at the bottom with a sharp edge of paper protruding from between its pages.

"The culprit," she grumbled and reached in to pick the book up.

Dried mud from an old dirt dauber's nest spotted the cracked leather cover. She chipped at the mud clumps with a ragged fingernail and brushed away the remaining dirt. Imprinted in faded gold letters were the words, "My Life in the Service."

Meliz frowned; it was odd to find JD's old World War II journal up here. Most of the boxes in the attic held items belonging to her grandmother, the relics of a woman dead and buried long before Meliz was even born.

She sat halfway in the sweltering attic on the top rung of a rickety wooden ladder. Sweat dripped off her forehead, and she wiped her face with the hem of her sodden T-shirt. The sun dipped low on the horizon and threw the attic into shadow.

Meliz shut her eyes, adjusting them to the sudden darkness. Unbidden tears slid down her cheeks. Even in the airless and cramped attic, her grandfather's presence lingered. His gentle spirit filled every square inch of this old house.

His face arose in her mind, lined and aged. The echo of his laughter rang in her ears. She longed to know again the lighthearted prodding of his sharp wit, the warmth of his kindness. Grief expanded in her chest and pushed its way into her throat. Meliz dashed her tears away with an impatient hand, tired of crying.

She flipped the book open. A black-and-white photograph and two folded pieces of paper fell into her lap. She studied the faded picture.

A teenaged JD sat with two other men on the trunk of a fallen palm tree. They turned solemn faces to the camera. The sandy beach and tropical foliage surrounding the three men placed their location somewhere in the South Pacific. The washed-out quality of the photograph intensified the feeling of heat and humidity they must have endured.

Though skinny and boyish, their serious expressions projected hard-earned maturity. JD was just a kid, right out of high school, when he enlisted in 1943.

Had the other two survived the war? She'd never met any of JD's old war buddies, and her grandfather seldom spoke of those days.

Meliz slipped the photo back behind the front cover and unfolded what had been a glossy magazine page now dulled with age. Taken from a post-war edition of *Life* magazine, the article featured a picture of a young soldier watching as Marines led two small children away. The rugged jungle landscape loomed in the background, and the grass lay broken and trampled at their feet. The juxtaposition of the fragile and shell-shocked children with the large, armed men surrounding them formed a powerful image.

The caption described the hundreds of war orphans left homeless and traumatized after the Battle of Okinawa. She focused on the profile of the young soldier, his anguish made palpable by his clenched jaw and rigid stance. Though untouched by the ravages of age, she recognized JD's prominent nose and thoughtful brow.

Meliz stared off into space. A scene flickered before her in the darkness like an old silent film: The children's hands slip from JD's grasp. A photographer's lens freezes the moment they turn from him. JD walks away. The children look back, their small faces devoid of emotion. Her grandfather struggles to contain his own.

Meliz blinked and drew in a deep breath. She refolded the article and flipped through the journal, noting the inspirational quotes printed across the bottom of each page.

She smoothed out the piece of paper with the jagged edge clearly torn from the journal. A quote by George Washington waxed philosophical and slanted cursive filled the page with grayed, ghostly letters. Meliz could discern only a few words in the encroaching darkness of the attic.

"Meliz."

She started, her concentration broken. She put the pieces of paper into the journal with the photograph and stuck her head out of the opening. "Yeah, up here."

"I can see that." Alberta laughed. She stood with hands on hips, head tilted back and a wide smile across her face. A neat bun perched atop her head and direct brown eyes gazed out from behind a sleek pair of cat-eye glasses. Slim, pressed khakis and sensible walking shoes completed the picture of intelligence and efficiency.

Meliz smiled in return. "The attic's too hot to sit all the way in, so I dragged the boxes to the opening and went through them here."

"A wise move." Alberta nodded with approval. "Your mother is on the phone."

Meliz climbed down the ladder with journal in hand. "Most of the stuff up there is Grandmother's, but look what I've found." She held up the little book. "JD's old World War II journal."

Alberta stopped in the process of opening the screen door and glanced back at Meliz with a frown. "That can't be. I know he included his journal with the archives."

"Have a look." She handed Alberta the book as they walked into the kitchen.

The industrial strength air conditioner hit Meliz with an icy blast, wicking the sweat from her skin. She shivered and picked up the phone.

"Hey, Mom. What's up?"

"Hi, sweetheart. We're home." Long years in the Southern California sun had worn away her mother's native Texas accent, until her voice held but a faint trace. "How goes the organizing?"

"Fine. Well, Bert's done most of the work," Meliz admitted.

"What would we do without Alberta?" Her mother sighed.

Meliz could not remember a time without Alberta's wry humor and firm hand guiding her grandfather's work. As JD's long-time assistant and coauthor, she was a member of the family and helped to form the bedrock of Meliz's life. When the call came late that awful night, she drew comfort from Alberta's steady voice, gruff though it was with emotion.

JD had died, slumped over the keyboard of his laptop computer. Ranger, his decrepit old German shepherd, whined at his feet. Her grandfather was dead only days after returning to this small West Texas town from her college graduation in New York City.

"Promise you'll be there," she had insisted over the phone. "You won't get all wrapped up in something and forget."

He dismissed her concerns with his worn, easy laugh. "When have I ever forgotten anything really important? Not to worry; Bert's got everything sorted."

JD had been there, gnarled as an old oak tree and beaming with pride. Now, he was dead. Guilt intermingled with grief and left Meliz doubly bereft.

"Take your time going through it all," her mother said. "Message Dad when you have a return date. He can book you a ticket home."

"I can get the ticket myself," she snapped.

"Of course. No worries. Old habits and all that."

"Sorry, Mom, I don't mean to be . . . It's just . . ." Meliz leaned back against the kitchen cabinet. An aching void opened in the pit of her stomach. "I'm lost. I can't stop crying."

"I felt the same way after my mom died, and your grandfather was with us for so many more years . . ." Her mother's voice trailed off, and she chuckled with sad affection. "Well, he cast a long shadow, as the marshal would say."

Meliz swallowed her grief for what seemed the millionth time. "Good ole Marshal Jameson," she murmured, turning her mind to a question she had long wanted to ask. "Why didn't you ever want to be a writer?"

"I never felt the itch. Medicine was always my calling. Anyway, who needs the pressure?" She caught herself. "Oh, sweetie, I forgot—"

"It's fine," Meliz reassured her. "I'm over the whole thing. Film's not exactly my calling, but I'm good at it, and the work keeps me out of that long shadow." She shook off her self-pity and straightened her shoulders. "I'll get back to you with my flight information. Okay?"

"Yep. Just let us know. Love you."

"Love you too." Meliz replaced the receiver on the base of the old rotary telephone.

The fans kicked on. Alberta must have already opened the windows because a dry gust of wind lifted the hair from her forehead.

As was JD's custom, the air conditioner switched off at dusk, and the powerful attic fans sucked hot air out and drew in the cooler evening air. The old-fashioned dogtrot style house creaked and moaned as if brought to life by the currents now coursing through its rooms.

Meliz crossed the breezeway and paused to gaze out the back porch. The sun hung just below the horizon, and the day wavered between light and dark. Silhouetted against the sky were the dim outlines of oak trees shading the house and the tall cottonwoods bordering the creek. She inhaled the pungent, smoky scent of creosote, and with it, a defiant melancholy.

JD's shadow had grown only longer in death. His bestselling series of westerns earned him a worldwide following, and words of condolence rolled in from around the globe. Meliz shut them out, unwilling to share her loss with the multitude. She owed nothing to nobody, as the marshal would say. Her mourning would not be rushed.

"Meliz," Alberta called out from JD's study.

She followed her friend's voice into the book-lined room and stopped on the threshold. Her chest constricted.

This study was as much the beating heart of her grandfather as had been the one in his chest, the rich smell of wood polish so pervasive it had clung to his skin like an aftershave. She imagined the room straining at its beams, stuffed with the ghosts of countless conversations, arguments, and laughter.

"Look at this." Alberta sat at JD's enormous mahogany desk and peered at the computer screen. The small leather-bound journal with the photograph and two pages lay in a neat row.

Meliz blinked back tears and squeezed into the desk chair with her. "What is it?"

"I was right. He did submit his journal, but only a transcript. The entries stop while he was in Okinawa, a little after the Japanese surrender. And there's no mention of this." She tapped her finger on the torn-out journal page. "I didn't even know he was in Japan at the time. He never spoke much of the war. And this magazine photo . . . the image is heartbreaking."

Alberta squinted at the screen and plucked at the keyboard. She brought up a website dedicated to the Second Combat Cargo Group in which JD had served. "This says their unit ended the war at Fussa, or rather, Yokota Airfield in Japan. They were engaged in airlift operations during the occupation. It looks like they were there for several months from around September forty-five to February of the following year."

Meliz read over Alberta's shoulder. Months in Japan, and JD never said a word, not even in passing. He had traveled to that country at least two or three times over the course of his long career for publicity and book signings.

"Strange he never mentioned being there right after the surrender." Meliz picked up the journal page and held it up close to her face. She leaned back in the chair and read aloud, "'Eighteen September, 1945, Fussa Army Airfield, Japan.'" She focused hard on the faded writing. "Is there a magnifying glass anywhere?"

"Are you kidding?" Alberta joked. "There's at least half a dozen scattered around here." She scrabbled through the desk drawers gathering an assortment of magnifying glasses in a pile on the desk.

Meliz picked up a large, silver-handled one. She angled the lamplight onto the page, reading. She grumbled in frustration.

Alberta looked up from the computer. "Anything?"

Meliz scowled at the page. "I don't know . . . It's hard to make out. Something to do with the journal, an officer. JD sounds scared."

"Not surprising. He was in a war zone."

"That's not it." Meliz walked to the printer and laid the page face down to make a copy. "Some officer didn't like an entry." She sat at the desk again and spent the next twenty minutes filling in as best she could on the copy.

"What a crappy speller," she muttered, scrutinizing each word.

Alberta smiled. "He was just a teenager, but I have to admit, his spelling didn't improve much with age."

Meliz sat up. "I got most of the words and fudged where I wasn't sure." She read the entry aloud.

"What on earth?" Alberta took the page from her and scanned it with a quick, practiced eye. "He's referring to those kids in the picture, right? I know the hat. He traded some of his Aunt Stella's hot sauce for it with an Australian soldier in New Guinea. It's part of his archives." She snorted with disbelieving laughter. "He must have been pretty desperate to leave his fate in Lois's hands. She was a tireless gossip, but hardly detective material."

Meliz flipped through the journal. Near the end, she came across stubs of paper where a razor had removed what had been there. "Here they are. Looks like that officer cut out two pages."

She read the entries before and after the missing one. The earlier entry was dated August 14, 1945. The one right after jumped to September 2nd, where her grandfather had written his final entry: a brief, sad eulogy for a friend whose plane crashed into a mountain over Japan.

"Can I see the transcript? Maybe he added something later."

"Of course." Alberta turned the laptop toward her. "Everything is yours. You can take whatever you need from his computer. In fact, the computer's yours too."

Meliz shifted in the chair, uneasy with her new status as primary heir to the Hawkins estate. Her mother had long ago waived any claim to JD's intellectual property, believing Meliz a better curator of his work.

She took the mouse, intent on scrolling through the file, but stopped and squinted at an e-mail window parked at the bottom of the screen. She clicked on it, and the message expanded. The two women leaned in for a closer look.

"What the hell?" Meliz sat back and glared at the computer.

"That old codger," Alberta blurted in disbelief. "A travel agent? Where'd he find one? I always made all his arrangements." She crossed her arms, offended.

Meliz pointed an accusatory finger at the screen. "Look. He had tickets, confirmation numbers, hotel rooms."

"How'd he think he was gonna get anywhere without me?" Alberta groused. "The man moved at a turtle's pace. The Philippines? Okinawa? It's not like the old folks' shuttle to a local casino. Silly ole coot." She dabbed her eyes with a shirtsleeve.

Meliz drew in a calming breath and patted her arm. "Maybe he hadn't gotten around to getting you a ticket."

Alberta harrumphed and scrolled through the e-mail thread. The succinct messages detailed a cryptic back and forth between JD and a travel agent in Tokyo.

"One of the biggest adventures of my life . . . Want to retrace movements of the 339th Airdrome Squadron . . . Most of my buddies from the war are dead . . . Old memories I'd like to put to rest . . ."

"Old memories," Meliz murmured.

That one stuck out from the others, a strange hint of regret. She knew veterans often carried with them the memory of traumatic events for years afterwards, sometimes for their entire lives.

"This has got to be about the journal entry. Right? A village, orphaned children, something bad happened. I know—"

A tight band of pressure encircled her chest. She pressed her hands against her diaphragm and drew in a deep breath.

It was Alberta's turn to give her arm a comforting pat. "Slow down. I'm calling your mother. Maybe she has some idea what this is all about."

Minutes later, the two women huddled over the desk waiting for Gwen's response to the jumble of news poured into her ear via Alberta's cell phone. The fans had switched off, and a cacophony of singing cicadas and croaking frogs provided discordant background music.

"I had no idea. He didn't tell me about any trip," was her disappointing reply.

Meliz slumped back in the chair. She was hoping her mother knew *something.*

"But I have seen that *Life* magazine photograph before," Gwen added.

"What?" Meliz straightened.

"I came across it stuck in an old photo album when I was thirteen or so. I showed the article to Dad. He said they were a couple of kids he found wandering around, lost and alone. He didn't elaborate, and I didn't press him. Never thought much about it afterwards.

"Listen, honey," she continued. "Dad didn't talk much about the war. Like every other returning vet, he grabbed the future with both hands. He wanted to move on, forget what happened. He came home and went off to school." Gwen cleared her throat. "Although studying journalism and English Lit didn't go over too well with his mother."

Meliz smiled at the familiar story and recited aloud her great-grandmother's words, "'Newspaper men ain't respectable, son, and writers drive themselves to drink.'"

They laughed. JD's memoir had made famous his formidable mother and passel of rambunctious siblings. Through the deprivations of the Great Depression and the sorrow of family tragedy, the Hawkins family endured with hard work and a healthy dose of humor.

"I'm going," Meliz announced, her color heightened.

As soon as the words were out of her mouth, she wished them unspoken. Her intestines twisted into a painful, and all-too-often, coil of anxiety.

"Go where?" her mother and Alberta asked as one.

Meliz licked her dry lips. "On his trip. Find out what happened to him. What he was trying to put to rest."

Silence followed this pronouncement. Gwen's sigh drifted out from the phone.

"You don't have to do this. Nothing could have kept Dad from seeing you graduate. If this trip was any indication, he felt fit as a fiddle. You have nothing to atone for." Her mother paused before adding with unnerving perception, "You have nothing to prove."

Tears slid down Meliz's cheeks. "You know I do, Mom."

Chapter Three

A mysterious bond of brotherhood makes all men one.
—Carlyle

1 Dec., 1943, Miami Beach, Florida—Boone is dead. I write these words, the first in this journal, and still cannot believe it's true. He cut school to go swimming at Shutter's Gorge and broke his neck on a submerged log. They brought him home, but he didn't live long.

My earliest memories are of us, always together. Younger than me by two years, Boone was more my twin than little brother. Until leaving home, I spent every waking day with him, his face more familiar to me than my own. Now he will never laugh or cry, ever again. He will never grow old.

The army gave me a five-day compassionate leave. Leo and the rest of the gang met me at the bus station. I had not seen any of them since joining up. On the ride over, I pictured the scene in my mind. Me being stoic and calm, a fighting man, not easily overset.

The bus swung onto Jefferson Avenue. There they all stood, gathered outside the station: Leo, rubbing his eyes, his glasses in his hands, Freda's face blotchy from crying, and the rest.

Dickens once wrote, "We need never be ashamed of our tears." In the end, I wasn't.

Momma's strength sustained us, as always. She fussed over me, saying the military wasn't feeding me right.

For her, I gave up joining the Marines. She wouldn't hear of it. "No son of mine is gonna run chest-first into a Japanese bullet. Not unless one of them generals is leading the way." Daddy backed her up.

She blamed Hemingway for me enlisting in the first place. "You know war ain't romantic, son. You know that, right? Why don't you go off to college now, like Leo?" I told her Leo would surely be drafted, and he'd have to go where they sent him.

I stayed alone in the room Boone and I had shared, unable to sleep without his steady breathing in the other bed. My sisters poked their heads in once in a while to see how I was doing. Their solicitude unsettled me.

There were two warring camps in our family: Boone and me up against our three sisters. That was, until Mason came along. He didn't even the odds much, though, him just now turning six. Still, we got some good licks in.

Here we were back down to two again, and I couldn't wrap my head around it. I expected Boone to walk in at any moment with a small, wounded creature needin' help or, more likely, a bitter complaint about our big sister, Lois.

After the funeral, I walked around to the horse shed to give old Trotter an apple. Momma sat on an overturned water pail, her face pressed into a dishtowel. The towel muffled her sobs, but I could hear them from where I stood.

Momma wanted no part of me going off to war. She hoped the whole thing would be over by the time I was old enough to enlist.

Yet, there she sat grieving over a dead son, but the war hadn't killed him. The Grim Reaper climbed up the trellis and slipped into a second-story bedroom window. It latched onto Boone when he awoke and followed him out that day with mischief on his mind. Nobody saw Death coming.

The morning I left, Momma hugged me tight, but there were no more tears.

**

Miami Beach Training Center, Florida, December 1943

I stood under the arched entrance of a white adobe building, one of many offices the military had scattered around this once sleepy tourist town. Salted sea air washed over my face and lifted my spirits. I had never been anywhere more beautiful than Miami Beach. Sure, I hadn't been many places, but this town beat by a long shot the overgrown training grounds and damp, rotted barracks of Camp Beauregard, Louisiana.

Since 1942, the streets of Miami Beach have hummed with the activity of thousands of soldiers. We lived in hotel rooms and summer resorts instead of barracks. They converted the pier into a recreation area for servicemen and, if we got lucky, servicewomen too. For a small-town Texas boy like me, Miami Beach had a sort of glamour that was missing from the tidy central square of my own hometown.

"Hey, JD." My buddy Eugene walked across the gravel drive toward me.

"Hey," I replied, brought up short by his sudden appearance. Still shaky from Boone's funeral, I had yet to master the manly stoicism of Gary Cooper or even the quiet strength of Jimmy Stewart. I feared the hollowness in my gut reflected on my face.

Eugene ducked his head to avoid looking at me straight on and mumbled, "Stanton told us your duffle was back at the room, but he hadn't seen you."

"Got in a little while ago and came here"—I jerked my head toward the doorway—"to report back."

He made a brave attempt to meet my eyes. "How's the family?"

"Best as can be expected," I managed. My voice sounded calm and collected, even to my critical ears.

He relaxed, relieved I hadn't broken down or something. "Castle and Freddie are at the beach. Some of the local girls set up a lemonade stand with cookies and donuts."

I cocked an eyebrow in disbelief, pretty darn sure it wasn't lemonade and baked goods that had tempted Privates George Castle and Freddie Brinks to expose their pale legs to the sun.

Eugene grinned. "Remember that girl Castle met on the pier awhile back, the Mexican one?"

"Cuban," I corrected him.

"Same difference." He shrugged. "He's meeting her there. They've been stepping out, but her family don't know it."

"He's meeting her on the sly?"

"Yep." He grinned again.

I pictured the girl in my mind: thick, shiny black hair, sun-kissed skin, and full red lips. The perfect curves of her figure and a particular skill on the dance floor drew more than one pair of admiring male eyes.

Josefina Ruiz had a bright smile and a kind word for everyone. Like every other guy here, I sure would've liked to know her better. I kept my distance, though. The only daughter of an important man was just a trap waiting to snap.

Her father, Renaldo, walked the streets of this town like he owned them. In truth, he kinda did. A well-known businessman with strong ties to Cuba, he had the reputation of a quick temper, never shy to use both his fists and powerful connections.

Her falling for Castle didn't surprise me. Movie star handsome and a swell from new money out west in California, Castle had all the luck. Too bad. There were some good Joes here in Miami Beach. Any one of them would have scrambled over the other to help Josefina on with her wrap, but not George Castle.

He played it cool, going on and on about his family's money, their big house, and all his women. George dropped the names of famous actors and the fancy places where they hung out together.

Turns out, none of his important friends or his daddy's money could save him from the draft. The Army Air Corps pulled him from his junior year at college and thrust him into the lower ranks with us commoners.

Castle started out with us in Louisiana, but I never warmed to him. He put on a regular-guy act, but it didn't fool me. He held himself above us lowly peasants. His playacting would have been pathetic if I hadn't wanted to punch him in his stupid mug half the time.

"Castle's gonna get himself into trouble if he messes with that girl," I told Eugene, pocketing the carbon copy of the readmission paper.

We walked across the circular drive and scrambled to avoid a greenhorn driving a supply truck. Safely on the other side, Eugene smirked and gushed, "Nah, not Lancelot. He's too smooth to get caught in a bind over a doll."

I grunted. Along with the interchangeable use of first and last names, everyone had a nickname. Lancelot seemed a natural fit for Castle, him being tall and handsome.

With the last name of Hawkins, and being the best shot in the company, they called me Hawkeye. I liked it, the nickname also being the moniker of the hero in *The Last of the Mohicans.* The name suited me fine, but George Castle given the honor of Lancelot was a constant irritant.

Sir Thomas Mallory's Arthurian Tales ranked right up there with some of my favorites. In my humble opinion, Castle didn't embody the ideals of chivalry for which the Knights of the Round Table were famous. Had to admit, though, he sure looked the part.

"Well, Genie, I guess we'll see what happens with that girl," I taunted.

He bristled. A slight, fair-haired boy with a dreamy head-in-the-clouds quality, Eugene Gibson got stuck with one of those jokey nicknames every man hopes to avoid. He hated the sound of it.

I bit my lip, regretting the unkind impulse. But his admiration for that snobbish rich kid whose bogus friendliness covered for his sense of superiority bothered me no end.

Nope, I did not like George Castle. Not one bit.

We stopped at Rico's Drugstore to buy an ice cream cone and kept walking on our way to the beach. The lowering sun hit me straight in the eyes. Its rays cast a brittle golden hue over the town, and a fresh breeze off the ocean brushed the hair back from my forehead. The normalcy of our surroundings made it hard to believe a war raged half a world away. That there were men like me mired in combat, some never to see another sunset.

"Hey." Eugene nudged my arm and nodded over at the cinema. "They're showing *The Iron Major*. We should go. Gladys," he said, referring to his sister, "wrote me she cried at the end. But she's pretty emotional . . . cried at *Bambi* too."

He looked down at the ground and kicked a small rock with the toe of his shoe. I figured Gladys wasn't the only member of the Gibson family to choke up when that hunter shot Bambi's mom.

I find sports movies boring for the most part, but grasped at the suggestion like a flea on a dog's back. My idea of fun didn't include watching George Castle string a nice girl along. I glanced at my watch.

"Twenty minutes to the five-thirty showing."

For the next hour and a half, we watched Frank Cavanaugh as portrayed by Pat O'Brien endure triumph and tragedy. Neither of us cried at the end, and we left the cinema and headed back to our quarters.

The muted sound of waves blanketed the darkness, and goosebumps rose on my arms as a heavy fog swept in from the ocean. The glow of streetlights lit a hazy path along the golf course where we walked. We'd rounded the corner onto a grassy verge of the hotel grounds when Freddie Brinks—nicknamed Fort Knox for obvious reasons—came running up.

"Come," he gasped. "Hurry . . . Lance . . . Lancelot . . . fight . . . bad . . ."

He ran back toward the hotel and out onto the fifth hole of the golf course without looking back. Eugene and I exchanged a quick, startled glance before rushing after him.

A car sat off the green. The harsh glare of headlights cut across the mowed grass. Two figures danced in and out of the mist and streaming lights. Well, one danced; the other staggered around flailing the air with punches.

We trained every day, and much as I hated to admit, Castle was a fine athlete. But he sure didn't know how to box.

I was quick and strong, but fell well short of Castle's six feet. Momma insisted I had yet to reach my full height, my father being a tall and lanky man. Her optimism didn't help much growing up. I spent a good part of my youth convincing bullies not to mess with me. That meant being resigned to getting hurt, fighting dirty when I had to, and making damn sure I took a piece outta the other guy—leastwise enough so's he'd think twice before picking another fight.

Men like Castle didn't learn that lesson. Their size intimidated bullies. George probably never had to defend himself. From the looks of it, he'd never been in a fistfight before.

Castle's opponent, though shorter, boasted a compact, muscled body and dodged his punches with ease. The man's footwork marked him as a trained boxer. His olive skin and shiny, dark hair marked him as a relation of Josefina Ruiz, probably a brother.

"We've gotta do something," Freddie declared, still out of breath. "He's gettin' killed out there."

I noted with some satisfaction this was true. Castle's lower lip protruded just enough to mar his perfect profile, and a cut above his right eye looked painful. I felt a little guilty for hoping the other guy would land him a facer while he had an audience.

"What happened?" I asked.

"That fella"—Freddie jerked his head toward Castle's foe—"come up to us on the pier and accused George of playing fast and loose with his sis—"

We all sucked in our breath as Castle took a punch that sent him reeling. I ran over to the car and nudged the kid sitting in the driver's seat aside.

I honked the horn and yelled, "Break. Round one to the champ over there."

Josefina's brother backed away. His buddies swarmed around him, wiping him down with his discarded shirt.

Castle looked up. His face, illuminated by the harsh glare of the headlights, held an expression as raw and unguarded as any I'd ever seen. He had recognized my voice, and it hit me, in that moment, that he knew how much I didn't like him.

Freddie and Eugene led him to the edge of the green. Castle bent over with his hands on his knees. His breath came in gasps between gritted teeth.

I didn't have a high opinion of him, but he wasn't stupid. Getting on the wrong side of an influential family wasn't something a calculating rich kid like Castle did as a rule.

"What the hell?" I exclaimed. "Why didn't you just walk away? You wouldn't be the first soldier to dally with a local girl."

Castle took a deep breath and straightened. "Believe it or not, I don't 'dally' with women." His face twisted, and he looked ready to cry. "Maybe I talk big," he admitted. "But . . . I . . . uh . . . well, Fina's pregnant."

This declaration landed like a thunderclap. It knocked Freddie off his feet as he stumbled back and hit the ground hard on his tailbone.

I sucked in my breath, shocked. "Well, I hope he beats the crap outta ya. I'd pound you to a pulp myself if he wasn't doing a better job. Leaving a girl pregnant—"

Castle lunged and shoved me hard against my chest. "You think I'd do that?" he shouted, looming over me, his face close to mine. "You think I'd leave her . . . Fina?" His voice broke, and his anger deflated as quickly as it had flared. He fought back tears. "Told her I'd marry her . . . wanted to marry her. But I'm not a Catholic . . ."

I glared at him. What a mess. This whole affair looked to be more complicated than the usual boy gets girl in trouble scenario.

"Well, first things first, forfeit—"

"No," Castle snapped. "He called me a dirty gringo, told me never to lay another hand on his sister. I'm not quitting."

I gritted my teeth. Shit stupid rich kid.

"Okay, hero, you want to land a hit against this guy, you're gonna have to fight smart."

Three pairs of eyes looked back at me expectantly. "He's a good fighter, light and quick on his feet. He has a solid left, but I have a hunch he can't take a punch as good as he gives. Here's what you do."

I motioned them to huddle up. "Keep out of range until you have the headlights at your back. He's a good deal shorter than you. The glare's gonna fall full in his eyes. That's when you rush in and hit him, but from here." I patted Castle on his stomach. "Punch out from your gut and hit him square on the jaw. Follow up with a left jab, hard as you can."

He crossed his arms. "Is that fair? The headlights thing?"

I rolled my eyes. "None of this is fair, man. You're not in a ring. There are no rules. He insulted you, and who knows what he's told your girl. You marry her, you don't want that asshole thinking he can take you on whenever he doesn't like something."

Castle clenched his jaw and nodded with conviction. The men swirling around Josefina's brother hurled taunts in Spanish. Their derision rattled me, and I wished he'd just give it up.

Castle walked to the middle of the green, unsteady on his feet. The brother danced around, shifting from side to side.

He lunged. Castle pulled back.

The brother's fist grazed his cheek, and Castle surprised me with a sly move. He faked a stumble and got the headlights behind him. The whole thing happened quick like. The brother squinted. Castle rushed him, landing a one-two punch to the jaw that sent the man sprawling.

He jumped right back up, angry but cautious. Success revived Castle, and the brother was now hesitant. Getting punched in the face hurts, and for what it's worth, Castle had a strong arm.

They circled each other a few more times, but the fight didn't last long after that. Both men exchanged hard looks and shouted insults before falling back to their respective groups.

The brother drove off with his buddies, and we helped Castle to his room. Freddie left to find ice. Eugene and I ran cold water over washrags for Castle to press to his swollen lips and black eye. His nose, still intact, stood out in refined contrast to the rest of his bloodied face.

To my surprise, his mouth crooked into a painful smile. He looked at me with an odd, relieved expression.

"Some fight, huh, Hawkeye?" He pressed the wet rag to his lips again and muttered, "Who'd a thought?"

**

The small Catholic church stood with doors open to the sea breeze. A couple of weeks had passed since the fight on the golf course. Except for the cut above his right eye, which still looked a little raw, George Castle's face could easily have graced a movie poster. In fact, instead of detracting from his good looks, the blemish gave his face a raffish cast.

He stood at the altar in his dress uniform, Josefina next to him. The simple white wedding dress and short lace veil highlighted her lovely features and elegant figure. Only a few of us knew the radiant glow on her cheeks was not just that of a bride, but also of a mother-to-be.

Her family gathered on one side of the church with important dignitaries in attendance, the mayor among them. As it turned out, Josefina had three brothers. Nino, the youngest, had given George the pummeling.

All the Ruiz men *except* Nino sat glowering from the pews. He looked as if this wedding was his idea from the get-go and George his personal choice as husband for his only sister.

None of Castle's family could make it on such short notice. That's what George told us, but you'd think rich folk could get across the country in two weeks' time.

What do I know? His friends made a good showing, though. Even the sergeant and our CO attended.

I stood to one side of Castle, still stunned at being his best man. The priest droned on, and I patted the pocket of my pressed khakis. I had not lost the ring in the thirty seconds since last checking.

I glanced over at George's solemn profile. The world was an

unpredictable place, and the war sure mixed things up more than usual. There's this famous quote about politics making strange bedfellows. Well, I think war does the same. Strip a man of his civvies and put him in a uniform and he looks pretty much like any other man.

There weren't many scenarios where I'd imagined myself standing up with a fella like George Castle—or even knowing him, for that matter. But turns out George ain't so bad, and I ain't so wise and discerning as I had once believed.

All this crossed my mind before the priest came to the end of his homily and asked for the ring. George turned to me.

I shoved a hand in my pocket, and my eyes flew open in an expression of shock. Panic flashed across his face before I winked and placed the delicate gold band in his palm.

"Had ya goin'," I whispered.

"Asshole." He quirked up one side of his mouth in a lopsided grin.

I grinned back at him and repeated his words in my head, "Who'd a thought?"

Chapter Four

And though hard be the task, keep a stiff upper lip.
—Phoebe Cary

"Are you going to write about your trip?" her mother asked as they packed in Meliz's bedroom back home in San Diego.

Early morning sun warmed the room, a rarity in the typically gloomy days of June. Meliz pulled her oversized "airplane" sweater from the depths of the chest of drawers and sat back on her heels.

"I'll update with pictures and videos . . . write about JD's wartime exploits. You know, fulfilling his last wish and all."

"And those old memories he wanted to put to rest?" Gwen probed.

Meliz stood and frowned down at the carpet. She hated ambiguity. It fed her anxiety. "Am I being stupid? His trip, the missing pages, those kids . . . All of it's connected, right?"

"I'm not sure about any connections, but Dad's imagination was never of the cloak and dagger sort. He loved a good mystery. But all of this secrecy, it wasn't like him. There's something strange here. I feel it too," Gwen declared.

She ran her hands over a pair of shorts, smoothing them into the backpack, and huffed in disbelief. "My God, he stuffed that entry into an old hat and kept the whole thing a secret for the rest of his life."

"He didn't even tell Bert," Meliz added, as if this fact established with certainty the uncharacteristic nature of JD's furtive behavior.

Gwen sat on the bed and clasped her hands in her lap. "You know, you aren't accountable for your grandfather's secrets."

"What?"

She looked up at Meliz. "You aren't responsible for JD's actions. He loved you, and you loved him back. That's all he ever cared about. He wouldn't want you to think you owed him or his legacy"—she enclosed "legacy" in air quotes—"anything. You don't have to be 'the keeper of the flame,' so to speak."

At the window, Meliz stared out on the quiet cul-de-sac. She bit back an angry retort. Her mother didn't understand.

Though Gwen and JD shared a close relationship, it did not extend to her wanting to follow in his footsteps; unlike Meliz, who yearned for a life of words and stories. Her mother couldn't grasp the bond this need created between granddaughter and grandfather.

JD's "legacy" fell to Meliz, whether she liked it or not. The burden weighed heavy, and she harbored some resentment her mother had sidestepped the responsibility so neatly.

She drew in a calming breath and sat next to Gwen. "If not me, then who, Mom?" She held up her hand to keep her mother from interrupting. "He *does* have a legacy, and we, I, profit from that. Planning this trip was literally JD's last act. It must mean something. I owe it to him . . . to us . . . to find out what."

"But—"

"Mom, listen."

"Okay, okay, sorry."

"Trust me. I've clawed my way out from his long shadow, and I don't intend to get sucked back in. But I've got to find a way to balance everything. JD's work was important. I don't want to lose that either." She choked up, limp with grief she knew her mother shared.

Gwen hugged Meliz tight and grumbled in her ear, "I wish you hadn't found that damn journal."

**

Meliz stood at the gate in the San Francisco Airport and searched for a vacant seat. She adjusted the daypack and small leather satchel slung over her shoulders with nervous fingers. The song, "Oh, What a Beautiful Mornin'," from *Oklahoma* ran on a loop through her brain. Summoned by her subconscious, the familiar lyrics soothed her frayed nerves.

The musicals of Rodgers and Hammerstein composed the soundtrack of her childhood. During the many summers at JD's ranch, blaring orchestral overtures shook Meliz and her cousins from their beds. They piled, sleepy-eyed and still dream-laden, into the smoky kitchen where JD served up pancakes and bacon. To this day, the smell of breakfast triggered in her mind the voices of long-ago musical stars of the silver screen.

A group of laughing women whisked past her and pulled in their wake a cold draft. Meliz shivered and wrapped her sweater tighter. Noises ricocheted around the cavernous building and combined with volumes of empty air to create a ceaseless babble of sound. She longed for a hidden alcove to regroup and fortify herself for the stresses of flying. Fear really, stress being too mild a word for the dread lodged in the pit of her stomach.

Meliz spotted a seat at the end of a row and plopped down, stowing in her daypack a bean and cheese burrito and bottle of water she had snagged from the food court. A gangly teenager slumped in the chair opposite, headphones on and eyes closed. Meliz sank into her seat and did the same.

She stretched out her legs and tripped a woman holding a baby. The woman stumbled and caught herself.

"Watch out," she snapped.

Meliz pulled off her headphones with a quick apology. "I'm so sorry. I wasn't looking."

Not much older than Meliz, the young mother sagged with exhaustion. "People need to pay more attention."

"I'm sorry," she repeated.

The woman nodded and walked off. Meliz met the bored gaze of the kid across from her. He shrugged and closed his eyes again, slumping even further down into his seat.

Meliz gave up any pretense at relaxation. She put her headphones back on and checked her messages. A steady stream of advice scrolled past with the flick of her finger.

Her many Hawkins cousins, with their penchant for family drama, had pulled Meliz into their confidences and conspiracies since childhood. Now adults, they busied themselves in each other's lives and formed a close-knit tribe. Meliz, the only child of only children, would have found life lonely if not for the boisterous offspring of JD's four surviving siblings.

They bombarded her with theories and suggestions. Everyone had an opinion on how to conduct her "little endeavor" as Cousin Tom had characterized this trip.

"Reading on cell phones can cause tiny horns to grow out the back of your skull, I hear."

The voice came muffled through her headphones. Meliz glanced up and snatched them off her head.

"Excuse me? Horns? What?"

From his perch on a low-slung wheelchair, an old man peered at her with intense hazel eyes through thick-lens glasses. "That's what I read. A study showed kids grew little horns at the base of their skulls from looking down all the time."

"Pops, really?" A much younger man stood behind his wheelchair. A rueful smile touched his lips. "A study?"

"Out of some Australian university . . . I swear." The old man held up his right hand as if taking an oath.

"Sorry, my granddad is a bit of a meddler," the young man told Meliz in the low-pitched, even voice of someone used to dealing with difficult problems. He parked the wheelchair next to her at the end of the row.

Meliz quashed with an effort the blush threatening to spread across her cheeks. A good decade older than her own twenty-two years, the man's prominent nose sat perched above full lips. Dusky hazel eyes, milder than his grandfather's, matched the deep gold of his hair. His teeth flashed white and pleasantly crooked. Feigning nonchalance, Meliz resisted the impulse to glance at his hands to see if they were boney and long fingered.

Wendy, her roommate, had dubbed his type "the handsome oddball." Meliz's dating history testified to its allure, though not its compatibility. Ever hopeful, she returned his charming smile with one of her own.

Meliz put her phone down and rubbed the back of her neck. "No problem. My neck does feel a little stiff."

A smug expression crossed the old man's face. "See, she's grateful."

His grandson grinned and nudged his shoulder with a gentle fist. Meliz looked away, a sudden tightening in her chest. She drew in a deep breath and checked her emotions.

"I'm gonna get a bottle of water and something to read. Do you want anything, Pops?"

"No." His grandfather patted a leather bag hanging from the wheelchair. "You go, Prescott. I've got everything I need."

Meliz deducted a point or two of hotness for the ultra-White name of Prescott. He walked off, and she pretended not to watch his trim, jeans-clad backside weave in and out through the crowd on the concourse.

"I saw you trip that lady. Too many people on their phones these days," the old man scolded. "What're you doing that's so important on that phone of yours, anyway?"

Meliz guessed him to be somewhere in his late eighties. She recognized his type. A couple of JD's old cowboy buddies had the same vibe. No matter how aged and weak they became, they still projected an old-fashioned masculine assertiveness that bordered on the belligerent.

"Planning my next bank heist," she deadpanned.

"That so?" He cocked a disapproving eyebrow, but admitted, "I have a cell phone. Prescott insisted. Said the thing was for safety, and at my age . . . well, you know."

"It's good to have. My grandfather had one too." Meliz didn't add that JD never went anywhere without it and was addicted to his Twitter feed.

"Your granddad not around anymore?" he asked with bluntness the elderly often felt entitled to.

"He died a few weeks ago." She kept her voice flat and emotionless for fear of crying.

"I'm sorry to hear it." The old man peered at her with sincere regret.

Meliz relaxed and answered in a more natural tone, "He was the best. Everyone loved him."

"Everyone, huh?" He snorted. "Anybody I'd know or you just saying that because he was your granddad?"

The old man most likely knew her grandfather's work. Ever since Marshal Clyde Jameson rode off the pages of JD's first novel in 1954 and into the hearts of millions, his books had never been out of print.

"Just because he was my grandfather," she hedged.

"Guess Prescott would say the same, but to be honest, most of my family tolerates me at best." He chuckled, and Meliz laughed as expected.

Prescott returned with a plastic airport shopping bag in hand. He stood in front of them, backlit by the enormous window and with his face partially in shadow. From beneath dark brows, he cast a quick measuring glance over Meliz.

Her skin prickled with irritation at his silent assessment. She frowned and narrowed her eyes, considering his athletic frame.

Marshal Jameson always claimed he could judge a man by the set of his shoulders. Broad and well proportioned, Prescott's shoulders slumped slightly forward. What would Marshal Jameson make of this? That he was bookish, protective, reserved perhaps . . .

She gave up. Like most Marshal Jameson catchphrases, this folksy piece of wisdom was lost on her. Meliz preferred faces and hands to shoulders anyway.

The intercom announced first class boarding. "That's our cue, Pops." Prescott stationed himself behind the wheelchair and hung the plastic bag on one of its handles.

The old man thrust out a thin, wrinkled hand. "I'm Jack Walker. I guess you're headed to Manila or you wouldn't be sitting here."

She took the proffered hand. Dry, parchment-like skin overlaid brittle bones. He surprised her with a strong grip.

"Meliz Lin, and yes, I am."

"Well, I'd ask your business if my grandson here wouldn't think me rude."

Prescott sighed, and Meliz looked at him with fellow feeling. She knew well the frustrations of traveling with an uncensored elder. JD had been a worldly and cultured man, but he often inhabited his good ole country boy persona with a little too much gusto.

"No, not rude. I'm on vacation."

Jack waved a friendly goodbye. "Well, see you on the other side." He grimaced, realizing the ominous sound of his words.

Meliz laughed and returned his wave as Prescott wheeled the old man up to the jetway. Another few minutes would pass before they called her group, and she pulled JD's journal from her satchel.

She traced the cracked leather of the cover with an absentminded finger. Her grandfather always projected confidence, sure of himself and what he wanted in life. Meliz bit her lip.

Anxiety had plagued her since childhood, and she never seemed sure of anything. She loved and adored JD, but was born a different creature altogether from her outgoing grandfather, and even her busy and accomplished parents.

She imagined the seventeen-year-old JD on his way to the South Pacific. His voice, raspy and warm, regaled her with all the war stories he had never told her in life.

No. She flipped the script running through her mind. His voice would be younger, a boy on his way to war, afraid, insecure, and full of romantic notions.

A tear escaped from the corner of her eye and trailed down her cheek. She sniffed and wiped it away. Perhaps they weren't so different after all.

Chapter Five

Even God lends a hand to honest boldness.
—Melander

Meliz closed her computer. The reading light burned overhead, a tiny, illuminated oasis in the quiet grayness of the cabin. She stretched out her legs, grateful to have plunked down the extra cash for Economy Plus. Thankfully, no weary mothers wandered through her small, untidy kingdom behind the bulkhead.

She could have afforded first class, but scorned the "tedium of the wealthy," as her grandfather often described the company of rich people. "All the best stories are in steerage, my dear," he often advised her. "The rich are boring."

JD always bristled when she reminded him he was rich. "You won't find me siding with that lot, ever," he railed. "Those greedy bastards got us into the Depression. And they'll get us into another one, mark my words."

Meliz smiled at the memory and looked out her window. In the surrounding darkness, she could just make out a shadowy ripple of clouds. A sudden disorientation tightened her chest. She interlaced her fingers and cracked her knuckles, releasing some tension.

In an effort to divert her mind from the gaping abyss below, she opened her computer to log on to her new, private website. Here, she intended to chronicle her investigation. Only her parents, Alberta, her cousins, and Wendy knew of it.

Meliz typed in her password, George Castle, a name that popped up a lot in JD's journal. She drummed her fingers on the tray table and contemplated the screen. Nothing came to mind. The urge to write had deserted her. On impulse, she logged off the website and opened her blog.

Since high school, she had plugged away at crafting clever anecdotes and poetic descriptions for her few dozen followers, most of them family and friends. But her fledgling efforts at writing came to a screeching halt when the world discovered JD Hawkins's only grandchild, that morning two years ago when she opened her blog to find her online following had grown at an alarming rate.

To this day, she cursed the respected PBS. Their *American Masters* series featuring her grandfather and his classic western fiction outed her. The obligatory home videos, one of JD playing with his little half-Chinese granddaughter, splashed across millions of television screens. It did not take long for the internet sleuths to find her out.

Her comment section filled with snarky remarks and critiques on her writing, most of them unfavorably comparing her to JD. More hurtful were the outright racists who resented her close relationship to an icon of modern American culture. The comments turned so ugly, JD published an opinion piece in the *Washington Post* disavowing those "fans" as un-American and unworthy of the sacrifices past generations had made on their behalf.

He ended it in perfect JD style: "Keep your sick words off my granddaughter and your grubby hands off my books. I don't need your filthy money."

He meant well, but for once, his words had not made her feel better. Disheartened and humiliated, she wanted nothing more than to retreat, to hide away until the crazies had moved on to their next target. Instead, she forced herself to keep posting, unwilling to be bullied. She restricted posts to film clips of class projects, and eventually all but the most hardened zealots gave up, and those she blocked.

Meliz perused her old postings and shook her head with a bitter laugh. She had never actively hidden her connection to JD. Until the *American Masters* reveal, she hadn't needed to.

Her multiracial heritage served as excellent cover, especially when it came to White people. They could never quite figure her out. If only she had a dollar for every time a White person assumed she belonged to some exotic, nonexistent Eastern European race.

This blinkered worldview frustrated Meliz, but it had also shielded her. She hoped to avoid becoming a cliché: the pampered grandchild of a famous and talented man. Meliz welcomed her anonymity, even if it resulted from racist assumptions. Her mind still reeled at how quickly those assumptions had turned from a shield into a spear.

"Thanks, fucking PBS," she murmured.

Meliz straightened in her seat and squared her shoulders. Fuck them all. She had a job to do.

Armed with the implements of her trade—a laptop and camera—Meliz was determined to track down JD's final story. She logged back onto her web page and wrote:

> *As the first entry on my super-secret website, I should write something of profound significance, but I have only trivialities on the brain. I'll tell you that my plane arrives in Manila around 10pm local time. At which point, I will be wide awake. The better to navigate customs, flag down a taxi, and get to the pension.*

I meet Garrett Rivera, a military scholar and the author of "Fallen Comrades: The Filipino Soldiers of Bataan," for lunch tomorrow. He was a visiting lecturer my junior year at school and is a professor at the University of the City of Manila. He's young for a tenured position, but the book was a bestseller. So now, he's kind of a star in academic circles.

There's not much out there on the combat cargo groups, or the Asian allies for that matter. Since many WWII veterans are dead, I have to rely on historians and academics. (Although Bert—thanks, Bert—is following up with a list of JD's old GI buddies). JD visited Manila once. I think the second time his unit returned to the Philippines. I'll have to look back through his journal to be sure—

"Sorry to bother you."

Meliz snapped her computer shut. Prescott leaned against the bulkhead. She'd seen him and his grandfather while boarding. The old man, small and frail in the large first-class seat, already slept, but Prescott had nodded as she passed them.

He stood in his socks, hair mussed up and eyes weary. "Your light was on, and I was hoping you had a couple of Advil or something." He glanced around the cabin. "Everyone's asleep, and the flight attendants are done in. I didn't want to bother them. I've got this persistent headache . . ."

Meliz nodded with sympathy. Her two seatmates were also asleep, twisted into awkward positions, the middle seat passenger wrapped so tightly in his blanket he looked like a huge cocoon.

"Yeah, no problem." She searched the messy space for a spot to put her computer.

"Here, let me." Prescott took the laptop and squatted with his back against the bulkhead.

"Thanks. I have some ibuprofen in here somewhere." She knelt and searched her daypack for the painted pillbox she bought one summer in Mexico. "Unless you want weed? It's legal," she chirped, mimicking the cheery motto of California's marijuana trade.

He drew back in alarm. "You didn't bring any on board, did you? You *cannot* take pot into the Philippines."

Meliz reassured him with a light touch on his arm. Her fingers tingled, and she jerked her hand back.

"Relax. I'm kidding. The one time I got high, I was super paranoid. To the point where I cried hysterically at perfectly innocent texts from my roommate. I haven't tried it since."

Prescott laughed. "Yeah, weed was never my thing, either." He leaned inward to look over her shoulder. "Sorry again about my granddad. He's always been outgoing, though intrusive is probably a better word."

They huddled together on the floor of the plane. Light escaped from the closed computer and illuminated the space between them. The warmth of his breath brushed her neck, and the hum of the engines enveloped them, as did the low, deep breathing of hundreds of slumbering passengers.

The moment stretched and suspended. Butterflies fluttered in the pit of Meliz's stomach. Her hand found the ceramic box and grasped it, breaking the spell.

"Here we go. How many do you need?"

He sat back on his heels and placed the computer on top of her daypack. "A couple. The pain's not too bad, kind of hanging around at the temples and won't go away."

Meliz pushed herself up onto the seat and opened the box. "Prescott . . . is that a family name?"

"Yeah, I'm named for Pops and my dad, who's the Second. I'm Jack Prescott Walker the Third. To avoid confusion, everyone calls me Prescott."

Meliz shook two small, white pills into his palm, noting his long fingers and the large veins standing out from the bones of his hand. A shiver raced up her spine and pinged at the base of her skull.

"Lin, that's Chinese, right?"

"Mm-hmm. My dad's family came over from Taiwan when he was a kid. Are you on vacation?" she asked, changing the subject.

Prescott stood. "No. Work, a board meeting."

"What kind of work?"

"Pops has majority ownership in a sugarcane farm and interest in several other businesses."

"I'm impressed he's so involved at his age."

Prescott flashed a fond smile. "Pops never let go of anything in his life. We're lucky he has to attend these meetings only once a year."

"You always go with him?"

"I'm general counsel for our company. The whole nepotism thing, you know," he replied with self-deprecating humor. "I'm really just a glorified companion."

Meliz laughed.

"This your first trip to the Philippines?" he asked.

"Yes."

He pulled from his back pocket a creased business card. "Don't judge me," he pleaded, flashing his rueful smile. "I have to carry these whenever I travel for business. If you need anything, give me a call. The Philippines is kind of our second home."

She took the card and thanked him.

Prescott rattled the pills like dice in his closed fist. "Well, maybe now I can get some sleep."

They exchanged an awkward little wave and he left. Meliz picked up her computer. She contemplated the blankness out her window for a long moment.

"He's into you." The voice came muffled through layers of blanket.

Her seatmate emerged just enough from his cocoon to reveal the bored teenage boy from the airport. "He's in first class. Those guys are all douches. They don't care about bothering the flight attendants. Seriously, you can't be buying that."

"I don't know, seemed like he really had a headache."

The boy snorted his contempt at so obvious a tactic and turned away, disappearing back into his blanket. Meliz laughed under her breath and opened the laptop. Her website had disconnected.

Instead of returning to her post, she pulled out JD's journal and found where she had left off reading. After struggling several minutes with the faded writing and her grandfather's terrible spelling, she snapped the little book shut and shoved it back into her bag.

Logging onto her computer once more, she brought up the search engine and typed: *jack prescott walker philippines sugarcane.*

Chapter Six

Arise, go forth, and conquer as of old.
—Tennyson

6 Nov., 1944, San Francisco, CA—We boarded the barge and were on our way to San Francisco by 1545hrs. The fog pressed in around us. The muffled sounds of fidgeting men and shifting equipment added to a feeling of depressed anticipation. When we arrived at the docks in San Francisco, Red Cross girls greeted us with cookies and coffee.

At 2000hrs, a band struck up "The Army Air Corps." We shouldered our packs and filed past the CO shouting out our names and shipment numbers as we climbed the gangplank onto the *USS General Hersey.*

They packed us in like cattle in the lowest livable part of the ship. I didn't like it one bit. There was better than 500 men billeted in a compartment below the waterline. The heavy, sweaty air made me gag, and the enclosed surroundings gave me the heebie-jeebies. I took my blanket and pillow and slept up on deck. It wasn't so bad.

7 Nov.—At 0740hrs we shoved off for God only knows where. Rumors were that our final destination was the Philippines. Others said the CBI (China-Burma-India) Theater, but the brass won't confirm anything.

We sailed under the Golden Gate Bridge. The view opened up into a spectacular panorama. Reality hit us all pretty hard as that iconic American symbol faded from sight. We were on our own.

16 Nov.—We crossed the equator. The crew initiated us into the Royal Order of Neptune's Realm. I got a certificate, but lost it. We all have KP or general cleanup duty, but there is not much to do except read.

21 Nov.—We passed Guadalcanal at sunset. The island looked hardly big enough to hold one army, much less two. We'll be in dangerous waters before long.

23 Nov., nearing New Guinea—I'm grateful to be within sight of land again. Japanese forces persist, but our troops have made good progress in reclaiming New Guinea. News is scarce, but we heard MacArthur went ashore at Leyte in the Philippines.

Our proximity to the Philippines brought to mind my buddy Joe Duncan's big brother, Kit. He joined up early in the war. He deployed to Luzon and retreated with MacArthur's forces to Bataan and Corregidor. After that, Joe didn't hear anything more from Kit. His name didn't show up on any of the prisoner lists. Joe told me they'd heard the Japanese had refused to cooperate with the Red Cross, and the lists weren't reliable.

Course news out of the POW camps is horrifying, but Joe and his family hope Kit is still alive. Though they fear what he might be enduring if he is.

Mrs. Duncan got a gold star from the army but refused to put it up on the service flag in her window. She told Momma a gold star would be a betrayal. Until she knows for sure Kit isn't coming home, she'll keep the blue star up.

Momma agreed. Told Mrs. Duncan she should hope until they knew for certain.

**

New Guinea, November 1944

I spent my free time aboard ship reading and writing. Those of us on general duty could do whatever we wanted once we finished our daily task. I found myself mostly alone in these pursuits, being one of the lucky few who didn't get seasick.

Those first few days out from San Francisco, the ship descended into a disgusting spiral of seasickness. I couldn't walk along the deck without slipping on a carpet of vomit. Hundreds of men hung over the railings puking their guts out into the ocean. The lower deck got the worst of it, what with the constant stream of upchuck falling from the deck above as one man would finish, only to be replaced by another, and so on.

I stayed mostly above deck. Though I ventured below once a day to give the poor sod in the bunk next to mine a drink of water and some saltines. He stayed in a fetal position the entire voyage and never even told me his name. I figured if he survived the trip, he'd have me to thank.

I kept the other reason for staying atop to myself. Though Castle and our buddy Frank Hoffman musta had some inkling of why.

Nobody but the crew manned battle stations. If we got into trouble, orders were to batten down the hatches and wait and see if we made it out alive. I didn't much cotton to being locked into an iron coffin and rendered helpless as the ship filled up with water.

Boone once pulled a bag of drowned kittens from the river. One of the most pathetic sights I'd ever seen, poor things, their claws bloody and with eyes staring and glassy. I couldn't think of a much worse fate than to drown in a confined space sealed off from the sky.

So, every night I slipped out of my bunk, hunkered down in a comfortable spot up top, and slept. I soon had company. More than a few men showed up above deck during the night. Soon, George and Frank did too.

The threat of enemy submarines lengthened our journey as the *General Hersey* zigzagged to avoid them. By now, we all hankered to get off this boat, but for the most part, the sea did okay by me.

I had witnessed some fine and beautiful sights out here. Dolphins and stingrays flew through the air and reappeared in my dreams, night after night. Most amazing of all were the whales.

About a week out from San Francisco, I sat on the foredeck reading Somerset Maugham's *The Razor's Edge* for the hundredth time. Daddy sent me the book when it first came out. I usually favored swashbuckling adventures, but Larry Darrell's suffering ignited in me a need for experiences that challenged my very humanity. Like Maugham's hero, I hoped one day to search for the real meaning of life, for a transcendent moment of clarity.

The waves beat against the hull, and the lowering sky cast a gloomy pall over the ship. Sea spray from over the bow misted my face. We slowed through the heavy waves. Even with my sea legs, I risked a headache or worse reading in the choppy waters. I closed my book and walked to the side of the ship.

We dipped into a large wave, and I grabbed the railing for balance. I was a strong swimmer, but my stomach lurched at the thought of falling overboard. Glancing down into the ocean, I about fainted from shock. Taper-shaped bodies skimmed below the surface, like huge torpedoes.

A whale broke the waves, its blowhole spewing air and water. Another one followed, and then another. I laughed with relief and heard the PA system crackle.

"Whales off the bow. Whales off the bow."

A group of men joined me. The magnificent animals pulled away from the ship and slowed. We released a collective gasp as the water exploded with breaching whales.

They sprung out of the ocean and fell back, slapping the surface hard with their enormous bodies. Some as big as buildings, I swear, over sixty, seventy feet long. My pulse raced with each tremendous, flying leap.

They were joyful. I do believe they were joyful.

The ship caught the trough and moved with stomach-churning speed up to the crest. A huge wave rolled over the whales, and they were gone.

The image of those whales stayed with me for days afterwards. They knew nothing of the war raging above them. They ruled over a kingdom vast and deep and unexplored by men. A whole other geography existed under the oceans, of mountains and valleys, maybe even lost cities, certainly the remnants of fierce sea battles.

There were two separate worlds on this earth, and I could no longer be certain ours was the most civilized. The whales' joyful beauty taught me I didn't need to suffer terrible things to experience transcendent moments of clarity.

**

We finally came in close to land and anchored near a place called Finch Haven, off the coast of New Guinea. About two in the morning, a whole lot of racket jerked me outta dreamland. Noises on a big ship were par for the course, and I slept through almost anything. Not this time—a group of forty men or so shouldered heavy packs and scrambled over the side in pitch-black. Not something you saw every day, even on a troop ship.

With the Japanese Navy lurking about, we kept the ship in complete darkness once the sun went down. I had excellent eyesight, though, and could see a couple of men from our unit among the group. We were too far from shore to let down the gangplank. I figured they must be boarding onto smaller boats.

I crept closer and peered over the side. Sure enough, two launches bobbed up and down in the water next to the ship. The boats struggled to stay steady in the rough surf.

"What's happening?"

I about jumped outta my skin. George and Frank had come up behind me. I shushed them and pointed to the group of men still waiting to climb over the side. Finally, they all disembarked and the boats pushed off from the ship heading into Finch Haven.

The next morning, we lifted anchor and left. The mystery of the missing men came up in conversation off and on during the next few days. Nobody knew anything. I asked around and found other groups had a couple guys gone without a word too. Of course, there were hundreds on board, and I couldn't talk to everyone. I made note of their departure in my journal.

We stopped again off New Guinea. This time at a place called Hollandia. A company of engineers got off, but no one else. Some rugged-looking Marines got on.

Frank, George, and I sat on deck, our backs up against the metal siding. The boredom of life aboard ship dragged out the days until they blurred together. I amused myself by wondering aloud what those men were about back at Finch Haven.

"Jeez, Hawkeye, enough already," Frank complained. "There's nothing screwy about it. They left at night so's the enemy wouldn't spot them. It's that simple."

"Why such a big secret? See any Japanese soldiers on this ship? And all of those guys were from different units. It makes no sense."

"I agree with Grumpy." George referred to Frank by his very apt nickname. "They were trying to leave without letting on. My guess, they're going in to shore up a division or something."

I scowled. George usually agreed with me.

Frank reared back, pleasantly surprised. He pulled a comical face and pointed his thumb at George. "See, if Castle sides with me, you *must* be crazy."

We all laughed. They were sick and tired of my theories. I let the whole thing go and filed the incident away in my mind under "Mysteries."

I had all these file folders in my brain, from "Officers I Disliked" and "Fine Fellows" to "Stupid Rules" and "C-rations." I figured that once we reached our destination, I would be filing stories under the likes of "Courage in the Face of Fire" and "Fallen Heroes." The stuff real authors wrote about.

George sucked on a cigarette and blew out a steady stream of smoke. Of the boys I'd started out with at basic, turns out only Castle and I ended up together. We said goodbye to Eugene, Freddie, and Bobbie when we shipped out to Warrensburg, Missouri, for more training. Later, we transferred to Syracuse, New York, where we were inducted into the newly formed 339th Airdrome Squadron assigned to the Eighth Combat Cargo Squadron. Both of these outfits came under the command of the Second Combat Cargo Group.

In Syracuse, the brass assigned me to mechanical training on the C-46 and C-47 aircraft. Both planes were cargo craft capable of pulling large loads, whether that meant equipment, men, or even livestock, over long distances and high altitudes. The objective of these combat cargo groups required us to be fully operational and ready to move at the drop of a hat. The Airdrome Squadron supplied all the tasks necessary to keep the planes up in the air and the men ready to fly.

I wasn't thrilled with my assignment; seemed a bit too tame for a writer trying to experience *real* life. I had hoped to get closer to the action. Captain Griswold, our CO and one of the finest officers I have met, laughed at the sentiment.

"Hawkins, this isn't like your typical land war," he informed me. "Nobody is safe. Our boys in the lead retaking these islands are always in harm's way, but this big ocean with its tiny landmasses is a challenge to secure, period. You just keep one eye up on the sky and the other fixed on the horizon. Cuz those Japanese soldiers, they don't quit."

I guess he was right, but that didn't make it any easier when they assigned Castle to a radio post with a C-46 crew attached to the Eighth. Being older and with three years of college under his belt, he had the advantage over me. I figured he'd stop coming around and start buddying up to the flyboys, but I misjudged him again. He continued to hang out with Frank and me.

George took another drag off his cigarette. He contemplated the letter in his hand. I could always tell when he got one from Josefina. His eyes, squinting through the smoke, held a faraway gaze.

He'd been lucky we shipped out from San Francisco. His whole family lived a little north of there in Marin County. Josefina and the baby, a girl named Rosa, were staying with his folks.

He got to spend time with the whole lot of them right before we left on Election Day, as it turned out. I was a bit envious, but in hindsight, the deployment went easier on the rest of us who hadn't seen our families in months. We were used to the distance and time apart.

Saying goodbye wears hard on the emotions. You can do it only so many times and maintain any semblance of manhood about you.

"Where do ya think we're going next?" I asked just to make conversation.

George and Frank grunted. Nobody ever knew the answer to that question.

General MacArthur had returned to the Philippines, like he said he would, but the fight had turned into the same long slog as with all these island battles. With us facing an entrenched enemy more than willing to lay down their lives if dying meant taking even one more of ours.

"Well, if MacArthur's in the Philippines," Castle suggested, "maybe that's where we're headed next."

Frank scoffed. He did that a lot, usually right before treating us to a screed on the follies of authority. He darted his eyes from side to side before saying under his breath, "I heard he walked onto the beach and then turned right around and walked back off."

"What do you expect him to do?" George asked. "Pick up a machine gun and lead a charge?"

"Yeah, maybe," Frank retorted. "They don't mind using us as cannon fodder. If those so-called great leaders got on the front lines themselves, they might be more careful with our lives."

George and I exchanged a painful look. Sometimes I wished Frank would just shut up. It's not like I blamed him for being resentful and all. After Guadalcanal and the staggering losses there, even the folks back home doubted the generals' decisions. But if we were to hold our nerve in the heat of battle, we needed to trust our leaders.

An airplane mechanic like me, I mostly got along fine with Frank. But ever since meeting up with him in Syracuse, he'd served up many a rant (he called them "discourses") on the corruption of the economic ruling class and their enforcers.

Believe you me. He didn't have anything good to say about either.

His full name was Frederick Mayer Hoffman, and he was Jewish on his mother's side. I didn't think he practiced the faith, though. In fact, I knew for certain he kept Christmas.

His dad's folks came from a small town in rural Washington, but most of his mom's family was still back in the old country. They were on Frank's mind a lot.

His parents tried to get them out a couple of years ago when things heated up with the Nazis. But no one came, and they've heard nothing since. I guess, like Kit's family, they just hoped for the best.

"Attention, men." The PA system popped and crackled. "All hands . . . we're shoving off for Leyte, the Philippines, with a three-destroyer escort."

A cheer arose from the men. Turns out Castle was right. We were off to the latest hot spot and bringing a whole lotta firepower with us.

Chapter Seven

Begin, be bold, and venture to be wise.
—Horace

The smell of fresh bread lured Meliz early from her bed, even though she had fallen asleep in the wee hours of the morning. She threw on a pair of loose-fitted hiking shorts and a linen blouse. With the leather satchel slung over her shoulder, she followed the comforting aroma to a bakery on the first floor of the building.

Meliz ordered a strong cup of coffee and a buttery *pandesal* and settled herself at a table on the shaded patio. The street and sidewalk shone wet from a night of rain, and the air dripped with moisture. A couple argued with quiet intensity at the next table over.

She crumbled a portion of the pastry on the ground, ostensibly for the birds, but in reality, as a superstitious offering to her personal travel gods for her safe arrival. Her laptop sat closed on the table as she perused a battered guidebook lent to her by the hotel staff. Meliz planned to visit some of the World War II sites in Manila before meeting Dr. Rivera for lunch.

Her mood darkened as she read the significance of many of the monuments. Meliz opened the computer and logged on to her website, writing: *I'm not surprised I knew nothing of the suffering of the*

Filipino people. The Pacific War always seems to get short shrift in the history books (not to mention popular culture). But from the moment the Japanese conquered these islands to when the Allied forces liberated them in 1945, the war had killed around 150,000 Filipino civilians—and that is a low estimate. They fought the main battle of liberation right here in Manila, the city laid to waste.

A single pulse beat hard against her temple, and she worked to slow her breathing—so much senseless loss of life. Somewhere between fifty to seventy million people died in the war. Meliz pushed the pastry away from her, sickened by the greed and conquest that had destroyed so many lives.

The urge to move, to purge her anger through action, propelled her from her seat. She gathered her belongings and left the quiet shade of the patio for the heat and bustle of Manila.

The taxi dropped her at the American Memorial Cemetery. A wide swath of green lawn marked by arching rows of white marble crosses lay before her, solemn and achingly sad. Unlike a normal cemetery, the vast majority of those buried here were young men, most not yet thirty.

The walls of the open-air galleries held murals and descriptions of the battles fought in the Philippines and throughout the Pacific Theater. Besides Meliz, only the groundskeepers and a couple bent with age and arms laden with colorful bouquets made tracks through the wet grass.

She walked the neat paths, tears perched on her lashes. Thousands of young lives ended here. Meliz imagined their stories cut short by a bullet, bayonet, or grenade.

How many gravesites had been visited by widows or children or grandchildren like her? How many grieving parents made the pilgrimage to this peaceful place to stand before the memorial of a dead child? Meliz wiped her eyes, thankful her grief was in the abstract, that she had no personal connection to this hallowed ground.

She took a moment to upload a video of the cemetery to her website and caught a taxi to the University of Santo Tomas Museum. Here, the Japanese established the largest internment camp in the Philippines. The exhibits revealed the inhumanity of the camp in unflinching black-and-white.

Meliz stood transfixed before a photograph of two men who sat in conversation on the concrete steps of a rundown building. They leaned in, heads close together, intent on what the other was saying, a portrait of normalcy. She had passed many such scenes living in New York City. Except, in this picture, the men were clearly starving to death.

Their shirtless chests caved inward, and the curves of their ribs protruded in a grotesque parody of the human body. The horror of their situation was made even more wrenching by the men's casual pose of neighborly conversation—just another day in the concentration camp.

Meliz shook her head in an effort to dispel the pressure building behind her eyes. She walked off her lingering sadness by touring the grounds and paused to write on a bench near the magnificent nineteenth-century building that housed the museum.

I am posting a link to the prison photography from the internment camp. The pictures are not for the faint of heart.

A short taxi ride later, Meliz stepped out onto the cobbled streets of the colonial Intramuros District of Manila. Few of the original structures in this historic part of the city still stood. Most of the buildings, along with the walls and gates that had encircled the district, did not survive the sustained bombing of the Battle of Manila. Over seventy years later, the government struggled to restore the area to its pre-war condition.

The aroma of spices and roasting shrimp drew Meliz with unerring precision to the restaurant's doorstep. Tucked away into a whitewashed building with balconies overlooking the street, tourists, students, and workers on their lunch break packed the tables. Servers whisked by with laden, sizzling trays, miraculously avoiding collision.

Meliz sat at a table in the courtyard and fidgeted, anxious not to miss Dr. Rivera in the crowded restaurant. She had not sat in on any of his lectures during his year as a visiting scholar, but felt certain she would recognize the slight, bespectacled Filipino from her attendance at a fundraiser for the survivors of typhoon Haiyan.

A few short minutes later, he walked with a brisk step and sharp eye through the ivy-covered arch in search of her. She waved and pushed her chair back to stand, bumping into a tiny woman with a heavy tray full of water glasses.

Meliz caught a tipping glass with one hand and steadied the woman with the other. "I'm so sorry. I didn't—"

"It's fine." The woman returned a tight smile. "No harm done." She sped away without another word.

"Smart move bumping into the waitress. I was sure to spot you," Dr. Rivera teased. "Quick save too."

"Well, you know, red belt in taekwondo." Meliz made awkward little karate chops in the air. "Lightning reflexes and all that." She rolled her eyes at her lack of subtlety and stuck out her hand. "Thanks for meeting me, Dr.—"

"Garrett, please," he insisted and took her hand in a firm grasp. "My pleasure, and anyway your research sounds intriguing."

She grimaced. "Research isn't the most accurate term for what I'm doing. My process is a bit more, um, random, more like fact-finding."

A server interrupted them, handing out menus. They sat, and Garrett helped her to choose. Meliz ordered *pancit*, a traditional Filipino dish of dry noodles topped with hard-boiled egg, vegetables, and shrimp.

Once the man left, Garrett settled back in his chair. "Even with fact-finding, a reference or starting point is important. Your grandfather's unit first landed in New Guinea, right?"

"No . . . I mean, yeah, they arrived first in New Guinea, but never got off the boat. JD was sloppy with dates. From what I can figure, they landed in Leyte around November 28, 1944. They stayed there a few weeks, and after that moved to Biak Island, New Guinea, where they remained for a couple of months before returning here. I'd hoped you might know what they did or how they operated."

Garrett nodded with a professorial clearing of his throat. "They did what the name implies, cargo, whether it was troops, weapons, or equipment. The planes, the C-46 and C-47, were incredible workhorses. They pulled some daring runs throughout the Pacific and over the Himalayas. These planes, their crews, and support units were instrumental in countering a mobile and fast-moving enemy. I believe the C-47 is still in operation."

He shrugged, dispelling any notions of scholarly omniscience. "Sorry, that's all I know about the combat cargo groups in general. I don't know anything about your grandfather's unit in particular, but I did read the scanned file you sent of his journal."

"All of it?" Meliz looked at him in disbelief. "It takes me hours just to decipher a few pages. The transcript would have been easier."

Garrett laughed. "I'm a teacher. Believe me. I've seen worse." He sobered and leaned toward her. "I prefer to review original sources, if at all possible. His journal is fascinating stuff. A study of JD Hawkins as a young writer, the emphasis he puts on the themes of courage and friendship and how those topics follow through to his succeeding works . . ." He sat back with a sheepish smile. "I'm sure I am not telling you anything you don't already know. I'm just surprised his war record wasn't a bigger part of his biography."

Meliz chose her next words with care. "I used to think he was kind of ashamed of his war years. His service wasn't something he considered heroic. JD was a great romantic in the grand romance sense." Tears started in her eyes. She traced the pattern on the tablecloth, avoiding his gaze. "You know, the young man searching for meaning and striving against adversity thing. The fact he wasn't on the front lines with a combat unit . . . well, it bothered him, like he didn't do enough."

Garrett nodded his understanding. "I get it. He wasn't tortured by the terrible things he'd seen and done. Very writerly."

"Yeah." She laughed, regaining her equilibrium. "But after reading his journal and finding the torn-out entry, I think it was something else. I mean, he did have a romantic view of the war, a need to be tested as a man. But . . ."

Garrett raised his eyebrows.

"I think he saw something that was hushed up." Her words spilled out in a rush. "He witnessed an event that hit him hard."

"This entry you mentioned, do you have it with you?"

She pulled from her bag the photocopy of the original journal page. "The writing is messy, but I've tried to clarify where the words were illegible."

Their food arrived while he read. Once finished, he placed the journal entry on the table beside his plate. "Well, that's certainly something."

Meliz swallowed a mouthful of noodles. "Isn't it? That officer sounds menacing."

"Yes," he agreed. "But your grandfather isn't afraid for himself alone. He's worried about this girl and her brother."

"I know."

Garrett frowned. "Regardless, it's strange he didn't tell the officer about them. That lieutenant pulled him into nothing less than an interrogation where any good soldier would have given a full account to his superior. Instead, your grandfather lied about what he'd seen and who was with him."

Meliz put down her fork. A tight, invisible band squeezed her chest. "What are you getting at?"

"From reading the journal, I got the impression insubordination would have been out of character for him. Your grandfather expressed the typical attitude most enlisted men had toward the brass, so to speak. There were admirable officers, and others he viewed with dislike, even contempt, but he was a good soldier. He believed in the rules and followed them."

"So, him lying means what?" The chatter of patrons, clatter of dishes, and background music fell mute as she focused on Garrett's answer.

"I'm not sure. Your grandfather might have reacted differently if confronted by an officer he liked or admired. He obviously doesn't know or trust this man, and he's not going to put his life or those of the kids at risk. Still, lying to a superior is a big breach of military protocol, and he knew it."

"He was afraid, worried the officer might come after him," Meliz countered, feeling the need to defend JD.

"Yeah, I hear you. But collecting journals and letters for censorship amounted to nothing more than standard procedure. It's not as if your grandfather was singled out. I've seen plenty of documents with blacked-out writing and blunt tips of pages where razors had removed them. They were fighting a war after all, and intelligence gathering meant serious business on both sides. Keeping as much information under wraps as possible was important and necessary."

Garrett rested his chin in his hand and stared down at the table. "Hmm."

"Hmm, what?" she prompted.

He sat up. "I'm not sure, but sending an intelligence type to issue a veiled threat to a rank-and-file enlisted man reeks of panic or, at the very least, alarm. The war was over, but whatever involved your grandfather . . . well, people were obviously spooked."

Meliz took a deep breath to lessen the tightness in her chest. She had allotted herself three weeks to dig up something. She did not intend to waste time. "I need to find out what happened to him."

He laughed. "Is that all?"

"It's going to be hard, huh?"

"You'll excuse my bluntness, but a lot of shit went down. That stuff either never got recorded or is buried so deep it would take serious digging to find documentation. And if the action was an unofficial, off-the-books operation, there's no telling . . ." He threw his hands up in a gesture of helplessness.

Meliz sat back and heaved a deep, dejected sigh. She caught her reflection in a mirrored wall. Dark, heavily lashed eyes stared back at her with disappointment.

"You have a lousy poker face," Wendy always joked.

Meliz could not deny that her emotions ran just below the surface. Like JD, she harbored a sentimental nature.

Straightening in her chair, she nodded with determination. "I've got to try."

He grinned. "Okay, then, I'll help you."

"Thank you," she replied with heartfelt sincerity.

"'No need to thank me, ma'am . . .'" he declared in a ridiculous attempt at a cowboy accent.

"'. . . my duty is who I am,'" they ended together.

He laughed, and Meliz nodded with weary acknowledgement. Marshal Clyde Jameson catchphrases occupied a unique place in popular culture. Her grandfather had scattered them throughout the series. In recent years, they popped up outside his novels as favorite source material for internet memes. Even decades after Marshal Jameson brought his last bad guy to justice, JD made up new catchphrases and texted them to her, resplendent with emojis.

"I'm guessing this isn't the first time you've heard that," Garrett said as they paid the check and stepped outside into the hot summer afternoon. Cars and bicycles bounced by on the cobblestone road, rattling loose hubcaps and fenders.

"Hardly."

"Well, *Long Ride to Morning* is my favorite," he informed her.

"I haven't read that one. But I've heard the phrase repeated on reruns of the old TV show."

The television series had been a sore spot with JD. It lasted four seasons in the mid-sixties. Titled *The Marshal*, the show starred Rex Stevens, a western B-movie staple from the previous decade. JD had angled for a bigger name and better talent, but the executives wanted the much-cheaper-to-retain Stevens.

"Puffed up, no-talent peacock," always followed any mention of the actor's name in JD's presence. Meliz disagreed with his harsh assessment of the man's abilities. Stevens's performance lacked nuance, and he missed the wry humor integral to the character in print, but he did convey the manly compassion and sense of upright duty at the core of Clyde Jameson.

The show was a big hit, but after Rex broke his back in a drunken fall down a staircase, the producers decided not to recast the character and cancelled the series. JD had the good grace not to show his relief whenever the subject came up, but often grumbled, "At least he couldn't butcher any more of my dialogue." The series never went out of syndication, a lasting source of irritation for her grandfather.

"You haven't read all the books?" Garrett asked, his tone a tad judgmental.

"There *are* twenty-eight," she countered in her defense, not revealing she had read only two. Her justification being that by the time she was born, JD had moved on to writing massive histories of West Texas. All of which she *had* read.

Garrett brought himself up short. "Whoa."

"What is it?"

"I can't believe it . . . I'm going to have to check . . ." He looked off into the distance.

"What is it?" Meliz repeated.

He refocused his eyes on her face and intoned, "*Everything Touches the Sky.*"

"Are you referring to one of the Marshal Jameson books?"

"Yeah, the next to last one in the series, number twenty-seven."

"So?"

"Well, the plot . . . I read the book years ago, when I was a kid. I need to find a copy." His wiry frame coiled for action. He poised, ready to take off.

"Wait." She grabbed his arm. "What about the plot?"

He blushed. "Sorry, I get carried away when I'm on to something." The gleam of excitement in his eyes was the same as in JD's when he was chasing down facts for a new book.

A sharp burst of jealousy surprised Meliz. Garret, someone she had just met and graciously allowed on her personal quest, now appeared to be a few steps ahead of her. She suppressed her resentment. "The plot?"

"Okay, well, *Everything Touches the Sky* is considered one of the best in the series, if not *the* best. The plot's bleaker than his usual style, and the book features an orphaned Comanche girl and her little brother. You know, like the kids he mentioned in the journal entry."

Meliz cocked her head to one side. "Sounds a bit far-fetched."

"I know. A little out there for sure. But why not dress up a traumatic event as fiction? Especially if he couldn't speak openly about the incident. Right?"

"Yeah, I guess." She let go of his arm. "I'll ask Alberta to check out the book. She's his collaborator."

"Of course, you would have the definitive set. But I might be able to run down an old paperback."

"Check its Wiki page. Most of the books have detailed summaries and lists of characters."

Garrett grunted his derision. "I don't like leaving my research to anonymous internet contributors, no matter how well-meaning." He glanced down at his watch.

"Can you do me a favor?" Meliz asked before he could leave. "Will you check your sources for anything unusual that happened in Okinawa sometime between August 14 and September 2, 1945—maybe on or near Bolo Point Airfield where JD was stationed? The missing pages are between those two dates."

"Will do." He winked a friendly goodbye and sped off, disappearing into the crowd.

Meliz smiled after him. His enthusiasm touched her. JD would have liked him.

She contemplated the ground, and her sight grew vague. The sun burned hot on the back of her neck. Why had she not told Garrett about the *Life* article with the photograph of JD and the children?

The image seemed to confirm the girl and her brother as central to the mystery. It might even support Garrett's theory about the plot of JD's book.

A shadow fell over her. She squinted up into the sky. Swift clouds raced in from the ocean to make their routine delivery of afternoon rain.

Her stomach clenched in a familiar little twist of dread. What did his secrecy hide? She could be making a huge mistake exposing JD to the scrutiny of historians.

Until the discovery of his tickets and itinerary, she believed her grandfather to be a man without a clandestine bone in his body. Yet, he had planned and schemed in secret. He held close the details of his little covert operation. He left those dearest to him in the dark, an action so unlike her gregarious grandfather as to seem incomprehensible.

Whatever haunted memory lingered in his past, it had tugged at him, never completely letting go. JD was a man on a mission, and now she intended to finish it.

Meliz shouldered the small leather satchel and turned back toward the main road in search of a taxicab.

Chapter Eight

Advantage is a better soldier than rashness.
—H.G. Bohn

A sudden storm plastered Meliz's blouse to her skin. The rain and heat had driven most people into air-conditioned stores and restaurants.

She flagged down a taxi and stared, transfixed, at the deluge, mentally adding "umbrella" to the list of things she needed to get. The taxi set her down in front of her hotel, the rain now a mere steamy haze.

The pension sat atop several businesses on a tree-lined avenue in a quiet, working-class neighborhood of Manila. The building's ornate latticework and bright pink paint resembled a top-heavy wedding cake and starkly contrasted with the exposed concrete walls of the businesses below.

The modest lodgings took up several floors and covered half a block. The bakery, a watch repair shop, and a woman's boutique formed its foundation.

Meliz inhaled the scent of gardenias as she walked down a narrow alleyway to the entrance at the back of the building. Laundry flapped in the humid breeze on the balconies of the neighboring apartments.

The gardenias' perfume followed her up a creaky staircase to the reception area where the chemical smell of bleach cleanser overwhelmed the delicate fragrance. Meliz got her key at the desk and went up another two flights to the fourth floor.

Three rooms occupied the short hallway, and two large bowed balconies overlooked the street below. Hot, heavy air shifted in from the opened French doors of the balconies. Clean and simple, she preferred these budget lodgings to the sleeker hotels in the more upscale part of the city.

"I scared off an intruder."

Meliz had not noticed the woman obscured by the French doors and standing halfway in the hall and halfway out onto the balcony. "Excuse me?"

"A man tried to get into your room. I scared him off when I left this morning." She nodded toward her own room at the other end of the hallway.

Meliz turned, her hand still poised with the room key in the air. The woman had delivered this alarming piece of news in a distinct German accent.

A few years older than Meliz, she sported a shaggy, blonde crop, unkempt in a blasé European fashion. Patched cutoff shorts exposed a long length of thin legs, and a loose, tank top revealed taut, sinewy arms. Like a stylish scarecrow, she held a cigarette in one hand and a coffee mug in the other. She flicked a length of ash into the empty cup.

"Someone tried to get into my room this morning?" Meliz attempted to clarify.

"Mm-hmm. Around ten thirty."

She dropped the key into her satchel. "Did you get a good look at him?"

"I didn't see his face. Dark green hoodie, jeans, and tennis shoes, that's about it. His hand was on the doorknob, but he ran off when I came out." She leaned against the frame where the French doors opened out onto the balcony.

"How did you know it wasn't his room?"

The woman took a deep drag on the cigarette and turned her head to blow the smoke outside. "Men aren't allowed past the second floor."

"Really? I hadn't heard. Why?"

"The owner is a former Catholic nun from Italy."

"Really?" Meliz repeated.

"*Ja*, really. She left the Church to marry, but is still very devout. The second floor is for men, and the third and fourth, for women only."

"How did you know? I didn't see a sign or anything."

"The rule is on their website." Her mouth twisted into a world-weary sneer. "I don't think the ex-nun would be so happy if she knew this attracted a lot of lesbians. Do you?" The woman stubbed out her cigarette.

Meliz laughed and stuck out her hand. "Well, thanks for scaring him off. I'm Meliz, by the way."

"Brigitte," the German woman offered in return, taking her hand in a firm grip. "Are you here long?"

"No. Well, I hope not," she amended, remembering her conversation with Garrett. "I'm doing some fact-finding on my grandfather who was here during the war, and I want to get out to Leyte."

Brigitte nodded, a sage expression on her face. "There is a lot more Japanese interest in the war these days."

"What?" Meliz tensed.

"There are more Japanese visiting the war memorials than in the past," she explained with the confidence of a local passing on helpful information. "I saw one of their tour groups just yesterday. Some of them looked old enough to be veterans. Ask around. Who knows? Maybe one of them served with your grandfather."

Frustration welled up in Meliz. The self-assured assumptions of stupid White people never failed to amaze her. How many times had she reminded those around her she was not "half Asian-half American?" As if her White mother was the only real American in the family.

Meliz longed to slap back with a quippy retort, to enlighten this blonde-haired, blue-eyed European of the heroic efforts and tremendous losses of the Chinese and Filipino fighters. There was more than one Asian story of the war. She clenched her jaw with suppressed fury.

Or maybe she should just ask Brigitte about her family's Nazi past. The woman was German, after all. How would that go over?

Meliz released a weary sigh. She could never do quippy, and her natural reserve shied away from directly offending anyone. At least Brigitte hadn't tried to place her ancestry in some mythical former Soviet Bloc country.

"I'm not of Japanese ancestry. My grandfather was a White American," she explained. "His daughter is my mother. My father is ethnic Chinese and also an American."

Brigitte's hip, worldly demeanor fell away. "*Dummkopf*," she exclaimed, and actually slapped her forehead with the now cigarette-free hand. "I am sorry, *ja*. I thought the war . . . and your grandfather . . . and you look . . . I am stupid. You must think stupid German, *ja* . . . stupid Aryan." Frustrated with her inarticulate response, she sputtered, "Fuck the Nazis."

Meliz laughed at this unexpected outburst. "No, I didn't think you were stupid," she lied. "I'm sensitive to the whole race thing. You know, always explaining what I am."

"Sure, I get it. My dumb mistake." Brigitte grinned with infectious self-awareness. "Maybe I'm not so cool."

"Oh, I don't know. You seem pretty cool to me."

Brigitte waved aside the compliment and pushed away from the doorframe. "Some friends and I are going out tonight, a club on the beach. Listen to music . . . dance. It will be fun. You can come?"

Her muscles heavy with jetlag, Meliz fought the urge to turn in early. She also didn't want to appear resentful. "Sure. What time?"

"I'll meet you back here at nine thirty, okay?"

"Yeah, great."

Brigitte disappeared down the staircase, and Meliz went into her room. She stood just inside the door and scanned the small area. Though nothing appeared disturbed from earlier that morning, a gentle prickling at the back of her neck sent her pulse racing and heightened her senses.

Meliz had shared with JD a love of mysteries. For her twelfth birthday, he gave her the complete works of Agatha Christie, and from there she branched out to Wilkie Collins, Ellis Peters, John le Carré, and more.

They tried to guess the solution to mystery movies and police procedurals so often JD invented an elaborate awards system to keep track of their mystery-solving prowess. "The biggest hurdle," he had explained, "is winning a Christie Badge. You can't win any other award until you get your Christie."

Solving police procedurals earned one a Marple Cluster. Later, JD added the Hercule Ribbon for more complex and cerebral puzzles. No real awards ever existed, but she loved the challenge, and the mysteries honed her observational skills.

Like her crime-solving heroes, Meliz paid attention to her intuition. She closed the door behind her and walked around the room noting the position of her belongings. The window unit hummed on low, blanketing the small space in a comforting white noise.

She opened the plantation shutters. A group of children kicked a soccer ball around the narrow alleyway behind the building. Wrought iron bars covered the pension's windows to discourage casual thievery in this poorer part of the city. A sheer wall dropped away from her room with no latticework or trellis to provide a foothold. There was no way anyone could get into or out of her room from the alleyway.

A flash of sunlight reflected off glass and drew her attention to the apartment building opposite. Windows, like hundreds of staring eyes, peered back at her. Who would risk a ladder or rope with all those potential witnesses?

Meliz turned back to the room and swept it again with a critical eye. The double bed stood flush against one wall flanked by two bedside tables. A heavy, decorative steamer trunk sat at the foot of the bed, upon which she had placed her daypack. Her large backpack rested on the floor, leaning against the trunk. Across from the bed stood a dark oak dresser, on top of which were her toiletries and an unopened water bottle.

On the desk were a notebook and a file folder containing maps of the Pacific Islands, the old photograph of JD and his two friends, and the *Life* magazine page. She had taken her laptop, camera, JD's journal, and the photocopy with her that morning.

Meliz flipped through the file folder. Nothing was missing, but her unease deepened as she struggled to remember in what order she had left the papers.

She paused, indecisive, in the middle of the room. The hairs on the back of her neck still stood on end. Meliz could not shake the feeling that Brigitte hadn't surprised the man trying to get into her room, but coming out of it instead.

Chapter Nine

Forewarned, forearmed; to be prepared is half the victory.
—Cervantes

A ping alerted Meliz to a text message. She swiped a thin coat of gloss across her lips and reached for her cell phone perched on the rim of the bathroom sink. The phone slipped from her fingers and fell onto the hard, water-splashed porcelain.

"Shit." She snatched it from the sink and quickly wiped the phone with a towel.

"Dammit," she cursed again, noting a new scratch across the screen as she read Alberta's message: *I checked out Walker Inc. as you asked. They look legit. The founder, Jack Prescott Walker, Sr., partnered with wealthy Filipino families after the war. As you suspected, he's a vet. They play his service up in the company lore, but there is nothing specific. I'll keep digging.*

Meliz typed back: *Thanks. Any luck with JD's old army buddies?*

A quick, answering ping: *Not much, almost everyone has died. I did talk with Eugene Gibson's son. Both Bobbie Stanton and Freddie Brinks were killed in the war. And your alias, George Castle, had two kids, neither of which I've had any luck contacting. No trace of Frank Hoffman either. I also put in a request for JD's army records, but they told me it could take several weeks to get them.*

Meliz ran a comb through her hair. She slipped some money and her ID into the pocket of her skirt.

Another ping: *Almost forgot. I read the entire website for the 2nd Combat Cargo Group and their Airdrome Squadrons. The information was basic, their deployment, stories, all limited to the officer or flight crew perspective, nothing helpful.*

Just like Alberta to be so thorough. Meliz typed a quick reply: *Wow! Thanks again. When you get a breather, could you look through our copy of "Everything Touches the Sky?" Garrett thinks the plot might reveal something about the incident. After reading the summary online, he may be onto something. The publishers haven't converted that one into an e-book. So, I can't get a copy. Sorry, I know you're busy.*

Alberta's response was short and sad: *Pile it on. I've been a little rudderless since your grandfather died. The more work, the better.*

Meliz sniffed and blinked back tears. She typed in return, *<3*

**

She met Brigitte at the reception desk. Meliz had changed from her shorts into a simple print skirt and white camisole. Other than lip gloss, she wore no makeup. She had learned her lesson long ago. The habit of rubbing her eyes, especially in sweaty surroundings, combined with mascara and eyeliner, resulted in raccoon eyes by the end of the evening.

Her new friend wore the exact same outfit: patched cutoffs and a tank top.

"It is all I have," Brigitte explained.

"I get traveling light, but one set of clothes seems a bit extreme," Meliz replied, amused.

She shrugged. "I have ten pairs of underwear. I'm good."

During the taxi ride, Brigitte regaled Meliz with a disjointed mix of interwoven stories of how she had met each of her friends, all involving a bar, or a bus stop, or getting high on a boat somewhere.

"On the beach" wasn't the most accurate description of the club, a squat, plank-wood building situated blocks from the water. The club's doors opened out onto a dark and smelly street. Sleeping gulls perched along the eaves like restless gargoyles, waiting for morning and the garbage truck.

Brigitte's friends formed an eclectic group. They stood together in a circle outside Deejays, and she introduced everyone in haphazard fashion.

Like a latter-day Marlene Dietrich, Brigitte struck a movie star pose and, in between drags, pointed at each person with her cigarette. "This is Hans, German, obviously . . . Minka, Ukrainian . . . Jubal, Australian . . . Um, um," she stuttered, pointing to a tall Asian man in a well-tailored suit.

He nodded and offered, "Hikaru Ikeda."

"*Ja, ja,* Hikaru, Japanese . . . and Julia, Austrian. And this," she pronounced with dramatic emphasis, "is Meliz, American."

A flurry of nods and shaken hands followed as everyone tried to remember names and countries of origin. Meliz suppressed a yawn and brought up the rear as they traipsed into the club and were engulfed in flashing lights and deafening music.

The rundown club tended toward seedy, but the music pulsed with a world beat and alcohol flowed cheap and abundant. Air circulating in from the open doors did little to lessen the sweaty atmosphere in the crowded club. Meliz wrinkled her nose at the odor of cigarettes and rotting trash drifting in from outside.

She found a barstool and ordered a San Miguel Pale Pilsen. The vinyl cushion stuck to her bare thighs, and she shifted, smoothing her skirt more securely under her.

A break in sets allowed her ears to readjust, and Meliz seized on those brief moments to talk to her group. Most of them admitted to vacationing, except for Hikaru, who stated business as his purpose in Manila.

After some mild resistance, she danced with Hans for one song but sat out the rest, preferring instead to people watch and catch snippets of conversation. Hikaru soon left, using an early morning meeting as an excuse. The rest partied on, drinking and dancing.

An hour later, the full effects of jetlag kicked in, and Meliz drooped over her lukewarm beer. She ached to catch a cab back to the pension, but could not leave Brigitte.

Her friend wove and stumbled in and out among the dancers, eyelids heavy and arms swaying over her head. Meliz suspected, from Brigitte's vacant look and general stupor, she had consumed more than just alcohol. The others appeared in the same state and paid her friend little mind. Except for the Australian, Jubal, who succeeded in slipping a sweaty paw under Brigitte's shorts before Meliz could intervene.

The chances of getting the German woman into a cab without protest slipped further away with each successive shot of tequila. Meliz pushed off the barstool and steeled herself for the scene to come.

She dove into the thrashing crowd. With a mixture of poking elbows and apologetic smiles, Meliz reached Brigitte in time to catch her as she stumbled.

"Let's get outta here," she urged with a gentle tug at her friend's arm. "Come on."

Brigitte grasped Meliz's hands and swayed. "Let's dance," she shouted, her slurred words sounding more like "letsants."

Meliz leaned in close and yelled in Brigitte's ear, "I'm exhausted. Let's go. We can party another night."

Brigitte pulled away. "You go." She patted Meliz's cheek with a lazy hand and turned, waving a goodbye over her shoulder.

Meliz groaned and made her way back to the barstool. This always happened to her. She had a magnetic attraction for the erratic and irresponsible, as if some cosmic force was forever trying her own reliable and cautious nature.

She would not leave Brigitte in her condition. Meliz dropped her head onto her crossed arms, resigned to the next miserable few hours.

"Fancy meeting you here."

Startled, she looked up into the clear hazel eyes of . . . "Jack Prescott Walker the Third," she announced to no one in particular, and stopped herself from adding, "of all the gin joints in all the towns," asking instead, "Did you just get here?"

A driving guitar riff forced him to shout. "Yeah, a few minutes ago." He nodded in the direction of the stage. "The lead singer is a family friend. He's the grandson of one of Pops's original partners."

"Bet there aren't many of those left—original partners, that is," she joked and then shook her head. "Sorry, bad one. I'm exhausted."

Prescott laughed anyway. "It's okay, and true. Pops is ninety-seven. He's the last of the founders."

"Wow. I did not think he was that old. He seems pretty spry. I'm surprised he's not here."

He laughed again. "Oh no, the old man's always in bed by nine o'clock. Which is somewhere you should be if you don't mind me saying?"

"I don't mind you saying at all," she countered, forgiving the implication she must somehow *look* like she needed sleep. "And I wholeheartedly agree, but my friend's shitfaced, and she won't leave. If I wait until she passes out, I'm going to have a hell of a time getting her into a cab. Anyway, I can't leave her."

Prescott's perceptive gaze homed in on Brigitte's swaying form. "Can I help?"

Meliz sized up the handsome face and trim figure dressed in a casual black T-shirt and jeans. He radiated reliable masculinity. He even smelled nice and appeared to be her best shot at enticing Brigitte away from the sleazy Jubal.

"Yup, I think you'll do."

Five minutes later, they stood on the curb, Prescott supporting a limp Brigitte while Meliz flagged down a cab. A rickety number with one headlight soon stopped. Meliz climbed into the back seat and pulled her friend in beside her. Prescott slipped in next to Brigitte and shut the door.

"Thanks, but you don't have to come with us," Meliz asserted. "You'll want to stay for your friend."

"It's no problem. I wasn't up to hanging out tonight. Anyway, you won't be able to get her to her room on your own."

Meliz relented in the face of this very accurate observation. Prescott told the driver their address, and they drove off in awkward silence.

Sitting between them, the blissed-out Brigitte ran her hand up Prescott's thigh, murmuring, "You smell good." He averted the maneuver by gently, yet firmly placing her hand back on her own lap.

At the pension, Prescott gave up any pretense of Brigitte walking and picked her up as they climbed the stairs. The lobby lights flickered and hummed while the night receptionist nodded off behind the desk. He gave Meliz the keys and attempted to enforce the "no men above the second floor" rule, but made a hasty exception when Prescott offered to hand Brigitte off to him. He waved them past the desk with a sour look.

Hot, sticky air from the open balcony washed over them as they reached the fourth floor and stopped at Brigitte's door. Meliz fumbled with the key in the lock before hearing it release. The door swung open, and she flicked on the light.

She paused on the threshold, struck by the clean and orderly surroundings. Meliz had expected a room as messy and chaotic as Brigitte's personality, but her friend had not exaggerated.

Instead of a steamer trunk, a low chaise lounge footed the bed, upon which Brigitte had placed her one piece of luggage: a large Thai sling bag. A comb and a twisted tube of hair gel sat atop the dresser.

"Pull back the covers," Prescott instructed before laying Brigitte on the bed.

Meliz placed the key on the bedside table, and they stood looking down at the sleeping woman. With a self-conscious smile, she checked Brigitte's pulse. A bit of overkill, but her friend *had* mixed drugs.

"How are her vitals?" Amusement shaded his voice.

She cast Prescott a sheepish look. "Amazingly strong and steady. She needs to sleep it off. That's all."

Meliz engaged the lock as they walked out and shut the door. She hesitated, troubled at not being able to throw the deadbolt.

"She'll be fine," Prescott reassured her.

They lingered for a moment in the hallway, the pension quiet and still around them. Prescott strolled over to the balcony.

He paused in the warm air drifting in from the open doors. "Nice little place."

Meliz joined him. "Yeah, my room's simple, but comfortable, and there's a bakery downstairs. Makes getting up in the morning easy."

He laughed.

That made three. He had laughed at all of her jokes, no matter how feeble.

They looked out the French doors toward the looming Manila skyline. The buildings stood in a jumbled array of shapes and sizes. They reminded Meliz of nothing so much as a random grouping of people on a subway platform.

"How long are you in Manila?" Prescott asked, still staring out at the city.

"A couple of days, then I'm off to Leyte."

"Think you'll have time for dinner while you're here?"

Lights from the cityscape glittered in the humid air, and the ever-present smell of bleach cleanser prickled Meliz's nose. Laughter floated up from the street below and held the promise of sex. She imagined the arguing couple from earlier that morning had made up. A shiver ran up her spine.

Prescott's easy-going personality lowered her defenses, and his strong, boney hands sent her pulse racing. She experienced the odd sensation of being both relaxed and aroused.

A few strands of gray lay sprinkled in at his temples. If she ran her hand through his hair and drew him close, he would kiss her. His arms would tighten around her, his kisses becoming more insistent. He would pull away only to trail his lips down her neck. Meliz would close her eyes and let the sensation wash over her.

They would go into her room. It could be so easy . . .

She sighed. Her imagination faded in the face of jetlag and temptation fell before the weight of exhaustion.

"Sure. I think dinner would be great," she answered.

The moment passed with a twinge of regret. She went with him to the lobby and watched as he descended the stairs and left.

"Can I have my computer and camera, please?" she asked the receptionist, having left them at the front desk as a precaution.

Half asleep, the churlish young man pulled her belongings from the shelf where they stowed valuables and shoved them in her direction. Without a word, he walked back to his stool and plopped down. He slumped against the wall and closed his eyes.

"Thank you," she said in an overloud voice, her tone sweetly sarcastic. She made a face in his direction and imagined jerking the stool out from under him.

Meliz rebuked herself for such spiteful thoughts and trudged up the stairs. She needed sleep before she actually indulged in one of her overheated fantasies.

In her room, Meliz pulled off the camisole and slipped out of her skirt. She stood over the desk and flipped open the file folder. The *Life* article with the photograph rested on top.

The edition in which the picture appeared came out months after the war ended and featured an article on its devastating aftermath. She imagined her grandfather buying the magazine from a newsstand, unaware of his presence within its pages. Perhaps he flipped through the publication over lunch or after dinner, doing a double take at his captured memory.

Meliz closed the folder, shutting out the stark image. Exhaustion pressed down on her. She gazed with longing at the bed, but forced herself to brush her teeth before giving in to sleep.

**

Meliz gasped and sat up in bed. A vague suspicion had startled her awake, resurfacing from her subconscious to knock loudly on her frontal lobe. She clutched at the crisp cotton sheet and worked to steady her racing heart.

A quick glance at her phone put the time at 5:42 a.m., less than thirty minutes to sunrise. She slipped out of bed and walked to the window, pushing aside the heavy curtains to look out on the grayness of predawn.

Meliz had seen in Prescott and his grandfather a gentle reminder of her loss. The sight of the fragile old man with his doting grandson closed her throat and tightened her chest. Simple curiosity had prompted her to ask Alberta to look into them. Her own hasty search revealed little beyond the most basic facts of their business.

She dropped the curtains and turned back to the room. In the airport . . . at the club . . . She rubbed her eyes. Fatigue and anxiety increased her uncertainty.

Meliz ran her hands through her hair. Her pulse had slowed, but a feeling of intense unease lingered.

"When you taste as good as a deer, you're skittish for a reason." JD had sent that catchphrase to her with a smiling deer face emoji.

Meliz compressed her lips and straightened her shoulders. "I'm not a stupid deer," she whispered, determined to cast off her indecision and trust her instincts.

Prescott had given the driver the pension's address, but she had not told him where they were staying. Meliz was sure of it.

Chapter Ten

Be strong, and quit yourselves like men.
—I Sam. IV: 9

28 Nov., 1944, Leyte, Philippines—We're here, got in at night with the sea black as pitch. Rain fell in torrents and soaked us to the skin in a matter of seconds. When the sun came up, we got a good look at the island. Ragged and beat-up, the beach overflowed with supplies: everything you could imagine, any kind of army equipment your heart desired.

Right about then, the air raid sounded. Shots fired from the 90mm anti-aircraft gun. The *General Hersey* threw everything it had up at them, except my GI boots.

I want off this boat bad. We are the only troop transport in anchorage and make a damn good target.

I can't sleep.

29 Nov.—Today we disembarked. Ducks transported us to shore. About fifteen or twenty meters out, the air raid siren went off again. Luckily, we weren't raided. Our P-38s must have intercepted them. When we got ashore, what a sight met us: equipment; wounded; engineers working on a road, up to their necks in mud; ducks hauling men and supplies ashore. Also the enemy, over the hill, about ten miles away.

They told us to hunker down on the beach. We sat on our barracks bags while the rain pounded down, all of us wet and bad-tempered. We put up pup tents about fifteen feet from the water. Some of the guys had to pull up stakes and go higher to keep the tide from washing them out. After that, they told us to dig foxholes. We had to stay in them most of the night, even though mine filled with sand and water by morning.

Our second day on the beach, and we are all resigned to being soaked to the skin. The rain never stops. And the mud . . . I could write a book on the mud of Leyte.

2 Dec.—Finally off the beach, though still in the little pup tents. I share one with Frank. We argue a lot. Sometimes, I want to slug him. Normally, I'd bunk with George, but he's in with Miller, who is also on a flight crew. They share a schedule, so it's easier that way.

Things are hot here: bombings, strafing, snipers, and patrols. Our guys killed a Japanese company about six hundred yards from the road. They worry troops behind the lines by slipping in among the tents and killing grunts as they sleep. We have to carry our weapon at all times.

10 Dec.—The days are too wet and muddy to write more than brief snippets of my day.

11 Dec.—We got a shock today. Almost two weeks on Leyte and we found out we're not even supposed to be here. They say our billet is in New Guinea. Six miles from the front, and now it looks like the brass is going to push us further back—all the way back to New Guinea.

They told us we would be moving to a more permanent position tomorrow. I guess that New Guinea angle was just a rumor.

**

Leyte, Philippines, December 1944

"I used to love the rain." I stared out the sodden tent flap. "Back home, it always arrived like an event, like a gift. The rain rolled in behind a cold front and wave of electrified air. You could see it coming from miles off, a blue curtain falling from the sky. Heavy showers washed away the heat and dirt and sweat of a summer day. Here, the rain is like a never-ending plague. It flows everywhere, into everything, leaching away life and color."

"Well, that's real poetic, Hawk." Frank sighed with a hint of weary scorn. "Why don't you write that one down?" I could hear the eye roll in his voice.

Frank and I were not exactly getting along. Seems like close quarters and a constant wear on our nerves didn't make for the type of camaraderie one usually associates with battle.

When faced with the enemy on the front line, the man next to you, no matter how annoying, is your best friend. When faced with the lower-level threats of intermittent and unpredictable strafing, bombings, and enemy infiltrators, as well as the constant rain and sucking mud, you're as likely to throttle your buddy as the enemy.

This was not the worst of Frank's gibes, so I let it go. In fact, Frank had dialed back the sarcasm and hostility about ninety-nine percent in the last couple of days.

Keeping dry might have had something to do with his improved spirits. Even though he didn't help much in making it happen.

I got the idea from the native huts. Those folks built their homes up off the ground, some several feet above it. We scoped out the highest spot at the edge of camp and moved.

Frank argued with me the whole time. He was getting on my one last nerve, but I could see his point. Who wanted to be the first tent a Japanese soldier came across? Thing is, no one on the outskirts of camp ever got attacked.

You don't kill the easiest target if you're looking to strike fear in the heart of your enemy. The Japanese soldiers went as far into camp as possible before making a move. But Frank would not stop nagging until I promised to set up booby traps around the tent.

I lifted some discarded cinder blocks and wood planks from the road construction site and built an elevated platform—large enough to hold the tent, if a little uneven. We took care not to dislodge it when climbing in and out. The platform kept us off the ground and everything more or less dry.

Other platforms popped up around camp, until the brass put a stop to the unauthorized construction. Some of the guys filched the good stuff instead of leftover materials. There's always someone ruining it for the rest of us.

"Hey, Hawkeye . . . Grump."

Castle squatted at the tent opening and flashed his movie star smile. I sat cross-legged with my journal opened in front of me. Frank reclined back on his blankets, but now sat up and nodded in a semi-friendly fashion.

Castle wore a rain poncho. He pulled another one out from beneath his and threw it at me. "You gotta come with me."

"What? No," I balked, reluctant to leave my nice dry tent while there were a few hours of daylight left to write.

We worked sometimes twenty-hour days. All the TAT equipment had to be loaded and unloaded every time we moved. Building that road through swamp and jungle with solid logs and sandbags left me too weary to lift a pen at the end of most days.

George stood, and the pooled rain in the crevices of his poncho ran off his shoulders in little rivulets. "Sorry, JD, my fault. They called our crew in for an operation, and Colonel Barnes asked for the best shots in the squadron. I said you, cuz it's true. Now, you gotta come with me."

"What do they want?" A weird sensation radiated out from the pit of my stomach.

"Don't know."

I glanced over at Frank, his expression now serious. All the spitefulness of the last couple of weeks dropped away. "Um, maybe they just need you for something" was his weak, mumbled offering.

"Well, we're not going to find out sitting here," George put in.

I slipped the poncho on over my head and pulled on my boots. Frank gave me a reassuring pat on the back as I stepped out into the downpour.

We trudged in silence to the waiting jeep. The late afternoon turned into evening as we drove, and the jungle pressed in around us. The encroaching vegetation dripped with moisture. My skin crawled at the thought of enemy eyes peering out at us from the undergrowth.

Our destination was Tacloban Airstrip, a few miles up the road. I had not ridden in a jeep since basic and passed the short trip in a dreamlike stupor.

We stopped in front of a large tent, and I followed Castle inside. A good-sized group of people milled about. I recognized several of the brass, including Captain Griswold and Colonel Barnes. Other than general troop inspections, we never interacted with the colonel. Castle joined the two officers deep in conversation with the flight crew.

I hung back. A group of men stood next to a row of benches. I studied them, trying to figure out why they struck me as strange. Rigged out in regular US Army duds, each one carried a rucksack and parachute pack.

Then it hit me. Despite their uniforms, and except for a grizzled redheaded American around which they gathered, all the men were Filipino. A heightened sense of anticipation surrounded them. Their expressions reflected calm resolve, but the intensity of their murmured conversation floated over to me from across the tent. The American left them to join Castle's group.

"Hawkins, Jones, Davis," Captain Griswold barked.

I hadn't noticed the two other guys standing in the near corner of the tent when I entered. They came up beside me, and we walked over to the group as if we'd come in together. We stopped, saluted, and stood at attention. I tried to mask the quick, shallow breaths that came on me all of a sudden.

"At ease, men," Colonel Barnes ordered. "I'm sure you're wondering why you were summoned. In short, we have a mission that requires sharp eyes."

The tightness in my chest eased a bit. Sharp eyes didn't sound as ominous as sharpshooter.

"We're putting a reconnaissance team into Mindanao tonight." He gestured toward the redheaded man. "There are several possible drop sites. Our contacts weren't sure which would be safest. You men are our best shots. You'll be scouring the island for the signal, a large bonfire."

They needed our eyesight, not our aim. I nodded, relieved. He handed us each a heavy pair of field glasses. They were all different. Mine was a Bausch & Lomb. Something similar to what I had seen used by the signal crewmen on the *General Hersey*.

"Make yourselves comfortable, men. You leave at 0120hrs. Dismissed."

We stood for an awkward moment, not sure where we had been dismissed to, when Captain Griswold intervened. "You can grab some grub in the Officers' Mess."

Castle left his crew and joined us. A number of the junior officers glared when we walked in, but no one challenged our presence. Hours more would pass before we left, so we all took advantage of the pot of hot coffee.

"Who's the ginger?" I asked George when we'd gotten off to ourselves.

He took a sip from his cup. "Dunno."

I set mine down with a clatter and glared at him. "Listen, I'm a lowly grunt, but everybody knows Mindanao is overrun with the enemy. Where the hell are we dropping those guys?"

"A lot of the island is rough and mountainous. Their main defenses ring the coast. The drop site will be somewhere in the northern interior."

"What are they? Spies?" There was a time not long ago when gathering important intelligence while dodging Japanese troops behind enemy lines would have appealed to my romantic sensibilities. But the last few weeks exposed to the general inhospitable environment of the islands had all but extinguished such heroic notions.

George cast a furtive glance around the mess. "Once we secure Leyte, Mindanao is next is what I figure. Those guys must be part of a native offensive or maybe an organized resistance."

I contemplated my coffee. My mind focused on another immediate concern. "How are *we* getting past those coastal defenses?" That they included anti-aircraft batteries was a well-known fact. Flying in low did not sound too smart.

A guilty expression spread across his face. "Jimmy's the best pilot we have. If anybody has a chance of getting us outta there alive . . ." His voice trailed off, and a chill of terror ran up my spine. Was this a suicide mission?

George laughed and placed a heavy hand on my shoulder. "Had ya going, didn't I?"

"Asshole." I slapped his hand away.

He chuckled again before answering my question. "Most of their defenses are concentrated near Davao. We're coming in from the north, making a diagonal sweep across that part of the island. We'll come in low to spot the signal. Once we have coordinates, we'll pass again, higher up, and drop 'em."

"Fuck, Lance," I protested in a fierce whisper. "That's nuts."

"It's okay. They make these drops all the time. And we have clouds and rough weather for cover."

"Making it harder to see the signal."

"Yeah," he agreed. "That's why we have you sharpshooter boys."

My heart pounded. I stood and took a couple of turns around the mess tent.

Our finest pilot, James "Jimmy" Deacon, had no equal. He'd flown the C-46 in operations throughout the CBI. Pulling the problem-plagued aircraft over "The Hump," as the Himalayas were nicknamed, with its rough mountain terrain and violent weather, was a feat to be reckoned with. Jimmy flew The Hump regularly and without incident . . . well, no life-threatening incident, or really, no incident ending in disaster.

George left in search of his crew, and I found a camp chair out of the way. I'd hardly shut my eyes before being shaken awake.

"Get up, soldier . . . time to move out." Ginger, as I had dubbed the redheaded officer, stood over me. Showered and shaved, he looked years younger.

"Yes, sir." I stood and barely caught the field glasses as they slipped off my lap.

I followed him out of the mess tent, my legs wobbly from sleep. I guess if I was being honest, it could have been fear.

We crossed over the landing strip to where the rest of the crew waited beside Jimmy Deacon's plane. The rain had slackened to a mild drizzle, but the lowering clouds promised torrential downpours to come. The lights around the airfield were out, and darkness banked up around us. I attempted to strike a casual pose.

Our group consisted of seven of the drop crew, five of the flight crew, and three of us spotters. A large craft, the C-46 Commando could hold up to forty troops and about as many wounded on stretchers. I had seen many take off overloaded with thousands of pounds of equipment on board, erasing any safety margin. And you wanted a margin of safety with the C-46. Believe you me.

Being a mechanic, my knowledge of the plane's many flaws surpassed that of even the crew. We'd worked most of the gremlins out of the model over the course of the war, but the C-46 wasn't nicknamed "the flying coffin" for nothing.

I signed up for the Army Air Corps in hopes of making it onto a flight crew, but I had never flown before. I strapped myself into one of the seats that folded down from the side of the plane in the cargo bay. George sat forward at the radio, the navigator station right behind him. The pilot and copilot commanded the cockpit, and a lookout stood in the astrodome hatch. He watched for anything that might come at us from above.

With everyone buckled up and the engines running, my stomach did flip-flops. I seemed immune to motion sickness aboard ship. I'd find out if that held true up in the air.

The purr of the engines and the even, constant whir of the propellers reassured me. I attuned my mechanic's ear to hear the slightest problem and sighed with relief at our smooth ascent.

The sigh turned into a yelp when the plane hit a rough patch. We dipped and the plane shuttered. My panicked hands clutched at the sides of the seat. Davis appeared to be the only other novice flyer aboard. We exchanged pained glances while everyone else took the abrupt movement in stride.

We cruised for a while. After some time, Ginger came back and motioned for the three of us to group up.

The plane flew level at this high altitude. I stood without much trouble.

"Hawkins and Jones . . . put these on." He handed us harnesses that slipped on like a jacket and buckled in front. "You two are stationed at the cargo door."

Jones and I stared back at him, our mouths agape. My heart skipped a few beats. The plane shivered, hitting more turbulence, and I stumbled.

Steadying myself, I stammered, "Excuse me, sir, wha-what?"

He suppressed a chuckle. "We've got one shot at this, men. We're going to open the door, and you will survey the island from there as we make our pass. Don't worry. We'll have you securely hooked in with a line. That's what the harnesses are for."

He motioned to Davis. "Your station is the forward-most window behind the cockpit. You won't have as broad a perspective as these two, but the view's good."

Davis blew out a long breath. He threw Jones and me a pitying glance before making his way forward.

A couple of Ginger's men got up to open the door. My eardrums bulged near to bursting as a rush of air filled the cargo bay.

"All eyes will be trained on the two of you," Ginger shouted over the din. "When you see the signal, don't yell. We might not hear you. Pump your fist above your head. Like this." He waved his fist in the air as if he had made a basket from center court.

One of his men hooked a line to my harness and tied the other end into a recessed insertion point on the inside of the plane. He helped me sit down a little behind the opening with my side leaning against the frame. He did the same with Jones, but at the other end of the door.

The wind pushed against me with terrifying force as the vast black ocean roiled beneath my feet. I settled the strap around my neck and brought the field glasses up to my eyes. The round lenses sat like twin bullseye targets on my face. I was petrified of seeing a shell speeding toward us.

The barest edge of the shoreline came into view as we descended with astounding speed below the clouds. My stomach churned, and I swallowed hard to keep its contents down. We bumped around at this lower altitude, but I forced myself to concentrate on the task before me.

I'd heard fear either sharpens the senses or paralyzes you. It did something of both to me. I could think, but my legs lay like dead weight against the cold steel of the aircraft.

Good thing Ginger gave us a signal to use, because my mouth tasted like a combination of sand and cotton. If I opened it, I would likely be sick.

In a rush of wind and rain, we flew over the island. I worked with systematic efficiency, scanning imaginary quadrants and moving on. Only seconds passed, before I threw my fist up in the air, and yelled too, for good measure. Across from me, Jones did the same. We had both spotted the signal.

A large bonfire burned in a valley of heavy jungle. The plane made a sharp ascent as Jimmy took us up for our final pass.

My eardrums stretched and tightened. An intense sucking sound filled the cargo bay. Anti-aircraft artillery exploded just off our tail.

The blast blanked my mind and shut down my senses. I floated for a split second in a blind bubble of silence. Next instant, I landed with a thud, sight and sound hitting me like a freight train.

The roar of another shell bursting above us further addled my brain. I clutched at my head. Ginger jerked me back into the plane. His men slammed the door shut.

"Hold on," he yelled.

Confusion reigned. I didn't know if we'd been hit, if we were going down. I stood, frozen with fear, gripping the side of the cargo bay, but the plane continued to climb.

Soon we flew into the clouds and out of range. I breathed for what seemed the first time since the blast and relaxed the painful tightness in my neck and shoulders. My ears hummed.

George walked back from his station, pale but collected. Jimmy apparently handed the controls over to his copilot, cuz he joined us.

I stood in my harness, still tied to the plane, and listened to the mumbled exchange. I'd be lying if I said I wasn't hoping they would abort the mission. The enemy knew we were here, and the terror of that exploding artillery had grabbed me by the balls and squeezed tight.

Ginger wouldn't budge. They needed to get in tonight. Another opportunity would not come again for many more weeks. Jimmy nodded, stoic, and both he and George returned to their stations.

I untied myself with shaking hands and shrugged out of the harness. The fire burned bright enough to see from the air, but through the alchemy of mathematics, the navigator pinpointed the drop site. Next pass, we would go right over it, fire or no fire.

Jimmy took us further up and out. Maybe as a ruse—to convince the Japanese we had done a once-over and wouldn't be back.

The drop crew stood as the plane turned around and headed back toward Mindanao. They opened the door and prepared for a static-line jump. This allowed for jumps at lower altitudes.

Each man hooked his line to the one running overhead. When they jumped, the parachute would open as the line disconnected from the plane. We were coming in at around three hundred feet. They would be in the air only seconds and, if lucky, land close to each other.

The bonfire burned in the distance. In a few shallow breaths, we would be right over the drop site.

Determination shown on the faces of the men ready to jump feet first into extreme danger. I stood in awe of their courage. Their homeland lay hundreds of feet below us, enslaved by the enemy. I silently wished them good luck and Godspeed.

Ginger stood at the open door looking out, his chute connected to the anchor line. "On my mark, men . . . one, two, three, now!"

They moved with swift and collected purpose to the door and out into the abyss. In a matter of seconds, they were gone. Ginger nodded, gave us a thumbs-up, and he, too, disappeared into thin air. I gripped the door handle and leaned over, counting the open chutes. I spotted five before Jones yelled, "Shut the damn door." I slammed the door shut.

The plane accelerated fast. We rolled to avoid an exploding shell directly in front of us, throwing me against the side of the plane. I staggered to one of the canvas seats and buckled up.

I could do nothing but hold on and pray. I did both in abundance.

We ascended at a steep incline. Another shell rocked the plane. The steel bolts beneath my seat bit into my clutching hands. It seemed like forever until the sound of anti-aircraft fire fell distant.

One of our engines sputtered and stopped, but I wasn't worried. The Commando could carry a payload over the Himalayas with one functioning engine. The plane was that tough.

George came back and sat down next to me. He grinned.

"Holy fucking shit, Castle," I cursed. "You get me into anything like this ever again and you're a dead man."

**

Dawn broke as I crawled into our tent. Frank stirred and sat up. "What happened?"

I had a mind to pay him back for all his bad temper and say they swore me to secrecy. But his eyes, squinting in the gray light coming in through a crack of the flap, pleaded, eager for any news.

We found ourselves in a hell of a situation, days vacillating between simple discomfort and abject misery. Who could blame him for feeling out of sorts most times?

I told him what happened, but big, making fun of myself. His laughter rocked the tent. He lay back on his pallet holding his stomach when I described my shock at where they expected me to sit. He choked when I told him how I had clung to the plane as we maneuvered to avoid being blasted from the sky.

I laughed with him, clutching at my sides. I gagged and crawled to the tent flap. Leaning out, I threw up into the rain and mud.

Chapter Eleven

When duty whispers low, Thou must, the youth replies, I can.
—Emerson

The rush of fear that had propelled Meliz out of bed eventually passed, but sleep eluded her. She spent the early morning sitting in her pajamas on the balcony trying to meditate, with little success.

Worry twisted her gut. She struggled to empty her mind and concentrate on deep and rhythmic breathing, but suspicions crowded her brain and clamored for attention.

When the sun's rays peeked over the tiled roof of the pension, Meliz gave up and got dressed. She knocked on Brigitte's door and dragged the groggy German off to breakfast.

In a tense, clipped tone, Meliz questioned her. Brigitte endured the interrogation with good-natured disinterest. If any words had passed between her and Prescott while Meliz was off hailing a cab, she didn't remember them.

"I guess I could have told him something," Brigitte admitted.

The morning heat pressed in around them. A veiled sun simmered in the pale sky; its burning touch filtered through overhanging leaves. She and Brigitte sat at a small round table on the shaded patio of the bakery. The aroma of cooking bread hung heavy in the air.

The two women drank tepid coffee and picked at a plate of pastries, their movements languid in the tropical heat. The coffee worked its magic, and Brigitte returned Meliz's intense gaze with a bright and focused one of her own.

"I am a bit fuzzy on the details," she confessed. "I don't even remember what this . . . this . . . who?"

"Prescott."

"Yeah, him. I don't remember what he looks like." Brigitte sat back in the wire-frame chair and sipped at the bitter coffee. "Why are you worried about him?"

"I'm not worried," Meliz protested. "Uneasy . . . maybe. I feel stupid. I almost slept with the guy last night."

Brigitte perked up. "Why didn't you?"

"Too tired."

"I don't think I've ever been too tired."

Meliz laughed and slumped back in her chair. Tension eased from her neck and shoulders. She clasped her hands in her lap and explained, "I'm sort of investigating a mystery, and it's making me . . . I don't know, paranoid is too strong a word, more like guarded."

"What kind of mystery?"

"My grandfather died recently, and I found his World War II journal with missing pages." A familiar lump arose in her throat. She swallowed her grief in what she hoped was a casual manner and continued, "There was another page he had torn out and hidden that referred to the missing ones. The entry was vague, a meeting with a strange lieutenant . . . a couple of kids, a village. He sounded scared."

Meliz paused to gather her thoughts. "It's odd. Without anyone knowing, my ninety-six-year-old granddad arranged to travel here. So, I'm following in his footsteps. Perhaps the hidden entry and his secret itinerary are somehow connected. I really don't have any proof, but maybe . . ." Her voice trailed off. She blushed, knowing how outlandish it all sounded.

JD's death had left her not only bereft, but also exposed. With him around, nothing could ever go too terribly wrong. She could steal from his bravado, raid his confidence, and face the world behind the shield of his stature.

Far from a man of mystery, he had been the one with all the answers. Now, whatever JD left buried in his past was up to her to uncover.

Meliz crossed her arms and shook her head with self-doubt. "I miss him. Maybe all I'm doing is hanging on a little bit longer."

Brigitte lit a cigarette. "My family's not close, but I liked my grandmother." She took a drag and exhaled. "You don't know what scared him?"

"Something to do with a village and kids, but he doesn't go into detail. That officer made him nervous, and he definitely didn't want the guy knowing anything about the children." Meliz shrugged. "The missing pages and even the hidden entry didn't seem like much until we found his itinerary. It all just kind of clicked into place, but now I'm not so sure."

Brigitte straightened in her chair, shedding her blasé façade. She snuffed out her cigarette on the half-empty pastry plate. "What else? Are any of his old soldier friends living?"

"I don't know. We are . . . well, my friend Alberta is looking into his army buddies. I've spoken to a military expert here. He thinks my grandfather may have written about the incident as a plot to one of his books."

"Books?"

"Um, yeah, he was a writer. You probably haven't heard of him," Meliz hedged, well aware Marshal Clyde Jameson's exploits were translated into many different languages. "JD Hawkins."

"Vhat?" Brigitte's eyes widened. As with inebriation, the German woman's accent thickened with disbelief and astonishment. "JD Hawkins? I heard he vas dead. You are his granddaughter, *ja*? Amazing."

"You've read his books?"

Brigitte deepened her voice to a manly register, "'No one gets the drop on me, because I ride . . .'"

"'. . . with Surprise,'" Meliz finished in chorus, Surprise being the Marshal's horse, a big appaloosa.

She laughed. Of course, this bohemian German woman would know a Clyde Jameson catchphrase. JD would have eaten it up.

"My brother had the first ten or fifteen books in the series. I liked that horse. Smart."

Surprise had pulled the Marshal and his deputy's asses out of the crapper more than once. In the old TV series, it was a toss-up as to who was more popular, the horse or Rex Stevens.

"My favorite book was"—Brigitte paused, searching for the correct translation—"*The Dance of the Kites.* The Marshal and his deputy, Cody, played dead; Surprise, too. The Stanton brothers thought they had killed them. They were unprepared when he captured the gang. That was a good trick." She nodded her approval. "Which book has the mystery?"

"Dr. Rivera believes book twenty-seven, *Everything Touches the Sky*, might hold some clues."

Brigitte paused, considering. "No, we didn't have that one. Jan, my brother, stopped reading them after a while." She flashed Meliz an apologetic smile.

"That's okay. I haven't read all of them either."

"Seriously?" Brigitte raised her eyebrows, her expression as judgmental as Garrett's.

Meliz bristled. "What the hell? He wrote the last one at least ten years before I was even born."

"JD Hawkins was your granddad," Brigitte repeated, impressed. "That's something. People love his books."

Meliz sighed. "I know."

"I need orange juice." Brigitte jumped up and walked inside the bakery. She came back with a large glass and took a long drink. She offered some to Meliz, who declined.

"What is the book about?" Brigitte settled back into her chair.

"I only know the general summary from the book's Wiki page. The Marshal and Cody stumble across a Comanche campsite burnt to the ground. Everyone is slaughtered except for a little girl. At first, Jameson thinks settlers massacred them. But the culprits turn out to be a renegade faction of the Comanche tribe in league with corrupt military officers, all of them trying to undermine a peace treaty and start a war."

"That doesn't sound like a Marshal Jameson book to me."

"It isn't, not like the others anyway. The plot is bleak and depressing and lacks much of the humor JD always infused in his stories. That book was supposed to be the last in the series. But his readers rebelled, and he wrote another, more traditional, one to satisfy the diehard fans."

Meliz's phone pinged. She glanced down at the new text message. "Dr. Rivera, um, I mean Garrett has new information." She grabbed her satchel. "I'm going to the university. Maybe I'll see you later."

"I'm coming with you. I can help."

Meliz responded with a diplomatic, "Hmm." She wasn't at all sure how this erratic, disheveled woman could help her. She might even be a hindrance.

"I've already missed my flight, anyway," Brigitte added

"What're you talking about?"

"I had a flight out to Malaysia this morning, but . . ." She laughed. "Well, you see."

Meliz did see. Brigitte had been in no state to get up and to the airport in time to catch an early flight. Her friend's drug-fueled night on the town might turn out to be a good thing. The Malaysian authorities did not play nice when it came to foreigners who broke their drug laws.

"I'm good at puzzles," Brigitte insisted.

Meliz couldn't figure a way to refuse without offending her new friend. "Okay. Let's go," she agreed and hoped she was not making a big mistake.

**

The University of the City of Manila lay a short walk from the restaurant where Meliz met Garrett the day before. A centerpiece of the Intramuros District, the campus buzzed with activity.

She walked with Brigitte across an expanse of lawn surrounded by buildings. The bustle of students scurrying in all directions filled Meliz with nostalgia. A sudden longing for the camaraderie and routine of academia struck her with unexpected force. She stopped to soak up the convivial atmosphere and to get her bearings.

"Which way?" Brigitte asked.

"I think it's that one over there." Meliz pointed to a tall, concrete building standing in stark contrast to the Spanish Colonial feel of the rest of campus.

They entered as a throng of students poured out into the hallways. The two women jostled their way to Garrett's second-floor office.

"There you are." He jumped up from his desk and ushered them into the cramped workspace.

Shelves with books and stacks of paper covered every inch of wall space. A partition bisected the room, separating his desk from that of another professor's. Humidity seeped in from an open window and tempered the frigid air blowing down from the overhead vent.

Meliz introduced him to Brigitte, and Garrett, in turn, introduced his officemate, Mia. She greeted them with a curt nod and continued with her work.

He unfolded two metal chairs next to his desk. "Sit down. Sit down." He clapped his hands together. "Now then, I have a lead." With a triumphant gesture, he waved a battered paperback copy of *Everything Touches the Sky* above his head.

The book was an original edition from the early eighties. The cover art featured JD's name and the title in bold, block font with a colorful illustration of Clyde Jameson astride Surprise. They stood on the crest of a windswept hill. Much like Sancho Panza to Don Quixote, Cody appeared at the edge of the frame on a much less magnificent mount.

Garrett sat down and swiveled to face them. "The plot came back to me in more detail as I skimmed through the book last night. I can see why the story didn't appeal to the teenaged me—much starker than the typical Marshal Jameson book."

"At least that horse is in it," Brigitte interjected, indicating the paperback now resting on Garrett's desk.

"Ah, Surprise? Sure. I suppose." He nodded, adding, "The horse *does* have a pivotal role in the story."

"Of course."

"What else?" Meliz prompted, impatient with the digression.

"Well, the book follows the Marshal's investigation of a massacre at a Comanche camp next to a river."

"Yes. I read the online summary."

"Then you know there are lots of twists and turns to the story, but I believe the intricate plot loosely parallels the competing schemes surrounding the Japanese surrender."

"The surrender? In what way?"

"Negotiations were fraught, to say the least. The Allies didn't trust the Japanese, and there were warring factions within the Japanese government itself. On the one hand, Emperor Hirohito supported surrender. On the other, an intransigent faction of the military wanted to fight to the literal death. It all made for strained talks."

He rested his elbows on the arms of the chair and steepled his fingers together. "Since your grandfather's incident occurred around the same time as the surrender, the Japanese intrigue might have provided a general outline for the plot, as well as giving us a possible clue to what happened to him."

Meliz could hardly imagine her nineteen-year-old grandfather somehow involved in anything as momentous as the Japanese surrender. "Is there more?"

"Yep. Last night I came back here and scanned the book into the computer—"

"The entire book?"

"Mm-hmm. It took me a couple of hours, but the digital copy allowed us to run a program on, ah, identifying literary devices—stuff like symbolism, alliteration, um, metaphor, you know. Mia here"—he nodded over at his officemate—"advised the students who developed the program, and she helped me interpret the data."

Mia stood and walked around Garrett's desk. She leaned back on the windowsill behind him and cleared her throat. "Our students developed the program as a collaborative thesis in comparative literature and computer science."

Garrett brought up a series of tables and graphs on his laptop. "Nothing super sophisticated, but it got the job done. There's lots of interesting stuff, but what stood out was something the program identified as 'religious subtext.'" He moved the mouse around and highlighted a table.

Meliz scooted her chair closer. "JD was never one for covert religious symbolism, or overt, for that matter." Her voice held a hint of skepticism.

"The imagery may not have been intentional. As you can see, we found the symbol of the cross figured prominently throughout the book."

Meliz and Brigitte leaned in to read the table. Everything from "crisscross" to "double cross" to "eyes crossed" filled the lined spaces.

"How does any of this relate to the actual cross?" Meliz asked.

Garrett did a double take at the screen. "Sorry, not this one." He scrolled further down. "Here it is."

This table listed phrases and words such as "sign of the cross," "crucifix," "crucified," and even the Latin word "*crucis*." Both women paused on the term "Green Crossing."

"What is this?" Brigitte pointed at the computer screen. "This doesn't belong here. It should be in the first table."

Garrett and Mia exchanged a knowing look. She gestured for him to explain.

"The phrase 'Green Crossing' shows up in the context of themes and plot threads associated with the Christian cross such as sacrifice and rebirth."

"This is all interesting, but what does it *mean*?" Meliz asked. "How does this relate to the Japanese surrender?"

Mia pushed away from the windowsill and thrust her hands into her pockets. "The Green Crossing is the name of the place where Marshal Jameson finds the massacred Indians. In fact, when he pulls the army and local authorities into the investigation, they refer to the crime thereafter as 'the Green Crossing Massacre.' In the book, it is a local river ford."

"Mia," Garrett told them, "made the connection between the Green Crossing and something that happened on Okinawa between the dates you're interested in."

"Have you ever heard of the Green Cross flights?" Mia peered at them through large, round-frame glasses, her eyes intense.

Meliz and Brigitte shook their heads.

"The Allies were suspicious and on edge when negotiating the surrender—as well they should have been. Soldiers and sailors throughout the Pacific were well acquainted with *kamikaze* attacks and suicide charges. And these tactics became more pronounced as Japan's fortunes faded." Mia paused before continuing, making sure they had absorbed the seriousness of the situation. "That diehard faction of the Japanese military wanted to go out in a blaze of glory. To avoid any last-minute insurgent attack, MacArthur gave detailed instructions on how the envoys were to proceed with presurrender negotiations."

Mia brought up old black-and-white photographs of World War II aircraft on Garrett's computer. They appeared white and had dark crosses on their tails, fuselages, and wings.

"These are the best-known images of the Green Cross flights," she told them. "MacArthur instructed the Japanese to paint the planes white and put green crosses on them to indicate surrender."

"These are Japanese planes?" Meliz clicked through the images of planes both flying and parked at an airstrip surrounded by American GIs on a day that looked blazing hot.

"Yeah," Garrett confirmed. "You can imagine the humiliation. The Japanese Air Force was the pinnacle of the warrior class. People revered the fighter pilots for their skill and courage. To paint over the *Hinomaru*, the red circle or sun disk, with the cross . . . well, it was pretty obvious MacArthur was aiming to assert the Christian religion over—"

"What *was* obvious," Mia cut him off, "was the need to easily identify any plane carrying the official envoys of the emperor. A plane not bearing these marks would have been considered hostile."

"How does this involve JD if he was in Okinawa?"

"These planes left Tokyo and landed on Iejima, a small island off the western coast of Okinawa," Garrett explained. "From there, American planes took the envoys to Manila to meet with MacArthur and begin treaty negotiations."

"Iejima? But JD was stationed at Bolo Point Airfield. I checked the map. The airfield was in Okinawa."

"Yes, but your grandfather wasn't only at Bolo Point. In his journal, he mentioned, right before the missing pages, that he drove north to Motobu Airfield with another man from his unit. Motobu was directly across from Iejima. You can see the island from the beach there."

Meliz walked to the window and stood next to Mia. She stared down at the grassy courtyard below. "I remember. His superiors sent him to Motobu for supplies. When he arrived at the airfield, everybody was celebrating the surrender."

"So what?" Brigitte piped up. "There were these Green Cross flights . . . Did something happen?"

"No," Garrett admitted.

"The planes landed on Iejima on August 19, 1945," Mia told them. "They stayed there while the envoys flew to Manila on American planes. Afterward, the envoys returned to Iejima and flew back to Japan on the Green Cross planes."

Garrett crossed his arms. "I don't know how, but the flights must have something to do with the mystery. The date, the location, and the Green Crossing can't all be a coincidence," he asserted. "I believe if there are answers, you'll find them in Okinawa. Maybe even on Iejima Island."

Garrett glanced over at the computer. "Shit, the time. I've got a class," he exclaimed and jumped up.

Meliz thanked them for their efforts, and the two women stood to leave. Before he rushed out, Garrett thrust the old paperback at Meliz. "I've got the whole thing scanned. I don't need this copy. Maybe you can read the series backwards."

She took the book. "Maybe I will."

Chapter Twelve

Excerpt from *Everything Touches the Sky*

The kid cried into her hands. "*Tami, tami,*" she repeated through her sobs.

Having no command of the Comanche language, I was helpless to comfort her. Dried blood caked the front of her dress. I examined her for wounds, but found none. Shock was what fueled her tears and shut down her senses.

Poor little thing, she couldn't have been more than seven or eight. I noted the soft deerskin dress and beaded moccasins. The Comanche prized their children. I figured they would be out looking for her.

I wrapped her in an old horse blanket. The thing smelled of dirt and dried sweat, but I needed to keep her warm. Fact is, I didn't have much else, having lost my bedroll and most of my pay at a poker game in Copper Creek.

Cody secured the horses and come up beside me. "All that red hair's got her skittish, Marshal. She's thinking you're the devil."

Cody's reasoning was often flawed, and there was more gray than red in my hair these days, but I put my hat back on, just in case. I took a gander at our surroundings.

"Where you figure she come from?"

We had ridden eastward through the foothills making tracks back to Texas. I had never known the Comanche to be out this far west. I guess you could never tell where they'd show up, them being horse folk.

Cody tapped my shoulder and pointed off to the southeast. I squinted, my eyesight not being what it once was. A thin curl of black smoke blended into the clouds over the far hill.

A good half hour later, we reached the hillside. We rode up and stopped at the top.

The grim sight that spread out before us didn't surprise me none. I'd had time enough to realize the girl wandered for miles, alone and bloody, because there was no one left alive to care for her. That did not make the viewing any easier.

Large oak trees and a stand of cottonwoods surrounded a peaceful clearing next to a river ford. The gathering looked to be a few families camped out.

Burned trees loomed ominously over bodies still smoldering from the fire. I tensed and placed a hand on my gun.

Cody come up behind me holding the girl. I told him quick like, "Don't let her see."

He shielded her eyes with his hat, but she wasn't looking at the river. She sat, as if entranced, her wide, glassy eyes turned toward a large prickly bush a few feet away. The girl cried again, "*Tami, tami.*"

I dismounted and walked over to the bush. Dread pulled me down with each step.

I knelt and pushed back the thorny branches with a gloved hand. Underneath lay a boy, younger than the girl, stretched out on his back and eyes staring open.

I pictured the scene in my mind—the girl and boy running for the hill, almost making the top before some filthy coward shot him in the back. She pulls him up under the bush to hide and holds him while he bleeds to death.

I bowed my head. Today, I learned a Comanche word. I figured it meant little brother.

Chapter Thirteen

Men ought always to pray, and not to faint.
—Luke XVIII: 1

15 Dec., 1944, Leyte, Philippines—We finished building a road to advance equipment further inland. The work was like slogging through hell. We enlisted the aid of two Australian soldiers with bulldozers. They were a big help. I worked alongside a captain and two privates. The privates worked like bulls. The captain got his hands dirty too, but he didn't have much to say to those of us in the lower ranks. That's not good. He should speak to every man in this army like he was a long-lost friend. You never know who's gonna have your back.

17 Dec.—We finally moved into permanent quarters a few days ago, three-man tents to be exact. George joined Frank and me in one. They are tons better than the pup tents. The camp even has a large mess where we can all stay dry while we eat.

The big mess tent reminded me of those used by the traveling church revivals that come through my hometown a couple times a year. They usually put up in a cow pasture. There's always a preacher, a band, and a choir. The whole setup stays for a couple of weeks, sometimes a month.

Boone and I got real religious during those times and went most nights. Momma and Daddy never went, but they sometimes let the girls go with us on the weekends.

Every night, the preacher got all wound up and called down the wrath of God on all us sinners. He talked about hell like he'd seen the place with his own eyes. Rivers of lava and the burning flesh of nonbelievers haunted our dreams.

Boone and I huddled on the wooden bench, scared out of our wits, and prayed for salvation. We never passed up a chance to be saved. When the preacher called for sinners to repent, we walked to the altar and knelt, begging for forgiveness. With tears streaming down our faces, he blessed us.

Course, the next day, we were back to our usual mischief, tormenting our sisters and playing tricks on Momma. Daddy always says the best part of being a Baptist is God's forgiveness. Doesn't matter when you ask for it, God always forgives. Even a lifetime of sinning can't keep a Baptist out of heaven. Not if he repents at the last.

Boone and I figured we'd have plenty of time for God's forgiveness. Guess you never can tell.

**

Leyte, Philippines, December 1944

We moved to a new location on Leyte called Tolosa. Captain Griswold was on a tear trying to figure out what we were doing here. Turns out, most of our squadron was on Biak Island, some said Finch Haven. No one knew where we were supposed to be. We'd heard rumors of another airstrip being built for our use here, but I'd seen no evidence of it.

Neither Frank nor I had put our hands on the engine of a C-46 since leaving the States. We needed the roads and infrastructure for sure, but none of it made much sense if we didn't have the planes or could put our training to good use.

The night before our move to Tolosa, a siren woke us around 2200hrs. We spotted a Japanese Zero bearing down overhead. Artillery fire drove the enemy away. That is, until 0300hrs when a flaming piece of shrapnel hurtled, like a fucking meteorite, past our tent.

The deadly steel buried itself into a palm tree not ten feet from where we slept. The tree burst into flames. I didn't wait around to see what was coming next but grabbed my helmet and carbine and jumped into my foxhole—Frank right on my heels. A few men who hadn't gotten around to digging one huddled under trucks or flattened to the ground like horned toads until the action ceased. We learned the next morning that our guys shot down three more Zeros within two miles of camp.

Here in Tolosa, the general atmosphere of tension was relieved from time to time with that of abject boredom. The camp sported nicer digs and the road allowed supplies and traffic to get through easier, but the battle at Ormoc raged not fifteen miles away. Japanese planes and snipers broke through the line on a regular basis, keeping us jumping in and out of our foxholes.

At Frank's insistence, I set up booby traps around our tent. I rigged up a bunch of trip wires connected to cans as an early warning system. So far, we'd caught a couple of sleepy privates blundering out of their tents for a midnight piss.

"What's Lance up to?" Frank lay on his mat. He had dragged it over to the tent flap where a strip of late afternoon sunlight streamed in. Natives wove the mats from palm fronds. They provided no cushioning, but were mighty helpful in keeping our blankets from getting too dirty.

"Don't know what he's up to," I replied, pretty sure Frank already knew my answer.

George had been gone three days. He flew out of Tacloban

Airstrip, but did not bother to let us know where to. Deacon's crew billeted with us here on Leyte, one of the few from our squadron that did.

"He'll be back soon, I figure. All his gear's here."

Later that same night, I wrote in my journal by the light of a small kerosene lamp scrounged up from the equipment shed. Cook "generously" siphoned off fuel from the stove for this purpose. Course, I had to give up two bottles of my Aunt Stella's hot sauce. I figured bland C-rations were a small price to pay if I could get in some writing.

The hour neared midnight, and most of the other tents slept. An occasional honking snore or murmured word floated out over the camp. I strained my ears at a faint stirring that coursed beneath the regular nighttime sounds of the island and heard the unmistakable hiss of urgent whispers. Booted feet ran in all directions.

A heightened sense of urgency electrified the camp and made the hairs on my arms rise up. Like aboard ship, being cooped up in a tent where I could be blindsided made me sweat with fear.

I put out the lantern, grabbed my carbine, and stuffed my pockets with ammo. Frank awoke as I pulled on my boots.

"What's going on?" he asked in that hyper-alert voice we all possessed even though seconds before we were off in dreamland.

"Don't know. I'm checking it out."

Frank scrambled behind me. I didn't wait to see if he followed. My eyes adjusted quickly to the darkness. I spotted four guys huddled together next to the mess tent. They startled and swore when I came up on them. Two rifles pointed in my direction.

"Ho, ho," I blurted in a fierce whisper. "It's me, Hawkins. What's happening?"

I heard the slow release of breath, and the men lowered their weapons. Frank came skidding up beside me, his helmet askew and grasping his carbine.

The group included Jacobson, Miller, Peabody, and Sauer. Even in the darkness, I could see the tense set of their shoulders.

Jacobson licked his lips. "Enemy snipers broke through the line and used a canoe to row down the river close to camp. They shot at the guards on the bridge."

"Anyone hurt?" Frank asked.

"Nope, but Captain wants us to double the guard. I'm getting men together. We're heading up there now."

"We're coming with you." I indicated Frank, who scowled at me casually including him.

"Yeah, okay," Jacobson agreed. "The more the merrier."

The bridge served as a checkpoint about a quarter mile up from camp. We jogged with everyone on the alert. I'd never had a chance to put my combat training to use, and I admit to feeling a bit keen on confronting those Japanese infiltrators.

Wanting to get into a firefight sounds crazy, but I'd been jumpy since landing on Leyte and doubted my mettle. We weren't a combat unit, but if the war came down to an invasion, orders would be every man to the front. This sneak attack offered me an opportunity to see if I could handle the heat of battle.

At the guard post, everyone hunkered down behind sandbags and concrete blocks. There were two machine gun mounts: one on the near side of the bridge and one on the far side.

That fellow, Davis, the one who flew with us on the mission over Mindanao, commanded the near side. He ordered Frank and me to shore up the far side, reminding us to "make it quick, cuz you're totally exposed over the water."

We made a terrifying dash across the bridge to the second machine gun mount. I flinched at the sound of our boots crunching on rocks, imagining what a round of gunfire could do to us. The last three feet or so, we dove and rolled behind the sandbags. Sergeant

Taylor, one of the two men already on guard, raised his eyebrows at our dramatic entrance.

Taylor had stormed the beaches of Guadalcanal and Saipan with the Marines. He sustained serious injury on Saipan. Doctors amputated four of the five toes on his right foot, and he received shrapnel to the abdomen. He recovered, but his injuries kept him from returning to his unit. Taylor pitched such a fit, the brass compromised and sent him to us.

A grizzled old veteran with tales of battle and death, the sergeant could not have been more than thirty. He had a habit of chewing on an unlit cigar and never flinched at gunfire.

"You boys come to help us drive off the enemy?" he asked through a shit-eating grin, his lazy eyes getting the measure of us. "You're in luck. Rosy here thinks there are seven or eight out there." He jerked his head toward the dense jungle not more than twenty feet from our position.

Rosy, also known as Ezra Rosen, sat across from Taylor and looked asleep. His chin rested on his chest, and his helmet had slipped over his eyes.

I startled when he spoke. His deep voice boomed out from the vicinity of his shirt collar. "It's been quiet. More than an hour since they ambushed us."

He lifted his head and pushed up his helmet. Standing, Rosy loomed over everybody. Broad shouldered and rangy, he assumed the tolerant, easy-going attitude big men often do. But I'd seen him move fast and hit hard when the situation suited him.

Right now, it suited both him and Taylor to sit tight and wait. We sat and waited.

Our nerves soon settled as the night progressed and the enemy gave no sign of trouble. At around 0230hrs, Taylor stood and grasped his carbine.

"Come on, Hawkins, Hoffman, let's check it out. I'm sick of waiting for these cowardly bastards to show themselves."

Eager as I was to test my mettle, this didn't sound to me like a smart move. I had envisioned manning the barricades against an onslaught. Going into the jungle in search of Japanese soldiers just seemed unnecessary.

Sergeant Taylor was in command, so I grudgingly got to my feet and glanced over at Frank. He threw me a resentful look. Can't say as I blamed him much. I wasn't too keen on this particular mission myself.

We made a hunched-over run for the jungle and crouched down inside the tree line to get our bearings. We all learned at basic how to scout. The three of us made a shallow arrowhead with Taylor running point. I held the left flank as we walked forward, making a slow sweep of the area.

Moisture dripped off the leaves and plopped onto my helmet. My eyes had adjusted to the darkness, but the jungle extinguished all remaining light, revealing my path only a few feet at a time.

Everything moved: trees, vines, snakes, bugs, everything. Like out in the middle of the ocean, the jungle did not stop living because men warred. My skin twitched, and I was as jumpy as a frog on hot pavement. I swung my rifle at the slightest sound.

"Settle down," Taylor ordered, his voice low and hard. "You can't aim at everything that moves. Use your judgment or you'll end up shooting a buddy."

My judgment? I suppressed a hysterical laugh. What did that even *mean*? Could a Japanese soldier fit behind a fern or flatten himself beneath a log? I figured he could be about anywhere.

The realization my judgment depended largely on luck hit me hard. Much as the darkness and dense jungle hid us, the heavy tread of our boots signaled our presence. If there had been any enemy soldiers about, chances were good none of us would have made it out alive. As it so happened, they'd most likely left after the assault on the guard post.

Taylor signaled a left sweep when Frank shouted, "Stop."

We froze.

"What the hell are you doing?" Taylor seethed.

Frank's face shone slick with sweat. He swallowed and pointed to a spot inches from Taylor's feet. "A tripwire."

Our eyes followed along Frank's outstretched arm. A weak shaft of moonlight caught the cold gleam of a steel wire. Taylor took a slow, careful step back. He set his weapon down and traced the wire while Frank and I kept nervous watch.

"It's connected to a stockpile of grenades," he informed us. "One of you, find me a stick."

We locked eyes, both of us reluctant to move. Frank raised his eyebrows as if to say, "I saw the damn thing; you get the stick."

I squatted and made a ridiculous spectacle of myself by rooting around an arm span from my feet. My luck held. Without moving an inch, I found a sturdy stick and handed it to Taylor. I stood, keeping my rifle at the ready.

Taylor pulled a handkerchief from his pocket and tied it to the stick. He pushed the homemade flag into the ground next to the trip wire. "We'll send the bomb boys in here at daylight. My guess, this isn't the only one."

My stomach roiled with fear, and I pursed my lips to keep from throwing up. The whole purpose of the raid had been to draw us out into a jungle jury-rigged with explosives.

"How're we getting outta this?" Not at all sure I wanted to move from my tiny island of safety.

"We retrace our steps as best as we can," Taylor said, his voice calm and even. He took in our pale, strained faces. "Easy, men, we're only a few yards in."

That walk stretched into one of the longest of my life. Taylor kept up a steady and matter-of-fact stream of instructions, so's Frank and I were able to keep a cool head. We took each step with care. With eyes glued to the ground, I could only hope our instincts were right and the Japanese soldiers had retreated after setting the traps.

Once clear of the tree line, we trotted double time to the machine gun mount. Even Taylor made a dramatic leap at the last to roll to safety behind the sandbags.

Rosy greeted us with a grunt, his eyes trained on the jungle and his finger on the machine gun trigger. "See anything?"

"Rigged-up grenades," Taylor told him. "The gunfire was a trick to draw us out. I'm betting those seven or eight enemy soldiers are long gone."

"Sneaky bastards," Rosy grumbled, not taking his eyes off the tree line.

At 0600hrs, we were relieved. Taylor left to make a report to Captain Griswold.

Weary to the bone, Frank and I returned to our tent to find George packing his gear. We stared at him in numb silence. The stress of the last few hours had whittled us down to our barest senses of sight and sound, and those functioned only in that we knew we were awake and on our feet.

I rubbed my eyes and tried to kick-start my brain. "What the hell are you doing?"

Castle straightened. "I could ask you guys the same thing." His eyes raked us over, taking in our muddy dungarees and unshaven faces.

"Guard duty," Frank mumbled.

"Well, sorry to say, you aren't getting much sleep this morning. We're moving out."

On cue, the PA system crackled and squeaked: "Attention, men.

We're decamping. Prepare to move out and reunite with the Eighth on Biak. Further instructions and assignments pending."

The rumors were true this time. We were leaving the front for Biak Island, Dutch East Indies. For the next few weeks, our unit would be far from the action.

Chapter Fourteen

Just draw on your grit; it's so easy to quit—
It's the keeping your chin up that's hard.
—Robert W. Service

Meliz waited at the information kiosk for Brigitte, who stood with the other passengers around the only baggage carousel in the building. Her friend had offered to grab Meliz's backpack, saving her the trouble of lifting with only one hand the heavy piece of luggage from a moving carousel.

She adjusted her sling, tucking the loose end of the strap up under the buckle. A painful twinge in her shoulder brought back those few desperate moments in the dark, deserted alleyway on her last night in Manila.

"You're lucky it's only a sprained shoulder," the baby-faced emergency room doctor had chided her. "What were you thinking?"

Meliz had not been thinking. She had just wanted to escape.

Even fleeting violence leaves its mark, and the focused brutality of her attacker lingered in Meliz's mind like a physical wound. She pushed the memory away, and looked out the window of the single-story terminal of the Daniel Z. Romualdez Airport in Tacloban, Leyte.

From its World War II beginnings, the airfield had morphed into a small, yet modern airport. Destroyed by typhoon Haiyan several years ago, the renovated terminal and runway was again open to commercial flights.

Searching the internet, Meliz found old, bleached-out photographs of the wartime airfield with its barren strip of land and ships unloading onto temporary causeways. She closed her eyes and conjured up an image of the place as it had been during the war.

In the waning months of 1944, fighters, bombers, and troop transports circled above waiting to land, while others queued in a long line to take off. Beyond the airfield, warships crowded the broad harbor, and a few short miles away, the Japanese still clung to this lush and war-torn island.

JD had been at this very airfield. Meliz imagined him standing up under a plane: He inspects an engine while joking with one of the crew, telling a funny story at his own expense. Propellers whir and engines rev, forcing him to raise his voice. He is laughing and at ease, but enemy fire looms as an ever-present threat.

Meliz opened her eyes to an explosion of color. She'd been imagining it all in black-and-white.

"Your bag weighs a bloody ton." Brigitte strode over, the pack resting securely on her back.

"At least I'm not totally useless." She indicated Brigitte's bag of underwear and her own small daypack, both slung over her uninjured shoulder. "Thanks again. It's lucky you could change your plans. This trip would have been a lot harder without you."

The German woman waved aside her gratitude. "What is a vacation if I cannot do what I want?" She nodded at Meliz's shoulder. "Does it still hurt?"

Brigitte had arrived at the hospital just as Meliz emerged from the exam room, her arm already in a sling and a bruise turning purple on her cheekbone. Overnight, the bruise had faded into what looked like a smudge of coal dust across her face.

Meliz took her arm out of the sling and lifted the strap from around her neck. She straightened her elbow and moved her shoulder with exaggerated care. "It's a bit stiff, but I don't really need the sling. The doctor told me to use my arm. I have to be careful for a couple of days. That's all."

Meliz's physical injuries paled in comparison to her shattered computer. The laptop had slipped from her satchel and smashed on the pavement when the thief tore the bag from her shoulder.

She needed a new computer, and their first stop would be an electronics store in Tacloban. Meliz gave the store's address to the taxi driver as they pulled out from the airport and onto a road skirting the ocean.

The air shimmered with moisture. Not the heavy downpour JD described in his journal, but a gentle mist that hung in the air and clung to the car's windows. A distant curtain of rain swept across the broad expanse of ocean, and Meliz shivered at the massive amounts of energy coursing above and below the waves.

A few years had passed since typhoon Haiyan (known in the Philippines as Yolanda) obliterated this northern part of Leyte. The photomontage from Garrett's presentation at the fundraiser chronicled the terrifying disaster. Not a building stood undamaged by the 165 mile per hour winds and massive storm surges that slammed into the city. Thousands of people had died and many were missing.

Haiyan was one of the strongest storms ever recorded at landfall. For a full hour, the pounding waves inundated Tacloban and submerged it beneath ten to fifty feet of water. The city disappeared from the map.

Meliz and Brigitte gazed out their respective windows, each lulled into a passenger's trance. The landscape passed in a soft blur of rain.

"It's amazing," Brigitte observed.

"What is?"

She nodded out her window. "How places come back. From the pictures, the city looked bombed out, broken trees, buildings gone, rubble everywhere. Now look." Brigitte gestured to the restored road and buildings.

Meliz said nothing. While at the American Cemetery in Manila, she had researched the wartime casualties per country. The Philippines lost over three percent of its population, both soldiers and civilians combined—this, in comparison to the less than one-half of one percent of the United States population, most of them military casualties. Meliz ran her hands through her hair, uncomfortable with her mental measuring stick of suffering, especially when so many had given everything.

"Maybe people are just that way," she finally replied.

"What way?"

"Forward looking, leave the past behind and all. Could be some places are better than others at rebuilding and moving on." She cocked her head to one side, considering. "Perhaps resilience is learned. I mean, in a cultural sense. There are places in the world, countries where people have suffered hardship after hardship. Maybe they just get better with practice." Meliz scowled out the window, uncomfortable with her phrasing. "Not the suffering part, but the rebuilding, moving on part."

Brigitte shrugged. "If you want to live, what else can you do but go on? People who have endured a lot may be better at moving on. But some of them give up too. It's hard to say why some survive and others don't."

Towering, slender palm trees stood like stalwart sentinels along the road. Meliz rolled down the window. A rush of damp air blew the hair back from her face. She breathed in the aroma of salt and fish.

Much of Tacloban hugged the coastline, exposing it to the full fury of a pitiless ocean. She could only imagine the terror of watching a wall of water rushing toward her and everyone she loved.

They made a sharp turn north and continued onto the Pan-Philippine Highway. On the outskirts of Tacloban, the taxi sped through a maze of streets. They drove past crowded neighborhoods of small concrete-and-plank-wood houses mixed in with storefronts and office buildings.

Life flowed around them in a colorful river of cars, trucks, and people. Men in shorts and flip-flops pedaled bikes pulling everything from produce to passengers. Motorcycles with elaborate covered sidecars squeezed past them at alarming speed. Like a rude guest, an occasional business suit interrupted the ease and comfort of tropical shirts and loose, fluttering dresses.

They soon turned onto a busy commercial street. Signs for cleaners, tailors, electronics, and various other stores crowded the narrow avenue. Meliz held her breath as the driver slipped with ease into a tiny parking space in front of the electronics store.

"Wait for us," Brigitte told him as they got out.

A little bell jangled when they pushed open the glass door and entered the cluttered store. Meliz passed Brigitte, who stopped to examine a rack of plug adaptors.

The woman at the desk assessed the laptop with an experienced eye, declaring the damaged computer unsalvageable. She offered to sell her a replacement, and Meliz settled on a small tablet with the programs she needed already installed.

They were soon back in the cab and heading for their hotel. Brigitte had consulted her numerous friends and acquaintances and declared uptown the best place to find lodgings. She booked them into a low-key inn off the bustling Burgos Street.

Reputed to be a foodie Mecca, the area boasted a lively nightlife.

Clubs and restaurants flashed by, but Meliz's eagerness to explore fell victim to exhaustion, and she only longed for a nap.

They turned off Burgos onto a side street as the sun broke through the thinning clouds. Colorful flowering vines crawled up the walls of stately homes and hung from the roofs. Meliz knew nothing about botany and regretted her ignorance in a setting so rife with plants. She could only identify the delicate white blooms of the sampaguita, the Filipino national flower. Meliz found its strong vanilla fragrance comforting.

The taxi pulled up to the curb of a large mid-twentieth-century bungalow painted white with a green roof and with stairs running up to a wide veranda. Flower boxes sat on the windowsills. Alongside the bungalow was a modern three-story version of the house with rooms opening out onto the running balconies of each floor.

Meliz paid the driver, and the two women entered the hotel. Generic lobby furniture greeted them, but the walls hung with unique and colorful cut-glass mosaics. A ceiling fan spun on the lowest setting—disturbing not at all the flies perched upon its blades.

Brigitte addressed the young receptionist, "We have reservations . . . Brigitte Müller and Meliz Lin."

Meliz leaned with her back against the reception desk, letting Brigitte do the talking. Her eyes panned across the lobby and stopped on a man coming down the stairs.

She admired his tall, slender physique dressed in a pair of dark, loose-fitting linen pants and a light, short-sleeved T-shirt. Meliz straightened in recognition.

Hikaru Ikeda, if her memory served her right. Meliz had exchanged only a few words with him that night at the club, but recognized his patrician features and head of thick, black hair.

She had observed him at the bar. A couple of times, he struck a casual pose with hands thrust into his pockets, tilting his shoulders to one side. When he walked, the position gave his gait a sauntering cowboy quality, a mannerism that had seemed to her at odds with his reserved personality.

That same movement drew her eye again, and Meliz felt confident when he reached the bottom of the staircase that the man was indeed Hikaru. He looked up and their eyes met.

His narrowed with momentary confusion, then opened wide as he remembered her. He stood straighter and smiled in greeting. Brigitte spotted him as well.

"Hikaru," she exclaimed. "Do you have business here too?"

He shook his head, and a lock of hair fell forward, brushing his dark, shapely brows. If not precisely handsome, his strong features and dignified bearing had a certain allure.

"No. I am on holiday," he answered in precise, accented English. He leaned against the reception desk and gestured to the bruise on Meliz's cheek. "What happened?"

"I was attacked leaving a restaurant."

"Oh?" He raised his eyebrows. "In Manila?"

"Mm-hmm. I had dinner with a friend." She shook her head in self-reproach. "Afterwards, I walked back to my hotel alone. It was late and really stupid. A thief jumped me and grabbed my bag. The shoulder strap broke and hit me in the face. That's how I got the bruise."

Her stomach lurched. The fear and helpless fury of that moment washed over her. The memory materialized in her mind, muddled and indistinct: a dark alleyway, a violent jerk, the sting of the strap across her cheek, the kind cab driver who stopped to help. She swallowed the resurgent dread.

"Very unpleasant," Hikaru acknowledged.

Meliz laughed at this massive understatement. "Yeah, very unpleasant."

"Did he take your belongings?"

"No. Everything fell onto the pavement, and my computer broke. He ran off. We've just come from buying a new computer."

"Very good."

They lapsed into an uncomfortable silence. Brigitte, never at a loss for words or curiosity, chimed in, "What are you doing here?"

"My grandfather was a soldier here and on Mindanao," he answered, explaining his interest in Leyte. "I want to see the memorials."

Meliz stiffened. "Which grandfather?" she asked.

"My mother's father." Hikaru eyed her with caution, sensing the shift in her mood. "He was sixteen and wounded on Mindanao and then captured by the Americans near the end of the war."

Meliz crossed her arms over her middle, bringing pressure to bear on her churning stomach. Maybe his grandfather was here at the very same time as JD, separated by a few short miles. Maybe he infiltrated the American camp, killing soldiers as they slept. Though long decades stretched between then and now, she tried, but failed, to shake off her resentment.

"We're going to see the sights too," Brigitte chatted, oblivious to the heightened tension between them. "Meliz's grandfather was a soldier here, JD Hawkins."

Meliz braced for Hikaru's reaction, Japanese being one of the many languages into which JD's books had been translated. She'd once even seen an episode of the old television show in a hotel lobby in Prague, the actors' lines dubbed into Czech.

She waited for the inevitable look of surprise, perhaps the title of his favorite book. Instead, Hikaru nodded with formal dignity. "My grandfather's name is Yamato Sasaki."

The muscles between her shoulder blades tightened. "He's still alive?"

"Yes. He is old, but never sick." Hikaru smiled, politely sidestepping further inquiry by adding, "I am sorry. I must go. I have an appointment."

"Maybe you can join us for dinner," Brigitte suggested on a cheerful note. "And tomorrow we are headed to Palo and the landing site of General MacArthur. You could come with us."

He paused, surprised by the invitation, but was gracious in his evasion. "Thank you, not tonight. I do not know my plans tomorrow, although I intend to see the MacArthur memorial sometime."

Brigitte waved her hand with airy aplomb. "Text me if you want to join us."

He returned a farewell wave and left.

They gathered their bags and headed for the adjacent annex. The hotel had no elevator, and they trudged up three flights of stairs to their floor. Drops of sweat trickled down Meliz's back, trailing beneath her cotton tank top. She lifted the hair off her neck and looked down the long balcony.

"I think it's this way." She turned and Brigitte followed.

Their rooms adjoined. Both overlooked a courtyard teeming with blooming vines and tropical foliage. The rain beat down again, and humidity rose from the ground, turning the garden into a steaming jungle.

Meliz swiped the key card and opened the door. Brigitte walked into the spare, tidy room behind her.

"Don't be angry with him."

"What?" Meliz spun around.

"Where do you want this?" Brigitte indicated her backpack.

"Anywhere." She swung one arm wide in an impatient gesture. "What do you mean?"

"You are mad at Hikaru because of his grandfather." Brigitte leaned the backpack up against a bamboo dresser.

Meliz dropped onto the bed and ran a hand through her hair. "So what?" she countered with a defensive shrug and winced at the pain in her shoulder. "He's visiting memorials, sightseeing at places where . . . well, I don't know," she said, her tone a mixture of defiance and embarrassment. "Japan started the whole thing. Maybe I don't think he has the right to mourn their losses here."

"Maybe he's not. He could be doing something else. You don't know." Brigitte's rigid stance clashed with her usual relaxed posture and easygoing nature. "I have been to Dachau and the American cemetery at Normandy. I know what the Nazis did." Her voice trembled. "In my hometown, there is a small war memorial with the names of our soldiers who died etched in stone." She swallowed. "Killing and dying in the name of something evil is a terrible thing, but someone loved them. And many were very young, like Hikaru's grandfather."

Anger expanded in Meliz's chest. Brigitte and Hikaru had nothing to do with a conflict that ended decades ago. But JD's journal had infused her subconscious, the fear and desperation of that time becoming real and immediate.

"I had another grandfather, my dad's father," she lashed out. "I never knew him. His health was broken in a POW camp in Burma. He survived the war and married late, but died when my dad was nine. He wasn't like Hikaru's grandfather. He was always sick and depressed. He never recovered from those years." She scowled down at her feet. "Yeah, I guess. So sad they were young, but soldiers on both sides were young and died. The Japanese just really fucked things up for my grandfather and my dad and millions like them."

"*Ja*," her friend shot back, "and they really fucked things up for millions of their own children too." Brigitte didn't slam the door on her way out, but it felt as if she had.

Left in her wake were coursing eddies of hurt mixed with anger. Meliz stood, contrite and intent on following her out, but sat back onto the bed. She didn't want to talk, even if only to apologize.

She picked up her daypack and dumped the contents onto the

bedspread. Garrett's copy of *Everything Touches the Sky* lay atop the pile. Marshal Jameson astride Surprise gazed with manly fortitude off into the distance.

Meliz flipped to the dog-eared page where she had stopped reading the night before. The Marshal and Cody had just come across the massacre at the Green Crossing.

Her phone pinged. Meliz read Prescott's message, and her stomach lurched.

Hope you had a good trip. Sorry about Pops. He can be a handful. We'll be in Tacloban tomorrow. Want to see you.

Meliz compressed her lips, angry at her initial impulse to slink off and hide. She dropped the phone into her bag without answering and shoved the rest of her things in with it. On the hotel notepad, she scribbled a quick message and slipped it under Brigitte's door on her way out.

Chapter Fifteen

The man at arms is the only man.
—Ibsen

24 Dec., 1944, Biak Island, New Guinea—We're on Biak, but we're pulling up stakes again and moving to Finch Haven.

Leaving Leyte took some doing. Part of our group flew out of Tacloban Airstrip. I'd only been to the strip at night and hadn't expected the amount of activity that appeared to be normal, everyday operations. I don't think any of us, except maybe Castle, had seen such a busy airfield. Bombers, fighters, and transports took off at least one per minute. Tons of air traffic circled the strip waiting for a chance to land.

Most of our unit boarded there, but those of us still waiting around headed over to Tanauan Airfield where three C-46s waited to transport us to Biak. When we pulled up to the airstrip, a formation of Japanese planes came out of nowhere.

We all hit the deck, jumping out of trucks and scrambling for shelter. I wiggled up under a broken-down Caterpillar dozer. Bullets struck the ground, blazing a deadly path down the airstrip.

After the "All Clear," we trudged back to the transports, but scattered again when one of the drivers spotted a lone Zero headed straight for us. The plane strafed us before I could crawl back under the Caterpillar. I dove into a deep rut and got covered in mud.

Bullets whizzed past me, leaving a trail of heat and fear. One of those small metal projectiles plowing into my temple and I'd be done for. Seconds of pure terror burned forever into my memory.

I had plenty of company in that muddy rut all right. But by the Grace of God, none of us got hit. And that's more than I can say for some of the other boys.

We took off, but got diverted by bad weather to Palau Island. This was where the costly Battle of Peleliu was fought and won less than a month before.

There were no quarters. We slept under the planes.

25 Dec., (Christmas Day), Biak—Got a letter from June. Couldn't have asked for a better Christmas present.

1 Jan., 1945, Finch Haven—New Year's Eve passed in a dreary manner. Homesickness plagued most of us, though we tried not to show it. We "celebrated" by listening to the radio, firing small arms, and drinking warm beer.

We just got here, and now they tell us we gotta go back to Biak Island. Captain Griswold suggested we change the name of our unit to the Globetrotters because we've moved, by my count, five times in the two months since deployment. At least we're all back together again. The squadron was happy to see us. I'm not sure how they managed without our support.

Moving the unit takes a huge effort and is a massive pain in the ass. We make the move in three stages: an Advance Echelon to assess the area, the Main Echelon, which includes the bulk of the troops and equipment, and a Rear Echelon, composed of mostly mess personnel and yet more equipment. The C-46 can take up to 40,000 pounds, but I swear we pile on more than that. It's nerve-racking to fly on an overloaded plane.

Good thing the Rear Echelon is still on Biak. Anyway, it's gonna take us at least two weeks to get the whole unit back there.

4 Jan., Biak—I'm with the Advanced Echelon. We flew the 900 miles to Biak and started the process of building a camp and getting used to a new environment yet again.

**

Mokmer Airfield, Biak Island, January 1945

I read June's letter for the hundredth time. In reality, it was a picture of her letter. V-mail, short for Victory Mail, is shipped as film and reproduced as photographs when at its destination. This process makes it easier to censor and transport letters. By necessity, the letters are short, V-mail stationery being one-sided with limited space for writing. June had sent hers by the cheapest surface route.

I've received two letters from her since deploying, each one as impersonal as the other. No matter how much I studied her words, no hidden meaning or endearments revealed themselves. She wrote about friends and her classes, but nothing that would make me think I was someone special.

A lot of guys must have asked her to write. The disheartening picture of her sitting at a desk dutifully writing letters and checking names off a long list kept me up at night.

I folded the letter and slipped it in between the pages of Kipling's *Just So Stories*. Momma read the book to Boone and me growing up. She skipped over words she didn't know. As a little kid, I never noticed, until I got older and heard her reading to Mason. I think Momma bought the book because she liked the title. It jibed with her outlook on the world that everything should be *just so*, a firm belief in the proper and righteous path.

The small book fit easily into my duffle. I drew comfort from its presence. To me, books were like talismans. They held a spirit or essence within them. This one overflowed with love, worry, certainties, and whimsy. The book was worn and ragged, and carried my mother within its pages.

Much as I turned to literature for inspiration, I didn't believe any book in existence could help me figure out June Harper. I met her the summer before my senior year when Leo and I worked for the state health department. That summer, the Trinity River flooded the bottom.

They hired us and a couple other local lads to combat the threat of typhoid fever by chlorinating all the inundated wells. The job was tough, but paid well. We had no supervision or reports to make. We loaded up Leo's Chevy with bags of chlorinated lime and headed out for the river bottom looking for wells. We pumped the water out of the casing of the flooded well and dumped in the lime. Users needed to wait a bit to pump water out again and discard the first few gallons before drinking.

Most of the wells were in areas populated by Black folk. You can bet they were a mite bit suspicious of us White boys putting a strange powder in the water. My guess, a lot more than a few gallons were discarded before they would use the well again. Can't say as I blame 'em.

We stopped to treat a well on the property of Charles Goodwin, one of the richest men in the county. He ran a community of sharecroppers that used the well. Mr. Goodwin happened to be there with his niece, June, when we drove up.

She came out of a sharecropper's house holding baskets of fruit and jams and such. I don't believe I'd ever seen such a pretty girl, a tall, willowy brunette with velvety brown eyes and full red lips.

I knew enough about knights and ladies to figure June practiced what's known as *noblesse oblige*. If anybody looked the part of Lady Bountiful, it was June Harper.

The day dripped with humidity. I sweated up a storm, and white lime powder stuck to my arms and face. I must have appeared like a scrawny-assed ghost standing there staring up at her on that rickety old porch.

She smiled down at me. "You look like a ghost." I figured refinement and good manners kept her from adding "scrawny-assed."

Leo would be the first to say I'm never struck dumb, but for the life of me, I couldn't talk. My throat closed up and left me speechless. A lucky happenstance, because the words that had formed on my lips were "Marry me."

She came down the steps. I had never felt so painfully my lack of height as when she stood two inches taller.

I found my tongue quick enough. Poor Leo, left to finish the job while I "helped" June deliver the rest of her baskets. She wouldn't let me into the houses. Told me my coming in with all my dirt disrespected the families. I took good advantage of the time in between the houses, talking to her and making her laugh.

I'm noted for my talking skills, and she laughed in all the right places. Mr. Goodwin gave me the side-eye from time to time, but fortunately, his sharecroppers kept him too busy to play chaperone.

After that, I tried to find out everything I could about her. Two girls from our gang, Freda and Mary Jac, were friends with the Goodwin crowd. I spent the summer popping up in a casual way at dances and hangouts where my spies told me she would be.

The more we talked, the more I liked her. She liked me too. I could tell. But the summer passed, and she went home with little more than a peck on my cheek as a goodbye. Couldn't figure it out, until Freda told me I was too short.

"Did she say that?" I demanded.

"No. But it's obvious a girl that pretty doesn't want a man shorter than she is."

The rejection cast me down, I can tell you. I tried to put her out of my mind all senior year. After enlisting, I still couldn't shake how just the sight of June struck me dumb. With nothing to lose, I wrote her, asking if she would write me back.

When her letter arrived on Christmas Day, I believed it was a sign. I ripped the envelope open, ready to read a declaration of love and devotion, but the bland contents depressed me. She could have written this letter to any old Joe.

I'd put on height in the last year. So much so, my dungarees grazed above my ankles. Momma wouldn't have batted an eye, but my new inches didn't matter much, not when it came to June.

What kind of girl turns down a boy she likes because he's too short? I wasn't stupid. I knew tall men were preferred. But if June Harper was that shallow, maybe she wasn't the girl for me—but only if she *was* that shallow. Could be Freda didn't know anything about June or what she really thought—

"JD." Frank jolted me from my musings by bursting through the tent flap and plopping down on his cot.

He'd been assigned to the Advance Echelon, same as me, both of us helping to set up the medical dispensary. I can tell ya, sorting through medicines is heaps better than moving the heavy machinery used in maintaining the aircraft. This choice detail came open when some of the guys working the medic tent were struck down with dysentery. Like ghouls, we benefited from their suffering.

Frank jumped up. He grabbed my arm and tried to pull me to my feet. "You gotta come see this."

I sat unmoved, agitation being Frank's natural state. "What is it?"

He dropped down again, but this time next to me on my cot. "Do you remember Mick Cassidy?"

You betcha, I did. A big brute of a man, Mick Cassidy liked to inflict pain on the weak and vulnerable. He had a short temper and a cruel streak, the kind of guy who'd lure a gull from the sky just to break its wings.

Even though he'd beat up plenty of men, the bird incident landed him in the brig on orders from the ship's captain. That injured bird gave the crew a serious case of the heebie-jeebies.

"It's like the *Rime of the Ancient Mariner*," I informed Castle and Frank at the time.

"That was an albatross," Frank objected.

"Water, water, everywhere, And all the boards did shrink; Water, water, everywhere, Nor any drop to drink," George intoned in a deepened voice and laughed. "We memorized the entire poem in school, and that's the only part I remember. Grumpy's right, though. The bird was an albatross."

"I *know* the bird was an albatross," I snapped, irritated at their smug assumption they knew something about literature I didn't. "Our situation is *like* that. Even a gull is too close for comfort."

The medics proved me right when they patched that bird up. The men rallied around the battered gull, feeding and cleaning up after it until it could fly again.

Something else about Cassidy—he had been one of the two men from our unit who disappeared that night off Finch Haven.

"I'm not likely to forget that bastard. What of it?"

"He's here." Frank jerked his head toward the tent flap. "In the infirmary."

"Cassidy? Here? What did he have to say for himself?"

"Nothin'." Frank shook his head with a puffed-up air of importance. "He's dead."

My senses hummed with suspicion. That didn't make any sense. The Allies fought and won the Battle of Biak before our unit even deployed. He couldn't have been killed in battle, leastwise not here.

"How'd he die?"

"I was in the dispensary cataloguing medicines when they came in . . ." Frank began.

The infirmary stood as a maze of interconnected tents with canvas flaps separating the different sections. Curtained off on all four sides, no one would know you were in the dispensary unless you made a noise. They put Cassidy on one of the gurneys close by, and Frank overheard the whole thing.

"Natives brought him in. They dumped his body at the camp boundary, and a guard stumbled across it."

"What did the natives say?"

"Nothin'. They were long gone by the time the guard found him."

"How'd they know it was natives brought him in?"

"Who else?" he snapped. "Does it matter? Anyway, I heard Captain Griswold order Sarge to question them."

"Captain Griswold was there?"

"Yep. Fit to be tied too. I mean, he didn't yell or anything. But I could tell by his tone Cassidy showing up dead unsettled him."

I could imagine. A man once under his command found dead on an island that hasn't seen hostilities in months would unsettle anyone.

"Is Cassidy still in the infirmary?"

"No. They moved his body to the equipment shed. They want to keep this hush-hush." Frank scooted closer and lowered his voice. "He didn't have any ID on him, nothing: no tags, no insignia. *Nada*."

I frowned. "So, if his old unit hadn't been here, he could have gone unidentified for a while."

"Maybe forever," Frank replied in an ominous tone. "He'll have to be buried sometime, and soon."

I stood. "Let's take a look."

Frank jumped to his feet. "That's the ticket."

I'm not sure what moved me to investigate Mick Cassidy's death.

He had been a rotten human being and wasn't likely to be missed. Poking around his body could get us into serious trouble, but the file in my brain labeled "Mysteries" fell open. The chance to discover what those men from the *General Hersey* were doing appealed to my inner detective.

We were still few in number, and the equipment shed stood half-empty and happened to be the lone out-of-the-way place to stash a body. The small metal building backed up to a grove of palm trees. Constant shade kept the temperature inside from reaching the boiling point.

The heavy air within stifled my senses, and the lingering odor of decayed flesh grew stronger as we wound our way around the boxes of K-rations piled high. We found him laid out on a stretcher, a sheet pulled over him. Flies buzzed overhead.

Frank and I stared down at the shrouded form of Mick Cassidy, not sure what to do next. A wave of nausea washed over me, and I closed my eyes to steady my nerves.

The pulp magazines my sisters read were trashy, being full of romances and love letters, but some featured great crime stories with private dicks in the mold of Philip Marlowe and Sam Spade. I didn't kid myself into believing I would ever be that cool or hardened, but I set my features into a fair imitation of cynical detachment and pulled back the sheet.

It was Cassidy all right. A large nose knocked sideways by countless fights stood out on his swollen, blotchy face. I would have known him anywhere by that broken, crooked nose.

Daddy and I came across plenty of decomposing carcasses when hunting back home. A lot depended on the weather. Decay on these hot and rain-soaked islands happened quickly. Cassidy had not been dead long—a few days, at the most.

An uncomfortable prickling crawled up my neck. If I had the

timing right, Cassidy was here and alive when we first arrived, and so was whoever killed him.

"What'd Doc say?" I swallowed my growing unease.

"He didn't." Frank squatted next to the body and squinted hard into Cassidy's face. I knelt beside him.

"What do you mean?"

"He wasn't there. Doc left for Finch Haven this morning. They needed him to help move patients." Frank gritted his teeth and turned Cassidy's head with his fingertips, exposing the back. He sucked in his breath. "Look at this."

A narrow, piercing hole tunneled into the base of his skull, blood and dirt caked around the wound. I had never seen such an injury before. "What makes a hole like that? Too small for a bullet."

Frank scowled. "Dunno. But pushing something sharp in at that spot would sure kill a man."

He pulled the sheet back further to reveal an impressive collection of tattoos. They were the usual fare: skull and crossbones, an eagle, a rose, and the name, Hilda, in Old English script.

Below his collarbone, on the left side and hovering above his heart, a small, faded tattoo stood out in stark contrast to the rest. Black interwoven lines formed a graceful pattern, like a sailor's knot. Unlike the others, this one displayed both intricate design and artistic skill.

I don't know why, but that tattoo touched something in me and made me sorry for the guy. I despised Mick Cassidy, but a violent death alone and far from home was a terrible thing.

"Hey, Hawk, check this out," Frank whispered, his voice tinged with apprehension. "On his wrists. Rope burns. He was tied up."

I sat back on my heels. If Cassidy had been bound, that meant he was taken prisoner. There were holdout Japanese soldiers on Biak for sure, and we all knew how the Japanese Army treated prisoners of war. But to kill a captive outright, execute him, chilled me to the bone.

Frank picked up one of Cassidy's hands. I admired his determination and fortitude. I hadn't wanted anything to do with Cassidy alive, and I wasn't about to touch him dead.

He turned the hand over, palm side up. "Look at this." On the wrist, at the base of the palm, another tiny tattoo peeked through the dried mud on his skin. The dark squiggly lines could easily be missed through the dirt and scrapes. The simple design looked like the number eighty-one, followed by two faded letters. I couldn't make them out.

We studied the tattoo until voices interrupted our confused silence. Frank and I exchanged a panicked look. We threw the sheet over Cassidy and dove for the cover of the K-rations boxes.

"Where is he?" Captain Griswold snapped.

"Over here, sir." That was Pete Cooper, our quartermaster.

The captain stopped uncomfortably close to our hiding place. I could almost touch his pressed khakis through the crack of the stacked boxes.

"Okay, men, get him on the plane." The captain's clipped tone demanded action. "Orders are to transport the body back to Finch Haven. Get moving."

We heard the stretcher being picked up, and the group left the shed, carrying Cassidy's body. Frank and I slumped back against the boxes and released our pent-up breath.

"Son of a bitch," Frank whispered. "That was close."

We waited a reasonable amount of time and slipped out unseen. Neither of us said anything on the walk back to our tent, both of us deep in thought.

Maybe Japanese soldiers captured Cassidy and killed him. But why strip him of his ID? How did the natives get ahold of his body? And what the hell was he doing on Biak in the first place?

"Hey, Hawk."

"Yeah?" I stopped, surprised to find us in front of our tent.

"Don't put anything about Cassidy in your diary," Frank insisted, casting a furtive glance around.

The brass picked up our journals once in a while to make sure we weren't giving away important intelligence. As if we could. They kept us in the dark better than they did the enemy.

I typically wrote down everything of interest to me. So far, none of my pages had caught their attention. Cassidy was different though. We weren't supposed to know about him.

Fear lodged in the pit of my stomach, and my nose twitched like a rabbit catching the scent of danger. Frank being all jumpy made me even more nervous. We had one piece of a puzzle and no way of knowing what the rest of it looked like or how to solve it.

Chapter Sixteen

Eternal vigilance is the price of liberty.
—Wendell Phillips

Meliz ducked into a café not far from the hotel, grateful to be out of the rain. A smattering of customers sat within, and she easily found a small, unoccupied table at a window overlooking the street.

The café's surfer décor gave off a Southern California vibe. Meliz settled in, at ease in the homey environment. She ordered a latte, opened her new computer, and pulled up her documents folder.

Meliz poised to write a long-overdue update. Indecisive, her hands hovered above the keyboard before dropping into her lap. Her mind refused to focus, and her thoughts drifted back to the argument with Brigitte.

Her anger was grief recast and redirected at innocent targets. She owed her friend an apology, but that wasn't all. She owed her the truth as well.

To hide her embarrassment, Meliz had withheld from Brigitte the whole story of her assault. She left out key information, specifically, the entire evening right before the mugging.

Meliz had set aside her suspicions of Prescott as the by-product of an overanxious imagination. She resolved to be more rational and arranged to meet him for dinner at a restaurant of his choosing. A gesture she soon regretted.

The private restaurant, a strange combination of stuffy nineteenth-century men's club and sleazy modern-day strip joint, seemed designed with the express purpose of putting her teeth on edge. Walls of dark wood paneling and furniture covered in leather upholstery signaled unrestrained masculinity. Stunning crystal chandeliers provided the dimmest of light and gave cover to hungry eyes and lecherous grins.

Every table was occupied by either a group of businessmen or an older man with a much younger woman. Servers, exclusively pretty women in sheer dresses and backbreaking high heels, glided between the tables and playfully slapped away groping hands. Meliz's skin crawled.

She experienced a strong urge to turn and run, but Prescott had spotted her. He waved her over to the table and flashed a reassuring smile at her uncertainty.

"Sorry about the place." He pulled out a chair. "But we've been members here since forever, and they serve the best traditional food in Manila. I promise."

His quick assessment of her mood and apology allayed some of her discomfort. Meliz sat at the table and made an effort to relax her shoulders.

"Where am I?" she asked and added with admirable tact, "This place is an unusual hybrid."

"To say the least," he agreed with a short laugh. "The club started out as a convenient meeting spot for businessmen right after the war. In fact, Pops is an original member. The place has changed over the years. Membership is required, but as you can see, it has, ah, evolved to meet other needs as well."

A waitress slinked over with confident allure. Prescott mumbled instructions, and she left with an accommodating nod.

"I hope you don't mind, but I've ordered *basi* wine. It's a local Filipino drink made from sugarcane," he explained. "The stuff has been manufactured here since before the Spanish conquest. In fact, the locals rebelled when the Spanish took over its production and forced them to buy their wine."

"How did that end for the locals?"

"Not well." Prescott shrugged. "They lost."

A twinge of irritation further dampened Meliz's mood. "That always seems to be the way of it," she observed, with a tight, cynical smile.

"The wine is a traditional Filipino favorite," he continued, as if she had not spoken. "This place has the best *basi.* They serve it by the glass and keep the bottle under lock and key, guarded like the crown jewels. I'm not a big wine aficionado, but I like its bittersweet quality."

The server returned with the wine. Meliz took a sip and forced herself not to grimace. She didn't like the taste, but the rich liquid ran through her veins and warmed her from the inside out. A half a glass later, her mind and muscles unwound.

Prescott ordered their food with the ease of long practice, and they shared an excellent meal of fried salted fish and *pinakbet.* Afterward, they each had a cup of the local brand of *Kape Baroko* coffee, a species of the coffee bean processed and consumed throughout the Philippines and Southeast Asia.

The alcohol, food, and coffee mixed to produce a breezy, sensual atmosphere, and the spark of attraction flared between them again. Any feelings of irritation or suspicion faded away with the exhilaration of a new flirtation.

Prescott regaled her with stories about his family, most featuring his grandfather's early attempts to establish the business. He admitted to Googling Meliz and discovering her connection to JD. The talk veered in that direction, though his curiosity stopped short of being intrusive.

He had read a few of JD's books as a boy, but westerns were never his thing. "I like biographies." He made this nerdy confession with a charming, self-deprecating shake of his head.

Prescott pushed a stray hair back over her shoulder, and his fingers brushed her neck. She drew in a quick breath and covered it up with a little cough. Meliz hoped he would offer to take her back to the pension, determined to act on the impulse overruled by her fatigue that first night in Manila.

He insisted on paying the bill and asked with appealing hesitancy, "Can I give you a lift back to your hotel?"

Meliz agreed and prepared to leave, but froze in mid-rise as a blur of wheels skidded to a stop at their table. She sat back in her chair, shocked to see Prescott's grandfather materialize with lightning speed out of nowhere.

"What are you doing?" Jack Walker, Sr. snapped, anger hardening his features.

Prescott frowned. "What do you mean, Pops? I'm out to dinner with a friend. You remember Meliz. We met at the San Francisco Airport."

"Don't treat me like a dullard. Of course, I remember," Jack Walker spat. He cut his eyes over at Meliz with a curt nod. She returned an uncertain smile.

Prescott leaned over to speak with his grandfather. They engaged in an intense, whispered conversation, none of which she could hear. Other diners threw quick, curious glances their way.

Meliz sat, confused and unmoving, until a young man hastened over. She recognized him as Prescott's family friend, the same one who had played in the band at Deejays.

He grasped the handles of the old man's wheelchair. "Sorry, Prescott. I turned my back for a second, and he disappeared. What's happening?"

"Nothing." Prescott spoke in a low and composed tone, but annoyance at his grandfather's display marred his usually pleasant expression. He touched Meliz on her arm. "Give me a minute, and I'll take you back."

"That's okay." She gathered her bag and stood. "I'll catch a cab."

Prescott protested, but Meliz backed away. "Thanks for dinner. I had a great time. Nice to see you again, Mr. Walker." She dashed off before he could insist further.

Meliz paused outside the restaurant for mere seconds. Worried Prescott would follow her, she hurried away, turning her steps in an unfamiliar direction. She wandered, angry and unfocused on her surroundings, her mind occupied with self-recrimination. Why hadn't she listened to her instincts?

The echo of a dark and deserted street penetrated her troubled mind too late. A man rushed her from out of the shadows, the lower half of his face hidden by a red bandana. His eyes burned with malice.

Meliz screamed and ran. The thief caught her by the satchel strap. He jerked her back, wrenching her shoulder. She screamed again and flailed her fists, but hit only empty air.

The leather strap broke and slapped her across the cheek. Her computer crashed to the pavement.

The thief ran away. He neglected to grab her wallet laying among the broken bits and pieces. An off-duty cab driver parked at the corner called the police. He gave her a tissue to dry her tears.

At the hospital, Meliz told Brigitte nothing of the confrontation between Prescott and his grandfather. Strange though it was, the old man's behavior had not prompted her hasty departure from the restaurant.

Her stunned gasp upon seeing Jack Walker's companion had gone unnoticed by the arguing men. The musician, Prescott's friend, was dressed in jeans, tennis shoes, and a dark green hoodie—exactly like the man Brigitte had described leaving her room back at the pension.

Meliz started and blinked at the sound of her phone alarm. She scanned the café with a self-conscious glance, aware she'd been staring blindly at the blank computer screen for the last half hour.

Straightening in the chair, she mentally prepared herself to meet Brigitte. Meliz hadn't received a text from her friend and could only hope she'd read the note and would accept her peace offering of dinner.

Brigitte's erratic behavior and affinity for drugs stood out in stark contrast to her own deliberate personality and self-restraint. Their opposing natures had given Meliz pause in allowing the German woman to join in on her quest. But Brigitte had proved a reliable and clearheaded friend, and Meliz was truly sorry for her insensitivity.

She shoved the tablet into her daypack and stood. A knot of worry twisted her stomach as she headed out the café door.

Anxiety, her old nemesis since childhood, had struck first in elementary school. Fear expressed itself in the tattered ends of her hair, chewed in an unconscious effort to relieve her worries.

When her parents consulted a therapist, JD railed against the decision. His generational prejudices rose up and clashed with his usually compliant daughter's medical expertise. He viewed with scorn any reliance on psychiatry, or "shrinks" as he not so delicately put it.

"She's a kid, for heaven's sake. People turn normal behavior into head cases these days. She needs to learn to trust herself. Listen to her gut."

For once, her beloved grandfather had been wrong. Listening to her gut proved difficult because it always told her to be afraid. Therapy had given her tools to help control her anxiety, but in stressful situations, her stomach still tied into knots.

Meliz drew in a lungful of hot, humid air, and the tension eased.

She wasn't worried about Brigitte. She knew her kindhearted friend would forgive her. Fear lingered as an aftereffect of the Walkers' strange behavior and the appearance of Prescott's friend.

A malevolent apparition floated through Meliz's brain, sowing doubt and confusion. She struggled to form a clear picture, grasping at vague clues and suspicions. She tried in vain to align them into a logical order.

At dinner, Prescott had not mentioned them coming to Tacloban, even though she spoke at length of her plans to visit Leyte to better understand her grandfather's war. Was Jack behind their sudden visit? Was Prescott privy to his grandfather's machinations?

Her gut told her that Walker, Sr. played a key role in the mystery of JD's missing pages. She wanted to believe her gut, but could not be sure it wasn't anxiety talking.

Meliz wove with absentminded precision in and out of the crowd along the busy sidewalk. She rarely thought of her paternal grandfather, a man she never knew. Perhaps the island setting had jogged loose a buried memory, for he arose in her mind, a somber figure in a suit standing in a tropical park, awash in black-and-white photography. Though he stood straight and dignified, sadness enveloped him. The war had killed her *yeye* as surely as if a bullet or bayonet had pierced his body.

Meliz set her lips in a firm, determined line. Now, over seventy years later, the war had also killed JD.

Chapter Seventeen

It ain't the individual, nor the army as a whole,
But the everlasting teamwork of every bloomin' soul.
—J. Mason Knox

Alberta's cell phone vibrated. She glanced at Ed with an apologetic shrug.

Her husband rolled his eyes with weary patience. "Go ahead. Take it."

She stepped out of the busy restaurant onto the sidewalk. "What have you got for me, Bob?"

Her inquiry into Walker Senior yielded little of note and led her to contact an old friend in San Francisco where Walker's company headquartered. Robert "Bob" Goode was an investigative reporter with a bi-monthly column, "The Goode Report," in the *San Francisco Chronicle.*

"Well, Walker was assigned to the Second Combat Cargo Group, same as your guy, except he was with another squadron. Nothing dicey there."

She groaned; another dead end.

"The weird thing is I couldn't find Walker's discharge from the army."

Alberta stood near the curb outside the popular local eatery. A small town, Silver Springs had its own set of local celebrities, Alberta among them. She smiled and waved to people while trying to focus on what Bob said.

"Okay. What does that mean?"

"All soldiers received discharges after the war, called a Report of Separation. But when I spoke with my contact at the military archives, he couldn't find anything like that for Walker."

"Maybe it's lost."

"Sure, I guess, but I think that's unlikely, particularly when he dug up Walker's enlistment card. This has general information—you know, date and place of birth, education, that stuff. The card lists his service record, his assignments, training, and so on."

"Can you cut to the chase, please?" She spied Ed's exasperated expression through the window.

"Sorry, forgot about the time difference. Well, long story short. The military has codes, usually numbers and letters, for different assignments. His was something called SR18."

"What does that stand for?"

"Good question. There was nothing in the archives. Next, I asked my contact at the DOD."

"You called the Department of Defense?"

"When I couldn't find out what service was attached to that code, I figured it was my next step."

"And . . .?"

"She told me the code didn't exist and not to call back."

"What? You mean, like never?"

"Ah, yeah . . . and she hung up on me."

"So, we've hit a brick wall?"

"Well, there are brick walls and then there are brick walls," he explained. "Her nonresponse or denial tells us something's there.

That's why I got back with my archives guy, and we searched the military databases for that code. We came up with thirty-nine other men and five women with the same designation."

"The men on the ship," Alberta mumbled.

"What?"

She told him about JD's journal entry. "More like a quick notation, but the coincidence is striking. Don't you think? Almost that exact number of men got off the *General Hersey* under cover of night at New Guinea."

"I'm not sure what to tell you, Bert. Eighteen is a number often associated with covert actions. They could have been some kind of commando unit. Honestly, I wouldn't be surprised if the records are scrubbed the next time we check." He paused. "Another thing," his tone serious, "Walker's company . . . the board meeting in Manila is scheduled for September. He may be there on business, but not a board meeting."

**

Nestled in the large, cushioned desk chair in JD's study, Alberta sent Meliz the new information, even though the sun had not yet risen in the Philippines. They exchanged brief texts before signing off so Meliz could go back to bed.

Alberta glared at her cell phone. Her mind churned over the possible ramifications of Jack Walker's involvement. His enigmatic presence nibbled away at her nerves, and she longed to do more to protect Meliz.

She wrestled with the idea of calling Gwen, knowing that Meliz would object to alerting her parents. Long association with the Hawkins clan gave her clear insight into the family dynamics.

Meliz's grandmother had hired Alberta to babysit five-year-old Gwen when she went back to nursing full time. At thirteen, the welcomed work came at a difficult time for Alberta. Her mother had died the year before, and with her father long gone, the family struggled to make ends meet. Alberta, as the eldest, was responsible for keeping her brothers and sisters from starving.

She was lucky to find a full-time babysitting job. In the mid-sixties, mothers who worked outside the home were unusual. Alberta checked herself.

Unusual for a White woman, but not for many women of color. Her own mother never stopped working. She took in washing and cleaned houses. She enrolled in a layman's nursing course and earned better pay as an in-home caregiver.

Her mother worked almost every day of her life. She had worked until her heart gave out.

Alberta sat back in the chair. On the computer, Dr. Rivera's file of JD's scanned book presented her with tables and graphs.

She clicked it closed and took off her glasses, rubbing her tired eyes. Leave it to academics to reduce everything to data points. Alberta remained unconvinced a bunch of related terms, literary devices, and symbolism added up to Iejima Island and the Green Cross flights.

"I guess it's as likely as anything else," she admitted aloud, sighing for dramatic effect. Her own careful review of JD's journal and correspondences had yielded no new clues to the mysterious missing pages.

Alberta leaned on the desktop, chin in hand. Her reflection stared back at her from the blank computer screen, a weird photo negative of her face.

"Hey, Bert, I'm going to bed." Ed poked his head around the study door. "Will you be much longer?"

"Just a few more minutes."

He walked off, Ranger close on his heels. The old German shepherd's claws clicked a lazy staccato on the hardwood floor.

Alberta took a sip of her lukewarm tea. She and Ed couldn't stay at the ranch much longer. There was a caretaker to be hired, but with Meliz's trip and Alberta's own oft-delayed book deadline, there hadn't been time to advertise for qualified candidates.

No one wanted the house to leave the family. Though the City Council had floated a proposal to preserve the ranch and open it to the public, there was no talk of selling it. To Alberta, the rooms already echoed, cold and empty as a deserted museum. The amount of life one gregarious old man had breathed into these walls amazed her. She stood, melancholy falling like a shroud around her.

Alberta's eyes alighted on a row of impressive leather-bound volumes. Adorned with gold lettering along their spines, they stood at attention on the bottom shelf of the crowded bookcase: all twenty-eight in the Marshal Clyde Jameson series.

She pulled *Everything Touches the Sky* from its penultimate place. Since she had Garrett's digital file, she hadn't bothered to disturb this special edition. Alberta ran her hand over the smooth cover and inhaled the scent of leather. She doubted if anyone had ever read these copies. The unused binding crackled as she opened the book and something slipped from behind the cover and fluttered to the floor.

The white envelope came to rest at her feet, starkly framed by the polished, dark wood. Alberta picked it up and sucked in her breath. The return address bore the name Kiko Tamaki on a letter sent several months ago from Nago, Okinawa.

She hurried back to the desk and typed in the name of the city. Located on the northern end of the island, Nago was popular with tourists and boasted unspoiled beaches and scenic hikes. The city also lay in close proximity to the World War II airfield of Motobu.

Alberta covered her face with shaking hands, reluctant to open the letter. The search for answers had been a game, a diversion from her grief. Whatever information this letter contained could make everything real: the children, the village, the motivation behind JD's secretive behavior.

She shoved the book away from her. Of all things, he hid the letter in that damn book. He hid everything from them . . . from her. He had skulked around, making plans, keeping her in the dark.

Alberta gripped the edge of the desk. This was all wrong.

JD didn't have secrets. He was open, emotional, moral, and kind. JD was her mentor and best friend. She knew him better than she knew almost anyone else in her life.

Alberta picked up the letter and turned it over in her hands. Her fingers tingled with apprehension.

Except he did have a secret, a secret rooted in shame. Of that, she was certain, and it made her afraid.

Chapter Eighteen

Excerpt from *Everything Touches the Sky*

Todd Jordan, the commander at Fort Cimarron, was the type of officer more concerned with the fit of his uniform than the welfare of his men. That hadn't always been the case. His predecessor, Colonel Bruce Lang, exemplified the best the army had to offer, a fine soldier and a good man. Even the most hardened among his troops shed tears when they brought Lang's body in, his head shattered by a stray bullet from a hunter's rifle. No sooner did they put him in the ground than the army promoted his much-less-beloved second and placed Jordan in command of the sprawling fort.

I'd butted heads with that prancing show pony more than once over the years, but mostly, I ignored him—easy to do with Lang in charge. All that had changed. Now Lang was dead, I could no longer avoid Jordan's small-mindedness and know-nothing bluster.

A little man, in both character and stature, Jordan enjoyed the trappings of command, the ceremony and deference paid his rank, but I had never seen anything greater in him. Duty, service, camaraderie—these played no role in his dealings with the men or those he was tasked to protect.

I didn't have any confidence in Jordan's ability to handle the massacre at the ford, but the matter wasn't up to me. With Indians involved, I had no choice but to report the killings to the army. Cody and I turned our horses toward Fort Cimarron and did our best to skirt the gruesome scene.

The little girl had cried herself to sleep. Cody passed her to me when his arm went numb. I held her in place, wedged between me and the saddle horn. Bundled up tight in the horse blanket, her head bobbed up and down in time with Surprise's smooth gait. Every time I looked down at her dark hair, a lump of pity rose in my throat.

I wasn't worried about how they'd treat her once we got to the fort. Lang's widow, Abigail, still lived there. She and her daughters ran the infirmary, her youngest having married one of Lang's junior officers. Abigail, as smart and levelheaded as had been her husband, would know better than me how to comfort the girl.

No, my pity arose from a gut-level feeling of distrust and unease, a conviction that justice for the girl and her kin would be in short supply. Jordan, though a preening idiot, did not strike me as malevolent. That couldn't be said for some of the other officers. Without strong leadership, the rotten and corrupt had gained the ear of their shallow new commander.

"Marshal, look." Cody alerted me to a group of five mounted riders coming our way.

I couldn't see who they were at this distance and loosened my gun in its holster. Pulling it out had never come easy. My shoulder muscles stretched taut, and the ache in my flexed fingers rudely reminded me of the weight of my years.

I relaxed when Cody let out a whoop and spurred his horse forward. A few more strides and I recognized the distinctive battered black hat and hooked nose of Sandy Reynolds. The sheriff of Cimarron and surrounding counties, Sandy was a bit rough around the edges, but strived to be a decent lawman. He and his posse appeared no more concerned than a bunch of old hens out for a Sunday stroll in the park.

"Well, *Marshal.*" His lazy drawl emphasized my title. Sandy gave the impression of an easygoing man, but he was jealous of his territory. "Looks like you've stumbled across an Indian killing." He gestured with a dismissive nod at the sleeping girl.

"You might say that." I eyed him, stony-faced.

There were four other men with him, or more like three men and a boy. The boy, pale and drawn, teetered on the verge of being sick. I guessed correctly it was him alerted the sheriff.

"But I'd say more like a massacre, wouldn't you, boy?"

"Yes, sir," he croaked and swallowed hard. "I didn't see the girl. Else I would've brought her in. I swear it, sir."

"I'm sure you would've, son."

My serious tone and lack of warmth shifted the mood. The men tensed and darted their eyes around, suddenly feeling exposed. Maybe they hadn't believed the boy or thought dead Indians didn't much matter.

"What are we gonna find, Marshal?" Sandy asked.

"A crime. And I got here the only witness."

Chapter Nineteen

Difficulties are the things that show what men are.
—Epictetus

9 Feb., 1945, Biak Island—Things are quiet here, though we've had our hands full keeping planes in the air. We're short parts and have to jury rig something fierce to get them flying. Chief rides the officers as hard as he can for what we need, but sometimes it can't be helped and we send guys up in an unsafe plane. I have flown a few times as an extra hand with supplies and wounded. Mostly, I'm on the line doing my part to keep the squadron running as smoothly as possible.

George has been acting irritable of late. I've taken to calling him Grumpy, like Frank, to snap him out of it. The insult doesn't have quite the sting it once might have, because Frank is unusually sunny these days.

Ever since Cassidy turned up dead, Frank's decided he's Sherlock Holmes and spends his down time "investigating." He hasn't had much luck, but he's right to be suspicious.

Word got out about Cassidy, and all the gossip and rumor forced the brass to release an official statement. The report concluded that he fell into Japanese hands and was unlawfully executed.

Believable enough, I guess, but Captain Griswold did not seem convinced. Nobody else here bought the story either.

I can't figure a way to get at the truth, but I encourage Frank to keep digging. The investigation makes him happy, and that's good for me.

We heard our troops made a push into Manila. George's crew flew wounded to a base in Australia. They said the fighting is like nothing they have ever seen. The civilians are taking a beating. Wish we could get them out of harm's way.

Germany was going, but they have hung on and pushed back—the Japanese too.

10 Feb.—George finally told me what's bugging him. Josefina is pregnant again, about four months along. I think he is happy and sad at the same time. Missing out on home life is tough. I complain June hardly ever writes, but I think if she were my girl, I'd miss her a lot more. I would be worried about a stateside Joe stealing her away. It happens. A lot of guys get "Dear John" letters. Who needs that?

21 Feb.—Haven't written in my journal lately because we've been busy with our unit newspaper. Yeah, you heard that right, a newspaper: the *Biak Bulletin*. I'm the editor. The brass hasn't authorized the paper, so we keep the whole operation under wraps. It's a one-page flyer, but we fit a lot on a page. I even have a cartoonist, name of Bradford Wainwright. Sounds pretty snooty, but he's just an ole country boy from Kentucky.

One of the guys found a mimeograph machine in the supply shed. We pinched some paper, and Doc lets us use the typewriter in the medic's tent after-hours. The cartoon is the hardest, because Bradford has to stencil it on and there's so little room. We put out our first issue, about fifty copies. It isn't much, but the men pass them around.

I write a serial about an old-time US Marshal, and we pepper the newspaper with inside digs at the brass. We try to keep the content as light as possible.

The newspaper's a diversion, and the guys enjoy reading it. The combination of boredom and backbreaking work that is life here on Biak Island is mind numbing. Now, with the paper and the brass sniffing around trying to find out who's responsible, life's gotten a bit spicier.

Couple of final notes: I got a letter from Leo. He sent it to Momma, and she sent it on to me. He's in Europe and has seen some tough fighting. Our buddy Joe Duncan is with him. Leo couldn't give me any details, but I got the gist of what he was trying to say. Hope he stays safe.

The Marines have invaded Iwo Jima. If past island battles are any indication, it is going to be a long, hard slog.

**

Mokmer Airfield, Biak Island, February 1945

"Hold the damn light still, will ya?" I complained in a whisper, trying to wrap the wax stencil around the cylinder.

Frank steadied the flashlight. "I swear I heard something."

His eyes darted around and he shifted, bumping my elbow and causing me to push the stencil out of alignment again. I bit back a sharp retort. Snapping at Frank never paid off. He only snapped right back.

It was hard enough to stay calm without his constant fidgeting and nattering. I knew as well as he did we'd catch hell (or worse) if caught.

Frank and I were in the middle of printing the second edition of the *Biak Bulletin*. We huddled together in the supply shed where we'd set up our printing press, such as it was. We carved out an obscure corner and used stacked boxes and a plastic tarp to hide the mimeograph machine when not in use.

I had learned the hard way that publishing a newspaper took

delicate management skills. We had a "staff" of six regular contributors and weeding out material never went over well. To include everyone's work was impossible. I tried to soften the blow by telling them their pieces would appear in the next edition, but we all knew each one might be the last.

The first edition made a big splash. The men loved it, but the brass didn't see the humor in it, none of it, and that put us in their crosshairs. Wished it'd been my masterful prose caused the excitement, but we all knew Bradford's work was what got the brass all riled up.

His comic made a funny, not-so-subtle jab at the miles of red tape it takes to keep everything stocked and the planes flying. We heard through the tin cans that Captain Griswold got pressure to flush out the culprits. Up to now, he had overlooked the insubordination.

"Got it," I whispered once the stencil sat straight on the cylinder.

Frank turned the crank. The rhythmic thump of the machine pulsed in the still air of the supply shed. The danger of discovery loomed largest during this part of the process. Any passerby would hear the noise, and the smell of ink was a dead giveaway.

We decided to keep each edition to fifty copies, to save on our supply of paper. The copy limit also cut the nerve-racking time spent printing the damn thing.

It didn't take long before we had a pile of newly minted *Bulletins.* I held the papers in my hands and inhaled the heady scent of ink. A quick read over the finished product gave me a sense of pride. Sure, the *Bulletin* didn't amount to much in the grand scheme of things. The paper may have been a rinky-dink little flyer with cramped words and a crudely cut-out comic, but it was my baby.

"Shh," Frank hissed, even though I hadn't said a word. He grabbed my arm in a vicelike grip and stilled like a frightened animal.

I heard them too. Opposing sets of footsteps meeting and

stopping right on the other side of the wall where we crouched. They were so close I could have touched them through the sheet metal.

"Evening, John." Doc Wilson's familiar Southern drawl came muffled through the metal barrier.

"Luka." Captain Griswold's crisp, military tone penetrated more clearly. "How are the troops this evening?"

"As can be expected; some persistent jungle rot and a couple cases of the clap."

The captain chuckled. "It never fails to amaze me how the men find women no matter where we are."

Doc cleared his throat. A brief silence followed.

"Was he buried?" Captain Griswold asked.

"Not sure. My guess, they put him out to sea. All my requests for information have fallen on deaf ears, as they say. HQ is not forthcoming."

"With me neither." I heard a hitch of anger in the captain's voice. "I was glad to see the back of Cassidy. He was a cruel man and an undisciplined soldier. But this is bad business."

"I couldn't agree with you more, but there's nothing to be done. Our orders were clear."

Captain Griswold did not respond, and we heard the shuffle of feet as they passed each other. A sigh of relief froze on my lips when the captain spoke again, "Don't suppose you know who's putting out this *Biak Bulletin*?" His voice sounded as clear as if he were standing right next to me.

Frank's grip tightened into a blood-stopping tourniquet. He held his breath and looked close to fainting. I felt a mite dizzy myself.

The one officer who for sure knew was Doc Wilson. I imagined him pivoting slowly on his heels, looking back at the captain, hands thrust into his pockets and a Sphinx-like expression on his face.

"I was wondering where they found a typewriter." The captain laughed. "Not to mention the damn mimeograph machine."

"A lot of the men use our typewriter after-hours," Doc answered with his usual calm. "You can fit more on a letter that way. I figure the culprit could be any one of them."

I admired Doc's answer—evasive, but technically truthful.

I could hear the captain's wry smile in his tone. "I won't put you on the spot. I have a good idea who's behind the thing. But our supply chain has tightened up since that comic caught the colonel's eye. I'll let sleeping dogs lie for now."

"Funny what a bit of pointed ridicule can do," Doc drawled.

"So long as it's just 'a bit.' Night, Luka."

"Night.

Their footsteps faded away, and I pried Frank's fingers from my numb arm. We breathed in a deep lungful of the stuffy supply shed air.

"Fuck, fuck, fuck," Frank blurted. "The captain knows."

"He *suspects*. That's all." I managed to keep my voice even. "We have to be careful. I'm sure Doc'll warn us to keep everything toned down."

Even through his alarm, Frank bristled at any suggested restrictions to his rights. "It's the goddamn First Amendment, Hawk. They can't tell us what we should and shouldn't write."

"Yeah, I'm pretty sure they can. I don't think the First Amendment applies much to soldiers at war."

We stood, our legs stiff from crouching. I jumped up and down to get the blood pumping again.

We threw the tarp over the mimeograph machine. I shoved the stack of newspapers into a medic's bag "borrowed" from the infirmary, and we slipped out of the shed unseen.

Activity at the airfield had slowed to an evening trickle. No one was about, and we turned toward camp. Darkness and humidity muffled the lights, and our footsteps sounded faint on the gravel path. A chill ran up my spine.

Everything stilled like an indrawn breath, that fraction of a second before exhaling. I knew the feeling from childhood. The quiet right before a tornado touched down.

A bomb hit the strip, and the air exploded, shooting a huge fireball up into the sky. The force of the blast threw us up and slammed us down onto the ground.

I landed hard on my back, my fall broken by the bag of newspapers. I lay there, addled.

Muted groaning reached me through the ringing in my ears. I pushed up onto my hands and knees. My head throbbed, near to bursting.

Frank lay stretched out on the ground, a bloody gash across the top of his head. I crawled on all fours and got to him just as he was coming around.

"Hold on," I bawled over my deafness.

I cushioned his head with the bag. My own head pounded as I staggered toward the radio room, waving my arms and screaming for help. Two more bombs fell, driving me to my knees, arms flung over my head.

Air Traffic Control headquarters burst into flames. Fire engulfed two big C-54s. Pandemonium reigned.

Someone grabbed my arm. "Are you hurt?" George yelled above the sirens and the roar of the fire.

"Not me. Frank." I pointed back in the direction I had come.

He pushed me toward the jeeps speeding up from camp. "I'll get him. You get checked out."

I tried to run, but my feet stumbled over the smallest tufts of grass. I could not keep my balance and fell as the first wave of responders flooded the airfield.

They carried me to a waiting jeep. Dead and wounded lay everywhere. A boy stumbled around, dazed. He held his arm from the shoulder down in his other hand.

I pointed and croaked, "Over there, over there."

I struggled to get up, to help, but they pushed me back down. The last thing I remember, they bundled that boy up and carried him off. I don't know if he lived or died.

**

"Ah, shit," Frank groaned, his eyes fluttering open. "I was hoping I'd wake up stateside. Instead, I'm still here staring at your ugly mug."

I had propped a chair up against a tent pole next to Frank's cot. Doc diagnosed me with a concussion, told me to lie down, and ignored me when I didn't. There were plenty of other men needing his attention.

Frank had come out of surgery over two hours earlier. He sustained a serious blow to the head, but it had not cracked his skull. A fact I found funny.

"With a head like yours, who needs a helmet, huh, Grumpy?" I grinned, relieved he had woken up cranky and irritable. Good ole Frank.

"Ha, ha, you're some comedian." He grimaced and fumbled with the bandages around his head.

"Don't do that." I slapped his hands away. "Doc put fifteen stitches in to patch you up. You won't be going home, but you could get furlough to Sydney."

He made a wavy, helpless gesture in the air. "Nah, if I can't go home, I'd rather stay here."

"Men." Captain Griswold appeared out of nowhere at the foot of Frank's cot. Dark bags hung under his eyes and a few new wrinkles creased his brow, but he stood straight and in command. I scrambled to my feet and saluted.

"Sit down, Private. You look done in."

I sat. Not only did my head spin, but my eyes liked to have bulged out of their sockets. The captain had the medic's bag slung over his shoulder. He dropped it onto the foot of the cot.

"I think this is Private Hoffman's. The bag was found with him and somehow made it to the infirmary in his company."

Frank choked. I squirmed and cut my eyes away. "Don't know, sir. That bag could be anybody's."

"Well, I was hoping it was one of yours." He glared at me. "There's a newspaper in here I think needs to get out. Can you do that?"

We glanced at each other out of the corners of our eyes. Frank wasn't talking. He'd passed the buck to me. If this were a trap, I would take the fall.

I straightened my shoulders. "Yes, sir," I answered. "I'll make sure the paper gets out."

"Good. The men could use a laugh about now." He left us with a brusque nod.

The tension eased from my neck and shoulders. We weren't a combat unit covered in blood, guts, and glory, but I believed Captain Griswold was the finest CO in the whole Pacific Theater.

Chapter Twenty

To dare, and again dare, and forever dare!
—Danton

"Your parents fuck you up and you still want their love and approval. That is crazy, *ja*?"

They lay across the bed in Brigitte's hotel room staring up at the ceiling. An empty wine bottle sat on the bedside table. Still stuffed from a dinner of chicken adobo, steamed rice, and stir-fried vegetables, they discussed their deepest fears and insecurities.

Meliz nodded. Screwed-up parents certainly sucked, although she could hardly relate. Her own loving and supportive (albeit nosy) family gave her little insight into Brigitte's struggles. She knew herself fortunate for never having reason to question her parents' love.

Her friend talked on, revealing the strained nature of her family life with unhappily divorced parents, a classically distant father, and an overachieving older sister. While Meliz listened, a feeling of shame crept over her; how petty and small-minded was her reluctance to include Brigitte. How trivial her own problems and anxieties seemed in comparison, just stupid counterintuitive by-products of unearned affluence and opportunity.

Brigitte stopped talking. A long silence convinced Meliz she had fallen asleep.

She sat up. The room spun even though Brigitte had drunk most of the bottle.

"Off to bed, then?" her friend chirped, and popped up onto her feet with surprising agility.

Meliz started and clutched her head. "How come you're not drunk?"

Brigitte snorted. "Practice." She pulled Meliz to her feet, and the two women hugged.

"Sorry again for being such a bitch," Meliz mumbled in her ear.

Brigitte shrugged. "I get it. Your granddad's journal has you spooked."

Spooked, but also strangely comforted. JD's journal had jolted her out of a stagnant morass of self-pity. The need to suffer for his art, his early aspirations, and obvious immaturity struck a chord with her own feelings of self-doubt. Each imperfect sentence, each clumsy expression heartened Meliz.

Her accomplished and world-renowned grandfather had been an insecure youth. It was good to know.

Meliz stumbled to her room and fell asleep fully clothed on top of the comforter, only for the insistent buzzing of her cell phone to wake her two hours later. She grabbed the phone and squinted at the screen.

Jolting up in bed, she typed back a hurried text: *Your friend has no idea what SR18 means?*

She waited a short minute before Alberta replied. *The DOD stonewalled him, and I can only speculate. But Bob thinks the designation might indicate a commando-type unit, soldiers who operated under the radar, maybe? They could have bunked with regular troops and been activated once in the field.*

This isn't a coincidence, is it? Meliz typed, her hands unsteady. *That group of soldiers leaving the ship in New Guinea, and now Jack Walker shows up here. A secret soldier? What's going on?*

Alberta's response was short and to the point. *I don't know. But Walker didn't have a scheduled board meeting. Please be careful.*

**

Meliz turned off the camera and loosened its connection to the tripod. A filmmaker's stalling technique, the action gave her something to do, a moment to collect herself and settle her emotions. The old woman sat, her hands clasped together in her lap, and waited with quiet patience for Meliz to finish.

"I'll get some coffee," the woman's daughter announced and left the room.

Brigitte leafed through a photo album, taking pictures of the ones that caught her interest. Many interesting things occupied this small house on the outskirts of Tacloban, not least of these being the old woman herself.

Garrett had messaged Meliz with her name, Tala Santos. A Filipino woman resistance fighter and the last survivor of her unit. She was ninety-three.

This should interest you, he wrote. *Some added history and local color for your project.*

Garrett could not have known how the woman's story would affect her. The old warrior's tale of valor and sacrifice left Meliz breathless with pride and admiration. Tala Santos deserved her own documentary, not as an addendum to JD's story. She amounted to more than "local color" or even historical perspective.

As a teenager, Tala had rallied and led her people in their darkest hour. She met brutality with brutality and never flinched. She sat now, wizened and shrunken, engulfed by a large armchair, the embodiment of survival. Tala Santos was an inspiration.

Meliz swallowed her emotions and screwed up her courage. She had a question to ask and feared the answer.

"What is it you want?" Tala's thin, raspy voice ruffled the air around them.

"Excuse me?" Meliz shook off her unease and refocused her gaze on the old woman.

"You want to ask something more. I can tell."

Her daughter returned with a tray of coffee, cake, and sliced fruit. The clatter of dishes followed as the women served themselves and passed each other the cream and sugar.

This simple domestic chore calmed Meliz's nerves. "My grandfather described a nighttime drop of resistance fighters into Mindanao. He mentioned a redheaded American—"

"Colonel Patrick," Tala broke in, "Justin Patrick. I met him, a fine man."

Meliz had researched Colonel Justin Patrick that morning in preparation for their interview. A hero of the resistance, he trained and established Filipino fighting units behind enemy lines.

"Yes, I read about him and of the resistance movement on the islands, but I was wondering about something else." She hesitated. The wrinkled brow lifted and faded brown eyes narrowed in question.

"Secret soldiers," she plunged in. "American commandos not associated with any particular unit. They were their own thing … maybe outside of regular command. Did you know or hear of such a group?"

Tala stilled. The flutter of one fragile hand signaled her distress. "Is the camera off?"

"Yes," Meliz assured her.

"And yours?" She nodded at Brigitte.

Brigitte glanced down at the phone in her lap. "Of course."

The old woman trembled, a gentle shiver, and stilled. Her daughter grasped her hand. "What is it?"

"There was such a unit. I didn't know them, but my comrades on Luzon told tales. They were … they did things no one else would do, terrible things." She paused, her eyes downcast. "War is terrible. I know. I have cut men's throats and shot many more. We all did bad—even unforgivable—things, but when the war was over, it was over. Not for them. They had to cover their tracks."

"They kept killing after the war?" Meliz wrapped her hands around the coffee mug for warmth.

Tala nodded, eyes fearful. "They did. Not just the enemy, but those who knew—anyone with knowledge of their actions. I was grateful they never operated on Leyte."

"Why worry about telling now?" Brigitte asked. "It happened long ago. If any of them are alive, they must all be in their nineties."

"Yes." The old woman drew in a deep breath. "But such times never leave you. There are things you fear, even if that fear is not rational."

**

"Must you hit every damn pothole?" Meliz complained. She regretted letting Brigitte drive.

"We are late. I told Hikaru to meet us at three."

"We can text him and let him know we're on our way. You don't have to wreck the car. Besides, the rental contract is in my name."

"I do not like being late," her friend declared, staring hard ahead.

The detour to interview Tala Santos, included at the last minute, put them behind the time. Lateness appeared to be the one thing the easygoing German could not tolerate.

They drove down a narrow track. Vibrant, intense greenery pushed in around them. Branches brushed the passenger's side of the rental car. A host of different trees lined the road. Vines and flowering plants spread across the canopy, and rays of sunlight dappled the pavement through the dense foliage.

Meliz contemplated the encroaching jungle. Tala's final words weighed on her mind. She tried to shake her disquiet and grumbled, "All these plants. I wish I knew what everything was."

"That"—Brigitte pointed to an orange flowering bush—"is a hibiscus. You see that tree, the one over there? The one that looks like two trees in one. That is a *balate* tree. They are parasitic, but good shade trees. That big palm is a *taraw* palm. There are spines along the leaf stem like shark's teeth."

"Are you kidding me?" Meliz laughed. "How do you know all this?"

"I'm a botanist."

"For real?"

"I do contract work for an NGO," Brigitte explained. "We preserve rare and endangered plant species."

"For real?" Meliz repeated, embarrassed she had never asked her friend what she did for a living.

"*Ja*, for real." Brigitte steered the car from the bumpy side road onto a smooth, wide highway. A few short miles and they turned into the parking area of the MacArthur memorial.

"There's Hikaru." Brigitte pointed out.

He leaned against a jeepney, his nose stuck in a brochure. Hikaru straightened as Brigitte pulled into a parking spot next to the colorful vehicle.

"Sorry, we're late," Brigitte called out as they walked toward him. "It was her fault." She pointed at Meliz and easily dodged a playful punch to her shoulder.

"No worry. I have not been waiting long. We were late leaving Tacloban."

"Did you come in that?" Meliz indicated the jeepney. "How was the ride?"

The jeepney symbolized Filipino resilience as much as anything else on the islands did. The residents made them from the surplus of World War II jeeps left behind by American troops. The locals had transformed many of them into unique minibuses with cramped seating and kitsch decorations.

"Uncomfortable," he answered. "My knees are bruised."

Meliz and Brigitte laughed. Hikaru drew back with a frown. "Did I say something funny?"

The two women glanced at each other. "Well, yeah," Meliz explained. "I mean, the jeepney is funny to begin with. And you're tall, and …" Her voice trailed off. She looked to Brigitte for help.

"It's funny," her friend confirmed in her matter-of-fact way. "Let's go."

The memorial sprawled across seventeen acres abutting a stretch of beach—Red Beach, named for the blood spilt there. They joined a steady stream of tourists entering the park.

Hot sunrays pushed through thinning clouds, but a cool breeze from the ocean brushed their faces. They walked with the crowd to the centerpiece of the large park: a sculptural recreation of MacArthur's landing on Leyte.

Built on heroic proportions, the monument included seven twice-life-sized bronze statues standing in a shallow pool. The statues were grouped together as each man appeared in the famous photograph by Gaetano Faillace. Children and adults waded in to take pictures holding hands with the giant General MacArthur. Meliz read a plaque explaining the historical significance of the scene.

She glanced up and laughed as Brigitte strode into the pool for Hikaru to take her picture. Her eyes slid past them out to the ocean beyond. Sparkling waves drew her to the beach. She stood on the grass verge just touching the sand.

JD had been here. He came ashore in a duck. A boy of nineteen, crowded in with other boys. Their collective fear and determination bound them together in the random brotherhood of war. Meliz closed her eyes and conjured up the pulsing sound of an air raid siren, the vibration of anti-aircraft artillery.

She cast her mind back over long decades. A beach lay strewn with weapons, crates, and wounded. Torrents of rain fell from dark, leaden clouds. On this fraught and turbulent day, Meliz searched for the teenaged JD.

She ran along the beach, weaving in between the paraphernalia of battle. A young Asian woman, she stood out among the uniformed men.

A soldier stopped her. "Who are you? What are you doing here?"

"I'm looking for answers."

"I don't understand you. Speak English."

"I *am* speaking English," she protested. "I'm an American."

Grief and frustration forced tears from beneath her closed lids. JD had been her anchor. While others questioned her place in the world—what she was and where she belonged—JD's iconic stature in Americana was unassailable.

He validated her inclusion. I belong with him. I belong.

Now he had gone, leaving behind a mystery. Was it a simple police procedural or a major crime? Would she earn a Marple Cluster or a Hercule Ribbon?

Would he still be the man she loved and trusted?

Where are you, JD?

"Hey, Meliz."

She turned to find Brigitte and Hikaru standing behind her.

"Are you okay?" Brigitte frowned with concern at her tears. "I called. You didn't hear me."

Meliz wiped her face. "I'm fine. I wish I had come here with JD, is all."

Brigitte hugged her, and Hikaru shifted his feet and looked out at the ocean. They moved on, buying ice cream cones from one of the vendors near the road. They sat on the shaded benches. Families with picnic lunches played on the broad swath of grass.

They toured the museum and lingered in the air-conditioned building viewing photographs of the battle and reading letters written by homesick GIs and staunch Filipino soldiers. MacArthur's speech upon landing at Leyte hung on prominent display. His words were old-fashioned, even for the times. Meliz imagined he had written them with history in mind.

"I have returned," she read aloud the first, and most famous, line boldly restating his earlier promise. But the phrase paled, in her opinion, to the dramatic and forceful words that followed: "We have come, dedicated and committed, to the task of destroying every vestige of enemy control over your daily lives, and of restoring, upon a foundation of indestructible strength, the liberties of your people."

The three friends stood in silent contemplation of what that moment must have meant to the Filipino people. To a nation subjected to years of brutal Japanese occupation, they must have been welcomed words indeed.

Rays from the lowering sun hit Meliz directly in the eyes as they left the building. She shielded them with her hand and admired the golden light bouncing off stray clouds. With the crowd rapidly thinning, she took out her camera and walked over to the statues to film them in the gathering dusk. A somber ceremony was in progress as they neared the memorial.

A small group of old men stood with a wreath before the plaque. At their center, Jack Walker sat in his wheelchair with Prescott gripping the handles. None of the men paid any attention to the tourists pressed in around them. Meliz began to film.

She inched closer, allowing the microphone to catch their words.

"We come here to honor our brothers who liberated this island . . ." She circled around behind and to the other side of the group, zooming in on the lined faces of the old soldiers, most of them Filipino.

She caught Prescott in profile. He turned and saw her.

His grip tightened on the handles. The pressure from his hands sped like an electric shock along the frame of the wheelchair. Jack Walker's head snapped up, and he glared at her.

Through the lens, his face hardened. Gone was the pushy, harmless old man who had accosted her in the San Francisco Airport.

In his place sat a killer.

Chapter Twenty-One

A man should be upright, not kept upright.
—Marcus Aurelius

22 Mar., 1945, Biak Island—It's been a month since the bombing of the airfield. We had twelve casualties: five dead, the rest wounded. No one can figure how the enemy slipped through without an air raid warning. The captain didn't crack a smile for at least two weeks afterwards. Course, he was the one who had to write the families. I don't envy him his job.

Even with all the cleanup and reconstruction, we got two more editions of the *Bulletin* out. I saw a big civilian muckety-muck reading one of our papers on a transport. He laughed and pointed something out to a general, who didn't look so pleased. I got a kick out of watching their reactions without them knowing I had a hand in it.

2 Apr.—Got a letter from Daddy. Jackson Carter, an old buddy of mine from the football team, was killed in Germany. That is the sixth kid gone, that I know of, from our town.

What will the place look like after the war? I imagine holes sucking air out of this world where people used to be: cold, invisible holes floating around town. You walk into one and remember, oh yeah, the time ole Jackson caught a thirty-five-yard pass for a touchdown, and we won the game. Ghosts creep me out, but maybe they're better than forgetting.

12 Apr.—President Roosevelt is dead. There are no words.

21 Apr.—We're moving again, back to the Philippines. I'm with the Main Echelon this time and won't get there for a few more days yet. Not sure what will happen to the *Bulletin*. Maybe we'll change the name to the *Dulag Daily*, except it won't be a daily—so maybe not.

Oh yeah, I'm a corporal now.

8 May, Dulag, Leyte—Germany has surrendered! Thank God! Thank God!

**

Manila, Philippines, May 1945

"I don't think I can eat another bite." I groaned and clutched at my stomach.

Frank, George, and I sat around a small table in a crowded restaurant Frank had insisted we try. Locals occupied most of the other tables, but there were a few off-duty military as well, including WACs.

We flew into Clark Field early morning from Dulag and spent the first half of the day eating our way through the city. By the time we sat down for lunch, I had eaten all sorts of delicacies from street vendors and stalls in the marketplace. I owed Frank ten pesos, but he knew I was good for it.

"Sure wish I could hollow out both my legs so's I could fit those cream cakes in." I grunted and contemplated the possibility.

George laughed. "You'd grow another four inches. I never knew anybody to grow so fast."

"Yeah, like a weed." Frank smirked.

I punched him in the shoulder, but not hard, too proud of my extra inches to take offense. Although shy of George's height, I had attained a respectable five foot eleven. I had gone through three different sets of dungarees, to where the quartermaster knew my name, rank, and serial number on sight.

"Yep," I countered. "And I'm just as tough to get rid of."

We laughed, reveling in the novel feeling of being together in a place that wasn't hot and miserable, a place where we could relax with no one telling us what to do. I looked forward to the rest of the day hanging out and maybe finding a hotspot or two at night. "What're we doing next?"

Frank had somehow got his hands on an old 1932 tourist guide of Manila. The book didn't do us any good, though, with much of the city destroyed. He ended up giving it away to a vendor lady in the market.

"I heard about a fine Oriental temple that survived the bombing not far from the harbor," George suggested.

I perked up at that. I had a hankering to explore Eastern religions. I knew tortured heroes often turned to mysticism to relieve their pain.

"A Taoist temple," a woman's voice interjected. "I believe it is a Taoist temple."

We pushed back our chairs and stood in unison. I recognized the petite blonde right off as a nurse I'd danced with at a native wedding a couple of weekends ago.

"Oh, hey there," I sputtered, sounding stupid. I had not expected female company, and running into women as often as we did now seemed mighty strange. "Um, guys, this is Sally, uh, Sally—"

"Merchant, Sally Merchant. And this is my friend, Miriam Acker."

The girl standing behind Sally stepped forward. I shot Frank a suspicious look, his insistence on eating at this restaurant now crystal clear.

Frank had the good grace to blush and greeted the ladies with a subdued, "Miriam and I have met."

You bet they had. Frank and she danced all night at that wedding. Of course, this being grumpy, tight-lipped Frank, he never said anything about the affair afterwards. I had no doubt he had arranged this meeting. So much for a guys' night out on the town.

We pulled up a couple of chairs, and they joined us ordering drinks. We all settled quickly into conversation. Both girls hailed from the Midwest and had an appealing mix of old-fashioned opinions and easygoing manners. Soon George was talking about Josefina and the baby due in July.

"If the baby's a boy, Fina wants to name him George Jr. But I'm not sure."

"Why not?" Sally asked. "Isn't it tradition for the first boy to carry on the family name?"

"Yeah, but I don't know. I kinda want him to have his own name." He made a noise between a snort and a laugh. "It's strange. After all this is over, I'll be going home to a wife and a couple of kids. Two years ago, I was single and without a care in the world."

The conversation tilted pretty one-sided. Sally lent him a sympathetic ear, and he took full advantage of her good manners. She nodded and made understanding noises in all the right places.

He rattled on about meeting Josefina and marrying her so fast, maybe too fast. How he worried what their relationship would be like once he got back and they were living together for the first time. Would he measure up as a husband and a father?

He'd never said any of this stuff to me.

I figured George was my best buddy. Trust was the foundation of our hard-won friendship, with each of us knowing the others' strengths and weaknesses. I relied on his judgment, never failing to pass a draft of the newspaper by him. He always knew when we had pushed the mockery too far.

Frank and I were collaborators and partners in crime, but he often rubbed me the wrong way and we fought a lot. His prickly nature made him unpredictable, and I couldn't be sure he wanted to hang on to me after the war.

It wasn't that way with George. I knew we'd always be close.

I determined to be a better friend, to ask him more about Josefina and Rosa, what his plans were once the war ended. I would listen and offer sage advice.

Someday he would stand up with me at my wedding. Someday he would listen to my doubts about being a good husband and father.

The rest of the afternoon turned out very fine. We toured the Taoist temple and the church of San Agustin, it being one of the few structures left standing in the historic Intramuros District.

I could not imagine another city so utterly destroyed. We'd heard rumors that Japanese troops had murdered tens of thousands of Filipino civilians. Just surviving must have seemed like a miracle to those spared. Now, they had started to rebuild, as people do.

Come evening, Frank and Miriam cut out on their own. Sally had other plans, leaving George and me to discover what nightlife Manila had to offer.

We ended up in one of the few bars operating in this bombed out city and were lucky to find stools in the packed place. The bar was of the makeshift variety and occupied the ground floor of what had once been an elegant mansion. Tables flanked a dance floor marked out in the large living room. The owners must have scavenged the heavy oaken bar, against which we leaned, from the rubble of the original business. The place buzzed with the release of pent-up tension.

Conversation swirled around us and drunken GIs stumbled over each other trying to pick up girls. A few soldiers disappeared up the grand staircase, their arms slung over the narrow shoulders of Filipino women. The bar served up more than alcohol, and the image turned my stomach.

Prostitutes had never been my thing, but I always figured they knew what they were doing. Here, I could not be sure.

Desperation fed this city barely two months out from a cruel occupation and devastating artillery barrage. I didn't like what was happening to those girls. I wished the military offered more than horny GIs to help them get by.

"We should be heading back." George gulped down the rest of his beer and pushed off the stool. "We can get a plane out tonight if we're quick."

Nonstop air traffic clogged Clark Field. Planes came and went at all times of the day and night, but we had no guarantee of a spot. We could wait all night and not get a flight out. Our pass ended at 0700hrs tomorrow morning. Getting a jump on a transport seemed like a smart move.

I hopped off the barstool, and my elbow hit the arm of a dark-haired woman holding a glass. The drink sloshed and some spilled down her crisp, white blouse.

She wore an American uniform, but no nametag, insignia, or any other identification. A hulking sergeant stood possessively over her. He glared at me from beneath a menacing brow.

"Excuse me, ma'am," I apologized, grabbing a towel from the barman and dabbing at the stain, nervous at the proximity of my hand to her breast.

The sergeant shot me an unforgiving scowl, but the lady answered with a gracious smile, "No problem, Corporal. It's crowded in here."

She reached for the towel, and I froze. On her wrist, at the base of her right palm, were tiny ink marks, exactly like those I had seen on Mick Cassidy.

Without thinking, I snatched at her hand and bent over her wrist, demanding, "Where did you get this?"

She jerked her hand from my grasp. The large sergeant grabbed my collar with a beefy fist and twisted it until I choked.

The woman and George acted as one to stop his other fist from connecting with my face. The woman shouted, "Stop. That's enough." The sergeant let me go with a rough shake.

A small audience pushed in around us. The woman stepped close and spoke in a fierce whisper, "Where have you seen this mark before?"

Lots of men would probably think her pretty. Only seconds before, her hazel eyes sparkled with a soft glow. Now, they glared back at me, hard as granite. She had transformed from cordial to menacing in an instant.

More people jostled in wanting a peek at the ruckus. They packed us so tight, I couldn't move.

"Where have you seen it before, Corporal?" she insisted, leaning in further.

Her eyes glittered with malice, and I reared back. Momma could sure pin us with a hard stare from half a mile away, but I'd never encountered a woman this intimidating.

I mumbled a weak reply and bit my tongue when George jerked me backwards by my belt. I fell into him. He wrapped his arms around my middle and dragged me outta there. People flowed into the vacuum left by our space, blocking the woman and her sergeant.

We ran.

Can't say in what direction. We raced flat out and didn't look back until twisting our way into a narrow alley. We stopped, bent over, hands on our knees, and gasped for air.

"What the hell were you thinking?" George snapped when he could speak.

He knew about the whole Mick Cassidy mess. Frank and I'd given him a full report when he got off duty that same day we'd examined the body. He didn't have much to say at the time, but agreed with Frank about not writing the incident down in my journal.

"She had a tattoo, same as Cassidy."

"What are you talking about?"

"That woman had a tattoo on the inside of her wrist. Cassidy had one too."

"A tattoo? Women don't have tattoos," he insisted. "It was probably an ink stain. She's a secretary or something."

Castle's calm, rational words usually made me think twice. Not this time—I could picture the look on her face, hear the venom in her voice. "Nope, you're wrong. She's the same as Cassidy, whatever he was."

Pretty sure no one had followed us, we relaxed. Castle walked back toward the main road. I followed him, keeping my eyes peeled for that harpy and her hulking guard dog.

We flagged down and hitched a ride with a farmer. He relegated us to the flatbed with some crated chickens and a couple of goats. George and I had made good our escape.

We stretched our legs out, backs up against the cab. The night lay dark and peaceful around us. The silhouettes of palm trees blurred as we sped past, and I inhaled the fragrance of earth and flowers.

Leyte had smelled of mud and more mud. Biak smelled of salt and sand. Here, on Luzon, I smelled life. The Philippines was free, and beneath all of the death and rubble, there was still life.

**

We didn't have much luck at the airfield, and had to wait for a plane leaving at 0525hrs. George swore under his breath.

Our arrival time would be a squeaker, and he feared any marks on his record. For a while now, I'd suspected him of wanting a military career. I couldn't figure the army for me, but Castle would make a fine officer.

We slept in the cargo hold of our assigned plane and were jolted awake by the painful sound of metal scraping on metal. George and I exchanged a quick, confused glance, jumped to our feet, and slid down the payload ramp.

Spewing flames and flying sparks met our eyes as a P-61 crash-landed and skidded off the runway. The crew bailed uninjured. Tracers and shells exploded in all directions, like fireworks on the Fourth of July. Men scattered, running headlong into each other in an effort to get equipment out of harm's way. The whole scene coulda been lifted from an old Keystone Cops film.

We stood like statues, helpless in the face of chaos. George ran his hands through his hair and barked with laughter. I joined in. Our laughter grew until our sides hurt, and we doubled over onto the tarmac.

Germany had surrendered. Maybe Japan would be next.

Anything could happen. The future lay before us, unmade and uncertain, but in that perfect moment, I laughed with my best friend.

Chapter Twenty-Two

We have met the enemy and they are ours.
—Oliver H. Perry

The camera could not shield her from the anger of one old man. Not the stone-cold killer she had imagined only seconds before, but a frail and frightened creature.

He shook his fist at her and yelled, "Stop filming. You have no right. Go away."

The old soldiers grouped around him peered at her through an array of sunglasses. Even though tourists snapped pictures and a TV crew filmed the ceremony, the men scowled at her in solidarity with one of their own. Prescott, his expression stoic, whispered something in his grandfather's ear.

Jack Walker turned away and did not look at her again. Meliz lowered the camera, her eyes still trained on his stern profile.

The Second Combat Cargo Group encompassed many units and consisted of thousands of soldiers. Most likely, JD and Jack never met. But her grandfather had seen him. Of that, she was certain. Maybe not to know it, maybe not even him individually, but as a group—the secret soldiers who disembarked that night off the coast of New Guinea.

What else explained Jack's sudden animosity but the fear of discovery? He knew who Meliz was and why she "vacationed" in the Philippines. He had known all along.

That frail old man frightened her. Tala had described a unit of soldiers uniquely suited to killing, pitiless. How would such a man mellow with age? He might be old and weak, but Jack was rich and powerful with a secret to protect.

A map of the Pacific Islands spread out before her mind's eye. Dashed marks of transport routes crisscrossed the blue expanse of ocean and made bold X's where the planes landed. In that maze, those ruthless men and her grandfather had intersected.

Meliz struggled to understand JD. She would have sworn secrecy and deception were alien to him, that his life was an open book, his stories of honor and justice a reflection of his own character. But over the course of these few days, uncertainty piled on top of grief, and Meliz feared a grandfather she had never really known.

On the drive back to Tacloban, her phone pinged with a text message. Meliz ignored it at first, her thoughts consumed with the confrontation at the monument. At last, she glanced down at her phone and gasped.

"What is it?" Brigitte asked, the car swerving as she looked over at Meliz.

In a shaking voice, Meliz read aloud the letter Alberta had sent:

Dear Mr. Hawkins,

I hope you get this letter. I hope it is you. My grandson is writing from my words. His English is mostly good.

I am the girl you saved. I am an old woman now. My brother died years ago. He had a wife and child. He had a good life. I have too.

My grandson likes your books, but in Japanese. His English is not so good that he can read books. He likes the ones about the cowboy. He was reading one last weekend. I asked him the title. When he told me, my heart stopped. Poor boy, he worried I was dying.

Do you remember that day? You must. That day my brother and I took you to the beach below our village. We looked out at the ocean, and you said, "Everything touches the sky." Of course, you spoke English.

You drew pictures in the sand. You drew clouds, a mountain, a tree, and the ocean, and you blurred the sand where they met. You pointed at the horizon and said again, "Everything touches the sky."

You thought I did not understand, but I did. Because it is true, everything does touch the sky. That was before all that was bad happened.

My grandson read the book to me. I could not believe our story was there. I know it is not the same. You changed many parts. There is more happening, or maybe I know only my little bit of it.

I do not know what I can write in a letter. The terror of that day still haunts me. Sometimes I wish I could tell what happened. Would anyone believe me?

Sincerely,

Kiko Tamaki

Relief and gratitude washed over Meliz. JD had saved a life . . . he was a hero. The girl, Kiko, now an old woman, still lived.

Hikaru, in the back seat, demanded an explanation for their excited chatter. Unable to control her emotions, Meliz let Brigitte fill him in on the details of their investigation.

"Tonight, we celebrate," Brigitte crowed when she finished

answering his many questions. She rolled down the windows and let the wind and afternoon rain pelt in on them.

Meliz didn't mind. She turned her face to the rain. It hid her tears.

**

A flush already warming her cheeks, Meliz stood with Brigitte and Hikaru just inside the doorway of the karaoke bar. She searched the room for empty chairs, letting her eyes adjust to the eerie red lighting within. Patrons packed the tables, spreading out from the club's central stage where a group of middle-aged men sang a Beatles tune. Strategically placed fans did little more than circulate the smell of beer and air-freshener around the crowded room.

The three friends had come from an excellent meal of red snapper with tomato and rice. Two glasses of heavy red wine, combined with the food, lulled Meliz into a warm and fuzzy state of relaxation.

Eying a likely spot near the back, she elbowed her way through the crowd and plopped down on a black vinyl couch. Her friends sank down beside her. Brigitte ordered drinks.

"To the letter," Meliz declared, and they clinked glasses.

"Okay, *ja*, okay." Brigitte slurred only a little even though she had already drunk one glass of wine, one margarita, and two mojitos. She scooted forward on the couch and raised her drink. "I haf a toast. Okay, *ja*, lift up your glasses. Okay . . . fuck Hitler!" She dissolved into giggles and said again, "Seriously, fuck that guy."

"*Ja*." Meliz hiccupped. The three clinked their glasses together again, laughing.

Meliz had counted Hikaru's drinks too. She determined the fourth to be his tipping point. Face reddened from alcohol, his groomed appearance had succumbed to the demands of sightseeing and barhopping.

Meliz sipped at her mai tai with thoughtful appreciation. The rumpled look became him, as did the ready smile and infectious laughter.

"Fuck Hirohito," he blurted with forced bravado.

To curse Hitler, the most reviled man in recent history, was one thing, but not so long ago the Japanese considered the emperor a deity. Some still did. Meliz admired his resolve.

"You bet. Fuck that bastard too." She raised her glass, and they all clinked.

Brigitte and Hikaru fell silent. They looked at her expectantly.

"What?" Meliz slurred, indignant. "You don't expect me to say fuck Roosevelt, do you?" She jabbed a finger at her chest. "*We* were the good guys."

Brigitte and Hikaru struggled to keep straight faces. They lost the battle and burst out laughing. Meliz grabbed a piece of ice from her drink and threw it at them. They ducked, and the ice cube hit the head of a man sitting behind them.

He turned. The three friends collapsed together, laughing harder.

"Sorry," Meliz apologized. "I was aiming for these two idiots."

"It's all right, mate. No harm done." The burly Aussie appeared to be somewhere in his late twenties. He nodded at Meliz and winked at Brigitte.

Brigitte perked up. She flashed a wide grin and jerked her head in the man's direction, mouthing, "What do you think of that?"

Meliz knew what to think of that. Her friend had a weakness for men and drugs and usually found both with ease, though her indulgence in one or the other never seemed to slow her down.

"Tell me a bad word in Japanese, and I will tell you one in German." Brigitte engaged Hikaru in the time-honored practice of teaching each other curse words in their respective languages.

"You first," he countered.

"Alright. *Schweinehund* is very bad, very insulting."

"*Schweinehund*? What does it mean?"

"Pig-dog."

"Pig-dog?" Hikaru shook his head, unconvinced. "Pig-dog is a bad word? I do not believe you."

"It is true," she insisted, nodding for emphasis. "What is a bad word in Japanese?"

"Not being courteous is bad, but there are insulting words too." He frowned and shifted on the couch. "I do not think I should teach you any. They are too impolite."

"That's the point." She laughed at his discomfort.

"I'll teach you some in English," Meliz offered.

"Everyone knows American swear words." Hikaru snorted. "You have nothing to teach us."

They found this hilarious and could not stop giggling. The three friends huddled together in their own private world. A world interrupted by a microphone shoved in Meliz's face.

"Your turn." The hostess's sweet expression belied the tone of her voice.

Her words vibrated with irritation at their breach of proper karaoke etiquette. Drinking and laughing were fine, but patrons must also acknowledge the efforts of singers with attention and applause.

They had done neither. Every eye in the place turned on them.

"Ah, no thank you," Meliz replied with a polite shake of her head. "I'm good."

The sweet expression transformed into a parody of the middle school mean-girl smile. "I'm sorry. If you don't sing, you'll have to leave." She gestured toward the door and shrugged her pretty shoulders. "Those are the rules."

"Fine, we'll leave." Brigitte waved a disinterested hand and scooted off the couch.

Fueled by alcohol and an intense dislike of bullies, Meliz grabbed the microphone. "The hell we will." She simpered at the woman with some exaggerated sweetness of her own and pointed the microphone at Hikaru. "You . . . with me."

He cringed; a comical expression of terror spread over his face. "No. I will leave."

She cast him such a baleful look, he reluctantly joined her in what seemed an endless walk to the stage. Silence descended on the club as they wove their way around the tables. A mixture of dread and anticipation filled the air.

The audience watched, enthralled by the drama, both embarrassed for her and eager for the rude American girl to embarrass herself. Several cell phones shot into the air, held at the ready.

She handed Hikaru another microphone. "You come in when the song indicates two singers. I'll sing everything else." He swallowed and nodded in nervous agreement.

Meliz lifted her chin in a defiant gesture, empowered not by the false courage of alcohol, but by years of hard practice. She sent a silent, long-distance thank-you to her *nainai*. That tiny, driven woman sang for two decades with the Los Angeles Symphony Orchestra Choir and trained Meliz's voice within a fraction of perfection.

She told the DJ her choice. The song was not one of her favorites, but was beloved by the karaoke crowd. With the opening notes of "All I Ask of You" from *The Phantom of the Opera*, the audience squirmed, now really feeling sorry for her.

Meliz sang the first notes in a rich alto and smirked inwardly as people's mouths dropped open. *That's right, motherfuckers. I can sing.*

She regarded the astonished crowd with smug satisfaction. She even threw a kiss at the awful woman who had put her on the spot.

Her voice soared into soprano range. Brigitte cheered from the back of the bar. The Aussie guy had slipped in next to her and whistled with good-natured enthusiasm.

The unexpectedness of her performance caught everyone up in a moment of shared fun. The stunned audience applauded and shouted their approval.

The crowd roared even louder when Hikaru sang. He stumbled over the first few lyrics, but his voice soon settled into an unpolished, yet warm baritone. Meliz raised her eyebrows at him.

The surreal moment expanded and enveloped them, as if they were projected onto an IMAX screen. She expected any second to break the fourth wall and speak directly to the movie audience of her own personal romantic comedy.

Isn't he cute? Do you think he's into me? Should I sleep with him? She imagined the audience encouraging her to go with her own plucky little heart.

Meliz almost laughed aloud when their voices meshed in perfect harmony on the final lyrics of the song. She *did* laugh when they finished, covering for the embarrassment of singing a love song with someone she barely knew. Someone everyone in the audience assumed to be her boyfriend.

They received high fives and pats on the back as they waded through the crowd to their table. No matter the warm reception, she would not attempt to sing again. No one liked following her up on stage. The woman had forced her to sing, and the audience responded with approval. That would all change if they perceived her to be hogging the spotlight.

"Vindicated," Brigitte cried and threw her arms around Meliz. "Look, the bartender sent us free drinks."

Sean, the Aussie, joined their little group as they continued to drink and laugh, now careful to applaud each singer. He boldly made his move, draping a strong arm across the couch behind Brigitte. He listened intently to her every word, and Brigitte responded by moving her hand higher and higher up his thigh as the night went on. Meliz noticed only in passing, far too enmeshed in her own predicament.

She sat shoulder to shoulder with Hikaru, their heads bent close together, his hand resting on the couch, intertwined with hers.

Brigitte stood and pulled her Aussie to his feet. "See you in the morning," she cooed, and left.

Taking her cue from Brigitte, Meliz made a bold decision. She grasped Hikaru's hand and led him through the crowd and out the side entrance.

Flowering vines trailed down from the eaves overhanging the deserted alleyway. The sound of waves intermingled with the smell of jasmine and the stench of two overflowing trash bins. Hikaru pulled Meliz into a tight embrace.

Theirs was a first kiss on steroids, a deep and clutching affair. The heat of the moment existed on a plane of pure physical attraction.

He pressed her up against the wall. The hard outline of his muscles imprinted on her body. Meliz reached down his pants. All restraint fell away in a frenzy of discarded clothing.

Hikaru yanked off his T-shirt and unbuttoned Meliz's blouse, exposing her breasts. His lips trailed down her neck. He slid his hands beneath her shorts and gripped her flesh, pulling her even closer.

Meliz's brain flickered and redirected its attention to her stomach. She stiffened. Hikaru hesitated and pulled back.

"This is unexpected," he muttered through his ragged breathing. His forehead rested against the concrete wall above her. "I should tell you—"

Meliz gulped and pushed him away. She covered her mouth and stumbled to the corner. A wave of nausea washed over her. She had stopped counting her drinks at five.

"Are you okay? Meliz, I'm sorry . . ."

She gestured him back. "No, it's fine. I'm feeling . . . stay there."

Meliz doubled over and threw up next to one of the trash bins. She leaned against the wall. A self-deprecating grimace twisted her lips. So much for sex with an almost stranger in a semi-public place.

She was no longer in the mood.

**

Hikaru wavered, indecisive and anxious to be of help. Meliz stood several feet away with her back to him.

A battered blue Toyota skidded to a stop at the corner, almost brushing her where she leaned against the wall. A masked man jumped from the car.

The man grabbed Meliz and lifted her off her feet. He pinned her arms to her side, bundling her up like a spider with a fly. She screamed and kicked out as he shoved her into the back seat.

Her scream jolted Hikaru from his stupor. Frozen disbelief morphed into panic.

He charged the attacker and rammed him into the rear door. The man slammed an elbow into his face and shoved him off. Hikaru staggered back.

The kidnapper jumped into the car as it screeched off. In a matter of seconds, Meliz was gone.

Hikaru gaped after the speeding car. He raced out into the street. Rear lights made a sharp right turn and disappeared.

He ran to the front of the club. A small group milled around the entrance.

"Help," Hikaru yelled, stumbling to a stop. "Help."

People frowned at him in confusion. Their eyes darted in all directions, fearful of what might be after him.

He stood shirtless, his expression panicked. His face throbbed from the blow.

"Help," he implored again, not knowing what else to do.

"Vat?" a familiar voice shrieked. "Hikaru, vat happened?"

He grasped Brigitte by the shoulders and shook her. "A man took Meliz. I need a car."

"A car? Vat is going on? Ver is Meliz?"

As if on cue, a souped-up old Mazda RX-7 rolled to a stop next to them and vroomed its engine. Sean called out in a cheerful voice, "Ready, Bridge?"

"Perfect." Hikaru jumped into the passenger seat. Brigitte dashed into the back.

Sean took his unexpected company in stride. "Okay, mate, happy to drop you wherever."

"No, no, Sean," Brigitte blurted in a rush. "A man took Meliz. We must follow him."

"Shouldn't we call the police?" he protested. "How are we gonna find her?"

Hikaru, his jaw set in a firm line, pulled out his phone and punched in a number. "I can find her."

Chapter Twenty-Three

Excerpt from *Everything Touches the Sky*

I'm an old fool, too slow on my feet and befuddled in my mind to do any good. Now I'm gonna die, and the girl with me. I should have turned in my badge last year after the incident in Del Rio.

But what would I do? Where would I go?

Cody's got himself a wife and five kids in Wichita Falls. He married Dagmar, a strong, plain Danish girl, a few years back. He tells me I should come live with them on their farm. They would give me a room overlooking the peach orchard. Never imagined I'd end up an old pensioner living off the good graces of a fella who's been my deputy for the past twenty-five years.

I had my chances at getting me a wife, but settling down wasn't for me.

Dying out here in these hills wouldn't be too bad if it wasn't for the girl. She was quiet now, but not dead, not yet. I made a sling for her on my back. I could feel the heat of her through my coat.

I should have seen the trap coming a mile away. My own stupid vanity not calling on help, but I had to be quick to save her.

With my skull cracked open and blood caked up in my hair, I dropped to my knees and laid the girl on the ground. She slept, but it was a parched and restless sleep.

Could be she won't ever wake up. I guess it was something they didn't kill her outright.

The pain numbed my brain, and I couldn't hold a clear thought in my head. It won't be long before I breathe my last. We'll lie here together until the scavengers and carrion-eaters scatter our bones.

Wished I could bury the girl, but she wasn't dead . . . not yet.

Chapter Twenty-Four

They can conquer who believe they can.
—Emerson

The car screeched to a stop in a deserted district of warehouses next to the harbor. A row of storage units stood illuminated by the sinister yellow glow of a blinking streetlight. Heavy fog crept in off the ocean and muffled the sound of boat hulls bumping up against the pier.

Meliz huddled in the back seat, her wrists bound with a plastic zip tie. She shoved a fist into her mouth to keep from screaming. The sound of her own sobs terrified her.

Her eyes darted around, searching for any means of escape. She clung with everything she had to a fragile sliver of self-control.

The men sat silent in the front seat, menacing and anonymous behind ski masks. The one in the passenger seat got out and opened the car door.

"Come here," he demanded.

Meliz could tell by his accent that he was Filipino. The driver never spoke.

She cowered back into the seat. "No."

He grabbed for her leg. She kicked his hand away and screamed, "Leave me alone."

"Be quiet, and you won't get hurt."

The man lied. He had hurt her already. Her injured shoulder throbbed. She kicked at him again.

He grabbed her ankle and yanked her from the car. The protruding footboard scraped her back. She landed hard on her tailbone.

The man jerked her to her feet and slapped her. Meliz gasped and cried out.

"American bitch, whoring in a back alley," he sneered. Derision dripped from his voice. He leered at her exposed breasts. She choked down a whimper.

"Keep your mouth shut and go home. Or a lot worse will happen to you."

The man pinned her back against the car. His hot breath singed her cheek. He fumbled with the waistband of her shorts and ground his pelvis against her.

A wave of revulsion washed over Meliz. Every vestige of conscious thought deserted her. She struck out with adrenaline-fed strength, flailing her bound hands and pounding her fists on his head.

Meliz shoved him away and turned to run. By sheer chance, her knee connected hard between his legs.

"Oof." The man stumbled back. His eyes bugged out like a cartoon character's.

He doubled over and clutched at his groin. Meliz, in utter survival mode, grabbed him by the shirt collar and rammed his head into the car. He dropped like a dead man.

She stared, trancelike, at his unmoving form for what seemed an age. A small portion of her brain clicked into gear and remembered the driver.

Meliz peered through the rear window into the eyes of the other kidnapper. Trauma telescoped her vision. His pupils dilated until blackness engulfed the hazel irises.

Fury wiped out any remaining traces of fear. "I know who you are," she mouthed.

The car jerked. She staggered back and tripped over the curb. Prescott ground the gears and sped away.

Meliz gasped for air. Relief weakened her limbs. She forced herself to remain standing.

She scowled down at the inert form of her attacker and poked him with the toe of her shoe. He groaned.

Meliz ripped off the ski mask. She'd never seen him before.

She wanted to bang his head into the concrete curb until it burst, but satisfied herself with kicking him hard in the ribs. "I can fuck anyone I want," she yelled.

Thud.

"In any fucking back alley I want."

Thud.

"In any fucking city."

Thud. Thud. Thud.

"In the whole fucking world."

She ended on a sob. Tears choked her.

Shaking from spent adrenaline, Meliz leaned against the corrugated wall of a storage unit. She needed to move. Get out of there.

She fumbled with her blouse, pulling it together as best she could. With her hands still bound, she couldn't reach the cell phone lodged in her back pocket.

Her stomach clenched with fear at the sound of a car turning into the driveway between the storage units. The headlights caught her, poised to run.

"Meliz!" Brigitte's head popped out the back window. "Meliz!"

Her friend jumped from the moving car and ran to embrace her. They sank to the ground. Meliz sobbed, her head resting on Brigitte's shoulder.

**

Hikaru paced outside the exam room. Brigitte and a police officer were with Meliz and the doctor. Sean, his large bulk folded into a wobbly plastic waiting room chair, read an old gossip magazine and sipped on a cup of vending machine coffee.

He looked up as Hikaru walked past him for the millionth time. "Listen, mate, I know how you feel. But all that pacing is just wasting shoe leather."

Hikaru stopped and ran his hands through his hair. He couldn't shake the image of Meliz illuminated by the headlights. Bare legs scraped and bleeding, hands bound, her tearstained face set with fear and determination.

"I'm telling you," Sean continued, "I work out with MMA fighters. I don't think they could've done any better. A concussion and two cracked ribs . . . Your little girlfriend, she nailed that bastard good."

Hikaru didn't correct him. Fatigue and relief overwhelmed his ability to explain their nonrelationship. He could barely focus his mind and admired the Aussie's superhuman composure.

Sean had handled the situation with calm, collected purpose. He called the police and checked the unconscious man. With gentle probing, he extracted from Meliz an account of the attack and her escape. He had even taken pictures of her bound hands before cutting off the plastic zip tie.

Hikaru sat next to Sean and slumped back in the chair. "They have been in there a long time."

"The chief's taking her statement. Bridge's, too. Then the exam . . . She was scraped up some."

"That is all. She said that was all, right? Bruises and scrapes." Hikaru struggled with his emotions. "I could not . . . did not stop him . . . I—"

"You can't do that, mate. You can't beat yourself up. You did good, quick thinking."

Hikaru shook his head, unconvinced.

"You're a bit banged up yourself," Sean observed.

Hikaru touched the side of his face where a large bruise spread from cheek to ear. The nurse had evaluated him and declared the bruise, while ugly, not life-threatening. He tugged at the too-snug, white T-shirt given to him by the hospital staff. It bunched up under his arms, but was better than nothing in the frigid hospital hallway.

The exam room door opened, and the two men stood. A police officer strode out, shutting the door behind her. She stopped to speak with them. "Do we have your statements?"

"Yes," Hikaru answered.

"This is bad business, Molly," Sean put in, "an abduction and assault. I have boats to run. A little discretion would be nice."

She returned a bland look. Even without the uniform, Molly Bautista exuded competence and command. A sturdy, middle-aged Filipino woman, she carried out her duties of police chief with unflappable calm and expertise.

"Will do, Sean, we won't scare the tourists," she replied with light sarcasm, her British accent the result of globe-trotting parents and English boarding schools. "We'll be treating this one with a good deal of discretion considering who she says was behind the wheel."

"Oh?"

"Jack Prescott Walker the Third."

Sean whistled through his teeth. "She identified him?"

"He wore a mask and never spoke." Chief Bautista gave a noncommittal shrug. "But she saw his eyes and . . . well, she smelled him."

"She what?"

"Smelled him, and I quote, 'He wears a distinctive scent, kind of clean and musky.' Her German friend, Ms. Müller, backed her up. About the smell, that is. Apparently, she, too, has smelled the man."

"What can you do with that?"

Molly grunted in frustration. "Not much. The Walkers are connected to the most prominent families on these islands." Sean raised his eyebrows. "Yes, mine included," she admitted. "That old man has his finger in every pot. Getting a warrant would be next to impossible even if she *had* seen the grandson. We've already made a few calls."

"You could question him," Hikaru insisted. "The old man yelled at Meliz. He and his grandson were at MacArthur Park this afternoon." He recalled the early hour and amended, "Yesterday, I mean. Yesterday afternoon."

"They left by private boat back to Manila an hour ago."

"Not one of mine," Sean objected.

"No, not a charter. The Ramos yacht."

He whistled again.

"You see what I'm up against now, do you?"

"The other man, he will know," Hikaru persisted.

A nurse walked by pushing a trolley of clanking bottles and hospital supplies. The chief waited for him to pass before answering.

"If he does give the grandson up, which is doubtful, the family will have alibis and witnesses already lined up. The guy's a petty thug and career criminal. He's no match for them. And there's the question of motive."

She cast Hikaru a measuring look. He dropped his eyes.

"Yeah, you see, don't you? Surprised me to find out she's JD Hawkins's granddaughter—"

"She is?" Sean interjected, astonished. "Man, I loved those books. Couldn't get into the histories though . . . too heavy."

"But that doesn't matter," Molly continued as if Sean hadn't spoken. "The idea of an old war mystery as motive is too far-fetched. I'll do my best, but the incident will probably go down as a run-of-the-mill assault."

Another officer approached them. "Chief, the suspect's come around." She bade them goodbye and walked off.

The exam room door opened again. Meliz and Brigitte came out, followed by the doctor.

"Get some rest, Ms. Lin. Fill that prescription. The medication will help you sleep," the doctor urged her before heading off down the hallway.

Meliz stood with a slip of paper in her hand. The nurse had cleaned and treated her scrapes. A red mark where the attacker had hit her overlaid the faded bruise from the mugging. The harsh hospital lights threw into stark relief dark smudges under her eyes.

Meliz smiled at the concerned faces of her friends. She waved the paper around. "I don't have the strength to get this right now. Can we just go back to the hotel?"

Chapter Twenty-Five

Excerpt from *Everything Touches the Sky*

The sound of dried grass parted by booted feet and a gurgling cough penetrated the blanketed darkness. A small voice cried out in Comanche, and a man's voice answered with soothing words in that same language. Cool liquid touched my lips and ran down the sides of my face. I coughed and opened my eyes.

"Hey, Marshal, good to have you back."

Cody bent close over me. He'd had that same gapped-toothed grin plastered across his face from the day I met him. I noticed for the first time the wrinkles around his eyes and the sagging flesh across his jaw line.

My own bones had turned stiff and brittle of late, but Cody? He was still a kid. If he has grown old, I must have one foot in the grave.

"The girl," I cried, panicked, and struggled to sit up.

"Steady there." Cody held me down with ease. "She's fine. You can see for yourself."

A Comanche man knelt beside me with the girl in his arms. She sucked on a corncob covered in honey. Stretching out a sticky hand, she touched my face, leaving a fingerprint-shaped dab of the sweet stuff on my cheek.

I winked at her. It hurt my head.

"We got a litter here for ya, Marshal. I don't think you should ride, or even stand."

"You can't drag a litter through these hills." I sighed with weary patience. Cody sure could be impractical at times.

"Hills? There ain't no hills. Leastwise not here. You're almost to the Green Crossing. Once we realized you and the girl was gone, we found you right quick. Though it looks like you walked a mite."

I couldn't figure it. I musta carried the girl over miles like a sleepwalker to the ford.

I barked in alarm as a cold, slimy sensation spread across my head. "What's that?"

"Calm down, Marshal. It's a Comanche remedy."

"What?"

"This fella here says it'll help with the pain."

My head bashed in, and I'd woken up in a world turned upside down. "Since when do you have any Comanche?"

"I don't." Cody chuckled. "He's kinda talking with his hands."

I stopped asking questions, cuz danged if that Comanche wasn't right. My head did feel better.

They lifted me onto the litter. "Where's Surprise?"

"Back at the fort. He's the reason we figured you'd gone."

My eyelids drooped, heavy with exhaustion. I mumbled, "How's that?"

Cody musta not heard me, cuz he didn't answer. I struggled to keep my attention on the matter at hand, but my thoughts drifted to a farmhouse in Wichita Falls. A bunch of kids ran wild, getting into mischief. A cool and peaceful peach orchard stood like a refuge round the back.

I could help with the chores and the harvest. Maybe even teach the kids their letters.

I figured there were worse fates.

Chapter Twenty-Six

Courage is the virtue which champions the cause of right.
—Cicero

The open balcony door welcomed an early morning breeze. Meliz huddled on a chair behind the curtains. The gauzy fabric fluttered and brushed against her bare skin. Dawn brightened, and light filtered into the courtyard below. The sun's rays moved across the garden, pulling color out of the darkness.

Meliz hugged her legs to her chest, chin resting on her knees. She hadn't slept. She had held vigil all night, unmoving.

Anxiety hung phantom-like at the edges of her subconscious, chanting its toxic mantra: Be frightened. Be watchful of everything, even the most unlikely of threats. This state of fearful awareness, this pseudo-vigilance, had proven a false guardian. Anxiety did not make her safer, only more afraid.

Meliz longed to call her parents, but they would insist she go home. She didn't want to go home. She wanted to know why this had happened to her.

Meliz shut her eyes, remembering a card her mother gave her long ago. Made of heavy pressed paper, the illustration on its cover featured a group of four women, an African queen, a French

Resistance fighter, a martial artist, and a World War I nurse. Inside were the words: Be wise. Be strong. Do not be afraid.

She opened her eyes.

The curtains of a first-floor window opposite hers twitched and drew back at exactly six a.m. Minutes later, Hikaru, dressed in running shorts and a T-shirt, came out. He checked his watch and put on headphones as he strode toward the hotel lobby, not bothering to look around him.

Who was he, really? Brigitte had regaled her with his heroics, how he had found her. But something felt off. His subdued demeanor, the turn of his head and downcast eyes, telegraphed more than just the aftereffects of violence.

And that "app" he had . . . tracking her cell phone . . . where did that come from? Her suspicious gaze followed him until he disappeared down a staircase.

"Trust your gut," Meliz whispered through gritted teeth. Unfolding herself from the chair, she slipped out of her room and tapped a sharp staccato on Brigitte's door.

A soft rustle of blankets and the patter of bare feet preceded the sight of her friend, naked and bleary-eyed, just inside the door. "Is everything alright?" Brigitte asked, her voice heavy with sleep.

"Yes, fine," Meliz reassured her, stepping inside. Her eyes darted around the room, stark and neat except for the rumpled bed. "Am I bothering you too early?"

"You mean Sean?" Brigitte pulled the embroidered duvet off the bed and draped it over her shoulders. "No. He had a four a.m. charter. He's long gone."

"I'm going to break into Hikaru's room." Meliz held up a hairpin. "Do you know how to pick a lock?

"Vat? Are you serious?"

"Look, Brigitte, something's off about him. I can't explain it. I'm just going with my instincts on this one."

"He's not a businessman?"

"Maybe." Meliz waved away the question. "I'm not sure. Do you remember where you met him?"

Brigitte nodded. "Of course, I met him right after I met you. He was in the bakery buying coffee."

"Shit. You're kidding me." Meliz, incredulous, rushed headlong for the door. She skidded to a stop. "Are you coming?"

Brigitte pulled on the familiar cutoffs and tank top. "Isn't he in his room?"

"He went for a run. Told me last night he never misses a morning."

"How do you know he has left?"

"I watched his room."

"All night?" Brigitte laid a gentle hand on her arm. "Are you okay?"

Meliz sagged, weighed down with fear and exhaustion. "No, I'm not," she admitted, squaring her shoulders. "I'm pissed."

Brigitte regarded her for a long moment. "Wait." She dug through her toiletry bag and held up another hairpin with a triumphant hoot. "You need two to pick a lock."

As luck would have it, Hikaru's room was in the original building with a regular key lock. All the rooms in the newer annex had magnetized card keys. Camouflaging their break-in would still be a challenge. Hikaru's room faced the inner courtyard, and guests in the opposing rooms had a clear view of his door.

At this early hour, no one but the hotel staff milled about. A house cleaner bustled past them with an armload of freshly laundered towels. They waited until she had gone and cut through the courtyard garden using one of its many charming and meandering paths.

Meliz and Brigitte stopped, hearts pounding and palms sweating, in front of Hikaru's room. The two shot furtive glances up at the windows and down the walkway. Meliz struck a casual pose and pretended to check her phone while shielding a kneeling Brigitte from prying eyes.

Brigitte swore under her breath as she wrestled with the hairpins. A curtain opposite twitched.

"Hurry up," Meliz hissed.

A combination of beginner's luck and an old lock released the mechanism. They heard a satisfying click as the door swung open. A quick glimpse up at the still-shuttered windows reassured them, and they scuttled into his room unseen. Meliz locked the door behind them.

He kept the room neat. Two bags rested on luggage racks, and he had pulled his rumpled covers up to approximate a made bed. A briefcase sat open on the desk.

"How much time do we have?" Brigitte hurried to the desk and rifled through the briefcase.

"He told me his playlist was fifty-five minutes. It's been twenty since he left. Say thirty minutes. That leaves us five minutes grace."

"I don't think we'll need it." Brigitte held up a laminated ID badge. A government seal with the words "Historical Investigation and Research Agency (HIRA)" and a portrait photo of Hikaru in a business suit covered one side. A magnetized strip ran across the back.

Meliz examined the badge. "This is an American seal, but I've never heard of HIRA. It doesn't sound real."

Their eyes locked, arriving at the same conclusion as one. "CIA."

The sound of a key in the door gave them only a second's warning before it opened to admit Hikaru. Meliz gasped, the badge gripped tight in her hand. Brigitte closed the briefcase and straightened a notepad and pen as if she had just wandered in to clean the place.

Hikaru stood in the doorway, sweat dripping down his face. He had a two-day's growth of beard and looked fit, muscular, and formidable. He also looked confused.

"What is this?" Meliz demanded, shoving the badge in his face. The best defense is a good offense and all that. She hoped.

"A badge for the HIRA, where I work."

The two women gaped at him, stunned. Not by what he had said, but how he had said it . . . in a perfect American accent.

Chapter Twenty-Seven

The fight is over when the enemy is down.
—Ovid

19 July, 1945, Dulag, Leyte—Today we signed for our points as of May 1st. I have thirty-four points with two battle stars. We've got more battle stars, but we're waiting for them to come through. Ole Bradford has enough points to go home. Whether we have a cartoonist or not doesn't matter anyway. We ran out of ink and paper days ago. The *Dulag Daily* is dead.

George is a daddy again, a boy. Josefina insisted on George Junior. Castle said he'd agree if she allowed Hawkeye as the middle name.

He was joking, I know. But I still felt proud.

1 Aug.—We received orders for Okinawa. Everyone's feeling a bit jittery. Word is we're gearing up for an invasion of Japan.

With the war in Europe over, our allies should be joining us in full force out here. Nobody is sure if that includes Russia.

I have a mind to meet me a Russian. They have some fine writers.

Moving is a huge pain in the ass. It's hard work, but I'm not complaining. Without the paper, time drags.

5 Aug.—We loaded up today. We leave for Okinawa tomorrow using our own planes for transport. I don't care too much for this trip. There's a typhoon brewing off the coast of Japan, and the planes are packed to the hilt. My plane carries seventeen men, with 300 pounds of equipment per man. We have a jeep with a trailer and a compressor in the trailer. It's a miracle these big planes even get off the ground.

We've heard rumors coming over the radio that Japan will surrender, but last night a group of flyboys told us they shot down two Japanese Bettys. We don't know what to think.

They've promoted Captain Griswold and assigned him to command headquarters. We're to get a new CO. We hear he's a real spit-and-polish type. I'm gonna miss the captain—major now. He is a fine man.

14 Aug., Bolo Point, Okinawa—Frank is hopping mad. They've assigned me to take a truck up north to Motobu Airbase. We're short all sorts of gear that didn't make it in with the Main Echelon and ended up at the other airfield. The squadron doesn't have a plane to spare.

I walked off the line, and Chief motioned me over. Told me to get my duffle and head up to Motobu with Joey Pitts, a kid and mechanic like me from somewhere in Maine.

Just in the right place at the right time, I figure. I don't blame Frank for being angry. Setting up camp is boring and backbreaking work.

**

Northern Okinawa, August 1945

The drive from Bolo Point to Motobu came in just under sixty klicks. In the time it took us to get from one to the other, word had spread of the Japanese surrender. Joey and I arrived at Motobu Airfield to the news and a crap load of celebrating GIs.

Motobu boasted a single runway built about four months ago as a combat facility to support operations in the battle for Okinawa. The place bustled with planes and trucks coming and going at all hours.

We had loaded the truck and were eating our rations on the tailgate when I overheard a conversation between two lieutenants sitting in a jeep next to us. They were part of a larger team conducting post-combat surveys of the island.

One of them sounded like a medic, and the other like some sort of crops expert. They talked about the civilians and the surveys in the south that had turned up massive devastation to the land and its people. Unlike Iwo Jima, which was uninhabited, Okinawa had a large civilian population.

Most of the heavy fighting centered in the south. The Japanese dug in good there and fortified what seemed like every hill and ridge. They conscripted civilians into the war effort and encouraged them to commit suicide in order to avoid capture by our troops. If these two officers were to be believed, somewhere close to a third of the people had died.

Listening to them gave me an idea. Most folks considered me a gifted talker. I've talked my way both into and out of sticky situations.

I approached them, saluted, and struck up a line of chat, asking questions about the surveys. "We've come up from Bolo Point," I told them. "That area is pretty scorched."

Lieutenant Byrd, the medic, nodded. "We're going to find less destruction in the north. The terrain is rougher than in the south, harder to fortify."

"My concern, sir," I replied in my best humble country-boy manner, "is the water. Much of the water supply is likely contaminated by artillery and sabotage."

"We have a water testing kit."

That was it, a water testing kit. I knew I had 'em. I filled them in on my experience with water purification, which consisted solely of pouring lime into wells, but they didn't need to know that. Embellishing came second nature to me.

My plan worked like a charm. Joey headed back to Bolo Point with the supplies, and I'd wangled me a spot on an environmental crew headed north. The lieutenants got clearance from my new CO for a four-day excursion up the coast to Cape Hedo, the northernmost point on the island.

Turns out, what really got me on that survey team had little to do with my silver tongue. More like a couple of officers who were only too happy to leave the grunt work to a lowly corporal. And dump on me they did. I took on the roles of driver, de facto water expert, and equipment packer/hauler.

I didn't mind. I always liked to drive, and the wind blew through my hair with liberating force.

It soon became clear Lieutenant Byrd's assessment was spot-on. The north had experienced noticeably less destruction than the south. The tropical landscape, mountains, and beachside cliffs stood mostly intact.

We bumped along a rough road, with temporary bridges built where the enemy blew up the originals. We stopped at any signs of people, camps, or villages.

Lieutenants Byrd and Murphy, who was actually a geologist, recorded the condition of the civilians and noted what infrastructure still stood. Murphy radioed the information back to Headquarters every few hours.

The job did little to tax our energy, because we found almost no people, camps, or villages. We ran into more of our own troops bringing supplies and relief in an effort to keep the surviving Okinawans from starving.

We spent the night camped out with a company of Marines. With them were two Japanese-American soldiers, not much older than teenagers. They hailed from Hawaii and talked just like me and my friends back home, but I couldn't shake how strange it was to see a Japanese man in an American uniform.

They weren't Marines. I could tell. I asked them their unit. They brushed me off and acted all cagey-like. But one of them told me they were with a company of translators, a whole group of them spread out over the Pacific.

"We're dispatched to talk villagers into surrendering," he explained. "I talked two hundred people out of a cave. Whole families ready to walk into the ocean and drown themselves."

This well-known pattern had repeated itself throughout the Pacific. The Japanese Army sowed fear of our advancing troops wherever they went. Telling locals our guys would torture, rape, and commit other violence against them.

The lies set my teeth on edge. The ones doing that were the Japanese.

The fellow's story made a big impression on me. Saving two hundred lives was sure something, I told him.

The Marines had a journalist with them. I didn't catch his name, but he worked for *Life* magazine. He didn't talk much and seemed more interested in taking pictures of the locals. I slept fitfully, and we left early the next morning, reaching Cape Hedo before noon without encountering a single soul.

Like balancing on the edge of a waterfall, I stood at the furthest point of the island, dizzy with exhilaration. Sheer, craggy cliffs marched right up to the ocean. Gigantic rocks jutted out of the water like the tips of huge spears.

The desolate and windswept point faced an endless ocean, and a feeling of complete isolation overwhelmed me. I walked around for half an hour, but met no people. We drove down a rough set of tracks in hopes of finding any sign of life.

One road drew nearer the beach, and gave us a full view of the cliffs. I jumped out of the jeep and scanned a hillside a few yards up from the dirt road.

A blur of movement caught my eye. I squinted through the field glasses at what appeared to be a collection of haystacks among the foliage. I brought into focus a village, a small grouping of shacks facing the ocean north toward Japan.

I yelled over to the officers lounging back in the jeep, "There's a village up there." I pointed up the hillside.

They turned as one and half-heartedly assessed the situation. Now we were at our destination, they itched to get back to Motobu and Headquarters.

"We'll radio in with the coordinates," Lieutenant Byrd grumbled, not moving from where he sat.

"Shouldn't we head up there and check it out?"

They shrugged in unison. "Don't think it'll make much of a difference if we do," Murphy replied.

I clenched my teeth in frustration. I had two days of leave remaining and sure didn't want to spend them hanging out at the Marine encampment or even the airfield. The brass always found a way to put us lowly grunts to work.

"I'll go," I volunteered.

"Well, that's fine, Corporal, but we're heading back to the encampment for the night and on to the airfield in the morning."

I considered my situation. Driving up and down these tracks had messed with my sense of direction, but I figured I could still find my way back. The encampment lay about twelve klicks south, a short jog for a country boy like me. I could check out the village, do a bit of hiking, maybe even hit the beach, and be at the camp before they took off in the morning.

I had never encountered such lackadaisical officers in my entire military career. They didn't even bat an eye at my suggestion.

"Suit yourself." Byrd yawned and rubbed his eyes. "But don't be late." They drove off, leaving the water testing kit, my carbine, and a duffle full of K-rations to distribute to the villagers.

The clearing lay maybe fifty yards up through the foliage. I sited out my path and climbed. A cool, stiff breeze off the ocean made pleasant work of the short hike.

The inhabitants barely glanced up at my approach. They had seen me long before I spotted them. I might well have been invisible, standing there in the middle of their little community.

The village resembled more a campground, with maybe six different families clustered in a small glade. Their crude shelters looked out over the ocean and would be damn uncomfortable in the rain.

Most of the civilians I came across, both in villages and military holding areas, were a people depleted, wrung dry of human emotion, what they had endured etched in harsh relief on their faces and in their ruined homeland.

This village appeared hardly fit for human habitation, but its residents hustled around busy with housekeeping and food gathering chores. I could only guess at what had driven them to this place or why they stayed.

Thank goodness for the children. Without them, I'd have stumbled around on my own. They rushed to my side and snatched with eager hands the K-rations from the duffle. I found interacting with kids the best way to get information. I focused on a bright, pretty little girl who was probably around eight or nine years old.

I went through my standard pantomime, making wavy movements and cupping my hands together in an effort to discover their water source. The girl caught on quick. She spoke to a young woman I assumed was her mother. The woman nodded, and the girl gestured for me to follow. We did not go far.

A short hike up the forested hillside, and I spied a spring bubbling up from beneath the thick undergrowth. Not much more than a trickle, these folks were lucky to have come across it even so.

I unstrapped the water testing kit. The girl perched on a rock and watched me work with a bright, inquisitive gaze. I used the standard tests for biological and chemical contaminants and soon determined the source of the villagers' energy. Their water was clean.

The girl waved for my attention. She looked her question.

"Clean," I pronounced slow and loud. "Your . . . water . . . is . . . clean."

She frowned.

"JD, you dummy," I muttered to myself.

I struggled with how to gesture "clean" or "good." I pointed at the water, nodded, rubbed my stomach, smiled big, and gave a thumbs-up. One of these must have translated, because she laughed and clapped her hands together.

We had passed a couple of gardens on our way up the hillside. "Where do you get your food?" I made an eating motion. She jumped up and ran off. I lurched after her, trying to keep up.

We skidded to a stop behind the stand of hovels where strings laden with all types of dried sea creatures stretched between the trees. She pointed skyward and made a flappy motion that must have meant birds. Seafood and fowl, not too shabby. Although the whole group combined, painfully thin as they were, couldn't have weighed more than a few well-fed grunts.

Back in the clearing, I found a nice dry spot on the ground and ate my K-rations. The children gathered around me and did the same. The girl translated my gestures to the rest of the group. I appeared to be a source of amusement, because they laughed often.

Their laughter sounded both familiar and strange. How many months since I had heard the happy sound of children?

I looked up at the bright blue sky with fluffy, white clouds scattered about. The villagers had chosen well. Protected by the hillside at their backs, the makeshift huts opened out on a magnificent view of the cliffs, beach, and waves beyond.

I focused hard on the horizon. Fuzzy, dark specks floated before me. I rubbed my eyes and tried again. Two of the specks solidified. I stood and peered through my field glasses. They grew larger, and their outlines formed two planes moving fast.

Bettys by the shape of them, but the color and markings were all wrong. Painted white, they bore green crosses on their tails, fuselages, and wings. As they drew closer, the planes became identifiable to the naked eye. The kids and some of the adults grouped around me, gazing out at the oncoming Bettys.

We all jumped and gasped when three Zeros dropped like birds of prey from the clouds above. They came out of nowhere and fired on the Bettys.

"My God," I whispered, "they're shooting their own."

The battle proved an unequal one. The fast, maneuverable Zeros pressed hard, merciless in their assault. The Bettys, unprepared for the onslaught, soon smoked and wobbled, losing altitude.

I imagined the pilots fighting for control, maybe preparing to bail. But even that avenue of escape crumbled when the Zeros collided in midair with the hemorrhaging Bettys. All five planes hit the water in a blaze of fire, steel, and smoke.

The attack was a murder-suicide and over in a matter of seconds. It seemed impossible anyone could survive, but I scanned the ocean for some hope of rescue. A flicker caught the edge of my lens, and I doubled back.

American aircraft, two P-38s, flew low and northbound on a similar flight path as the downed Bettys. They passed over the wreckage, rolled back southbound, and buzzed right over us. I raised an arm in salute.

I panned back and forth, searching for anything that might explain what had happened. Black smoke still curled up from the water, but the waves already churned the debris under and out into the deepest ocean.

The villagers' faces reflected back at me my own confusion. Several of them pointed up at the sky and over at me. I held up my hands, saying aloud, "I don't know."

Maybe the two lazy lieutenants would have an explanation in the morning. Right now, I wanted to get down to the ocean. I signed my question to the little girl. "How do I get to the beach?"

She jabbed a finger at her chest and ran over to her mother. The woman didn't give her permission so readily this time. She shook her head and turned away, but the girl would not be put off. She pulled at her mother's arm, talking nonstop. The woman tried to ignore her, but finally gestured over to a group of boys.

The girl jumped up and down with delight and called over to them. A little boy detached himself from the group and joined her. They appeared to be brother and sister, with the boy a couple of years younger. They headed down the slope toward the road without looking back, expecting me to follow.

I had anticipated a path leading to the sandy beach I spotted from the clearing. Instead, the children turned off the road down a steep trail of loose dirt and rocks. It twisted and turned sharply, making for a difficult descent. I suspected the kids were playing a trick on me by leading me astray. I was wrong.

The path stopped at a secluded beach with an emerald-green inlet bordered by large caves on each end. The children stood puffed up and proud, presenting me with the most beautiful part of their home. They smiled at each other, gratified by my expression of amazement.

I had the remains of a Bit-O-Honey bar in my pocket and split off a rectangle each for the kids and one for myself. We sat on the sandy beach and chewed the sticky candy. I talked to them and drew pictures in the sand. They laughed and nodded, not understanding a single word I said.

Despite their dirty faces and thin frames, the wonder of childhood shone in their eyes. The thought of what they had suffered so young struck me with force. I sure hoped life would get easier for them.

The kids showed me tide pools where rare and colorful fish swam. To my delight, an octopus shot through the water, just below the surface, and squeezed into a tiny crack.

We picked up shiny rocks and built a fire ring. They helped me gather driftwood, and I shared my K-rations with them as we sat around the campfire. They left right before evening fell.

Alone on the beach, the fire now reduced to embers, the stars spilled unchecked over a cloudless expanse. The heavens moved across the sky, and I slept as they made their age-old journey into morning.

Chapter Twenty-Eight

Almost everything that is great has been done by youth.
—Disraeli

"You're an American?" Meliz practically bared her teeth in fury. Yet another man who wasn't what he claimed.

"Guilty." Hikaru grinned.

"Asshole," Brigitte spat. "Definitely CIA."

"What?" The smile dropped from his face. "No, I'm not. That's crazy."

Meliz opened her eyes wide. "Crazy? Like faking a Japanese accent and pretending to be a businessman." She threw the badge at him. It wobbled in the air like a wounded butterfly and landed with a pathetic plink at his feet.

"Did you have anything to do with my assault?" she demanded, her voice breaking.

Hikaru reared back and threw up his hands. "God, no, Meliz, I would never do that. You have to believe me." He stepped toward her.

She backed away. "Why should I believe you?"

He stopped. "I found you. If it wasn't for the track—"

"Oh, sure, the *app*," she cut him off, putting air quotes around "app."

"You could be in on it with that old man," Brigitte interjected. "They grab Meliz. Get away. You show up just in time. Big hero."

"I don't even know them . . ." Hikaru shook his head in exasperation. "Listen, guys, believe it or not, tracking apps are not James Bond stuff. They're easy to get and required by my agency when I'm out of the country." He walked to the closet, and the two women stiffened in alarm. "I'm getting my computer," he reassured them, pulling it down from a shelf.

Hikaru set the laptop on the desk and logged on. He typed something and turned the computer toward them. "This is why I'm here."

Meliz and Brigitte leaned forward. An e-mail from JD lit up the screen. Meliz picked up the computer and sat on the bed. She read the message.

JD Hawkins *<Marshal2Texas@gmail.com>*
to HIRArequests

Dear Liz,

I've hit a brick wall with my research and hope you can help me. I'm investigating the Green Cross flights that ferried Japanese officials on August 19, 1945, from Japan to the island of Iejima off the western coast of Okinawa. I believe another such flight left Japan on August 17, 1945, but never made it to the island. Is there any documentation, either Allied or Japanese, official or unofficial, letters or articles, etc., that even alludes to the possibility of such a flight? I would appreciate any assistance you can render me.

Sincerely,
JD Hawkins

The e-mail sounded like JD. He was usually blunt and focused when doing research.

A thrill of discovery shot through Meliz. Garrett and Mia had been right. The Green Cross flights were connected to the missing pages.

She quashed her excitement and asked, "Why would this e-mail send you all the way out here . . . and at the same time as me?"

"I'd already scheduled this trip when you posted your travel plans. A vacation to the South Pacific seemed a little too coincidental. My boss, Liz, and I thought that maybe you were on the same trail as us. I changed my itinerary by a few days to coincide with your trip."

A pained expression crossed Meliz's face. How could she be so stupid? After posting a brief tribute to JD on her blog, she noted her "vacation" plans before signing off for several weeks.

"What an idiot." She could have slapped herself. Instead of being clever, she'd left breadcrumbs for anyone to follow. Brigitte cooed and patted her hand.

Meliz smiled at her friend and shook off her self-recriminations. She turned a demanding glare on Hikaru. "What do you mean by 'same trail?'"

"That e-mail sent up a red flag. I don't know how or why, but your grandfather's query pinged a decades-old intelligence request."

"Yeah, we know, CIA." Brigitte sneered, determined to connect him to the spy agency.

"No, I'm not CIA. I'm a historian."

"Intelligence request?" Meliz prompted.

"More of an alert . . . to let them know if anyone asks for information regarding a Green Cross flight on that specific date, August 17, 1945."

"Let who know?"

"Well . . . the CIA," he admitted with a guilty frown. "I talked with a low-level somebody at the Agency, just procedure."

"Really?" Meliz narrowed her eyes with suspicion. "Your organization, the Historical Investigative something-or-other, reports to the CIA so often it's procedure?"

Hikaru hesitated. "No. I mean . . . listen . . . can I get a towel? I need to wipe off this sweat. I don't have a gun stashed anywhere. You can relax."

He walked into the bathroom. Meliz and Brigitte exchanged an intense, uneasy look. They heard water splash in the sink. He came out pulling on a clean T-shirt.

Meliz averted her eyes. If he intended to distract her with his muscled midsection, he would be sadly disappointed.

"My agency is under the Library of Congress. We're not . . . obvious. We investigate historical issues for the different branches of government, but also for independent researchers, like your grandfather. He used us a lot. I even fielded some of his requests, but he preferred to work with Liz."

"You *have* read his books."

"All of his Texas histories. They're amazing, vivid and full of love for the place. I read a couple of the Marshal Jameson series when I was a kid." Hikaru shrugged. "They weren't my thing, but I liked the horse. That horse was like a super smart dog."

Brigitte squirmed and looked at Meliz with a "maybe he's not so bad" expression on her face.

Meliz rolled her eyes. "None of this explains why you're here."

He pulled out the desk chair and sat. That she had ever believed him a stuffy businessman amazed her, his reserved demeanor now replaced by ease and informality. She had recognized the incongruity that first night at the club and again upon meeting at the hotel. Intuition she had ignored.

Meliz compressed her lips. He would not fool her again.

"We have a decent discretionary budget. Sometimes my boss gets a bug in her ear and wants to know what's going on. We'd never come across an intelligence alert that old. And after your grandfather died—"

"Your boss sent you off on a trip to the Pacific islands to satisfy her curiosity?" Meliz interrupted, unconvinced.

"No. First, I researched the hell out of the thing. I got nothing from the CIA or the FBI, and my overseas requests came up empty-handed. You can see for yourself."

He took the computer from her and pulled up a folder labeled "GreenCrossHawkins." He handed it back to Meliz. "I keep my e-mails grouped by project. Everything is there."

Brigitte plopped down beside Meliz, and they scrolled through the e-mails. There were a multitude from archives, libraries, and universities in Japan, the Philippines, and throughout the Pacific region.

A familiar name surfaced. Meliz clicked on an e-mail to Dr. Garrett Rivera.

In the message, Hikaru did not mention the Green Cross flights or her grandfather. He asked for any documentation regarding the Japanese surrender, in particular, the preliminary meetings with MacArthur in Manila on August 19 and 20, 1945.

The request was general in nature, and Meliz understood why Garrett had not made the connection between Hikaru's research and her own. What she didn't understand was Hikaru's interest in the Manila talks.

"Why this?" She pointed to the query.

"Sometimes I come at a subject sideways, so to speak. Here, let me show you." He waved Meliz and Brigitte apart and sat in between them. Taking the computer, he brought up a table laid out in rows and columns with intersecting dates and events.

"Your grandfather didn't just ask about the Green Cross flights, he mentioned a specific date, August 17, 1945. The intelligence alert also referenced that date. This was strange, because the episode is well-documented. The Japanese delegation landed on Iejima Island on August 19 and from there went on to Manila to meet with MacArthur. That's where I started, in Manila with MacArthur."

Hikaru paused. When they had no questions, he continued, "I discovered a communiqué from MacArthur outlining instructions for the surrender. They spelled out, step-by-step, what type of aircraft the Japanese delegation was to fly, what the planes should look like, flight path, etcetera."

"JD knew the August 19 flight had taken place," Meliz interrupted with an impatient wave of her hand. "He was interested in August 17."

"I'm getting to that. In his communiqué, MacArthur mentioned a date the planes should leave Japan and arrive on Iejima . . . *August 17*, weather permitting. Even some old personal letters from soldiers on Iejima mentioned expecting the planes earlier, but they were delayed for whatever reason."

"Meliz's granddad did not ask about a delayed flight," Brigitte objected. "He wanted to know about another flight that *didn't* make it."

Meliz stood, discomfited by the warmth of Hikaru's thigh pressed against her own. She walked to the window, the blooming garden beyond now host to waking guests.

"You're right. JD thought there was another flight."

Brigitte joined her at the window. "No, he didn't think. He *believed.* That is different. He wanted proof of something he already knew."

Meliz looked at her friend in admiration. "Right again. He wanted verification."

"Someone told him?" Hikaru stood, drawn to the window and the two women.

Silhouetted by the morning light, they formed a picture of concentration poised on the brink of understanding.

"No." Meliz was suddenly sure. "He saw what happened. JD

witnessed a Green Cross flight on August 17, and he wrote about it in his journal. Those are the missing pages."

**

"You must call your parents." Alberta expressed concern, but also frustration. Meliz had put her in a difficult position. "I can't keep this from them."

"I know. I'm sorry," Meliz apologized. She sat cross-legged on the bed in front of the computer screen. "I can't leave yet. I have to . . . I . . ." She ran her hands through her hair and heaved a deep sigh. "I needed you to understand. So . . . so—"

"So I would take your side when your mother calls," Alberta finished for her. She knew this maneuver well. Meliz often flew trial balloons past her grandfather before telling her parents of any unpleasantness.

Meliz grinned. "Am I that obvious?"

"You're not *that* obvious," Alberta returned with a smile. "Or maybe just to me."

Meliz sobered. "I thought of *Yeye* the other day." She stared off over the top of her computer. "I'd like to know more about him. Dad hardly ever mentions him . . . kind of like JD never talked about the war." She looked back at the computer screen. "I know it makes him sad, but I want to have some idea of who *Yeye* was."

Alberta studied the young woman staring intently back at her. Meliz's face presented to the world a visual repository of her dissimilar ancestors. The mix had produced a graceful compromise between the Chinese and European chromosomes. June shone through in her flawless complexion and Gwen in the shape of her face. Meliz's dark, thickly lashed eyes were a replica of her father's, and she had inherited her *nainai's* soaring singing voice, along with JD's sense of humor.

Alberta's heart constricted. Damn this country. Always forcing one to choose, or choosing for one.

If the internet trolls were anything to go by, Meliz's Asianness set her apart, even from her own family. They cruelly assigned her the role of other and denied her the full richness of her heritage. Alberta suspected that Meliz's determination to uncover JD's mystery was also an attempt to reclaim her own multilayered story.

She understood this struggle all too well. Alberta also yearned for validation, a constant ache behind her breastbone. She salved the pain with work and research. With every new book and accolade, she pushed back against those who would reduce her to mere pigmentation.

"You should ask him about your *yeye*," Alberta declared with a defiant nod. She wanted nothing more than to shield the girl from the brutal vagaries of an unjust world, but it was clear Meliz could protect herself. "Take all that belongs to you."

Meliz laughed. "Thanks, Bert." Dark circles smudged the delicate skin under her eyes, but she emanated strength and a budding sense of relaxed self-confidence.

"Did you get a hold of Kiko?" Alberta asked, having included Kiko Tamaki's address and phone number in her earlier message.

"I spoke with her grandson, Ren," Meliz replied with a sad shake of her head. "We're the same age, you know. He was surprised to hear from me. They thought after JD died the whole thing would be forgotten. Anyway, he spoke with his grandmother and we arranged to meet at her home in Nago."

Alberta nodded and added, "Oh yeah, Hikaru Ikeda is legit. We've used the HIRA a lot in the past. I found the e-mail." She glanced at her notes. "I'll follow up with his boss to make one hundred percent sure, but I've dealt with him before." She signed off with another admonishment for Meliz to call her parents.

**

"Sometimes, I pretend to be a Japanese businessman when I travel," Hikaru told Meliz when they were alone. "I'm good at it. And being anything other than an American is easier, especially in Asia."

They sat in a secluded spot on the rooftop garden of the hotel annex. Brigitte had slipped out, citing a lunch date with Sean.

"With the information from your blog post, we were able to piece together your itinerary. And, well, Liz has some connections too." He grimaced with embarrassment. "I staked out your pension, trying to figure out my next move, when I ran into Brigitte in the bakery." He threw her a significant look. "You know how she is."

A fond, indulgent smile spread across Meliz's face. "Yeah, I know."

"She struck up a conversation, filling me in on the people she'd met and how you were all gathering at Deejays that night. I was already doing my Japanese thing . . ."

Hikaru had apologized so many times, Meliz lost count. He insisted everything else he told her was true. His grandfather fought for the Japanese, and after the war, emigrated to the US. His other grandfather spent his adolescence in an internment camp in California. Hikaru grew up in San Francisco.

Meliz leaned back on the bench and closed her eyes. His voice droned on, deep and soothing. He spoke of the Japanese surrender and the warring political factions within that country, details of which Meliz had recently become familiar.

Even after the devastation wrought by two atomic bombs, most members of Japan's Supreme Council opposed unconditional surrender. The Japanese were set to inflict extreme casualties should the Allies invade *Kyūshū*, the southernmost island of Japan. They'd hoped this strategy would win them a negotiated peace while holding onto territory and preserving Imperial rule, as well as avoiding war crimes trials.

The Japanese destroyed much of the documentation related to the war. Historians found research in the area difficult. They disagreed on the confluence of events that pushed Japan's intractable leadership to surrender. In the end, Japan did surrender unconditionally, sparing hundreds of thousands, perhaps millions, of Allied and Japanese lives.

Meliz opened her eyes when Hikaru stopped talking. He gazed out at the roofs and treetops of Tacloban.

She studied his profile and thought it a noble one. A strong forehead and prominent nose sloped down into a full mouth. Meliz touched the place at the corner of his eye where the skin was just beginning to wrinkle. He grasped her hand and kissed it.

Meliz wanted to trust him, to reclaim those passionate moments in the alleyway before the brutality of her abduction. On impulse, she stood and straddled his lap, looking down into his upturned face.

"I'm not sure what this is or where it will end up. But right now, I just want to go back a little in time. Okay?"

The sun beat down on them through the leaves of the potted trees. A drop of sweat fell from her lips onto his. He breathed her name and pulled her close.

Later in her room, Meliz flopped onto the bed and released a long sigh. They planned to travel to Okinawa the next day. She would discover the truth at last, but not alone. Brigitte and Hikaru would be with her.

Chapter Twenty-Nine

All actual heroes are essential men, And all men possible heroes.
—E.B. Browning

22 Aug., 1945, Bolo Point Airfield, Okinawa

- 17 August around 1500hrs, small village/settlement, Cape Hedo, Northern Okinawa.
- Two Bettys painted white with green crosses shot down by three Zeros
- The planes rammed in a *kamikaze* manner
- All five planes fell into the ocean and were destroyed
- No survivors
- P38s overhead
- The Bettys headed southbound–origin Japan?
- Destination? Iejima?
- Got back to Motobu (18 Aug)–heard the white planes with green crosses indicated surrender
- Will land on Iejima with Japanese delegation
- They were delayed and will arrive 19 Aug
- No mention of the downed planes
- The village burnt to the ground

- What happened?
- 19 August–the Green Cross planes landed on Iejima
- Saw them fly by, even from Motobu
- Can't figure any of this out

**

Bolo Point, Okinawa, August 1945

"Are you sure?" George asked, after I worked up the courage to tell him. "They were Americans?"

I was never so sure of anything in my life. Every detail of that morning burned into my brain like a brand on cowhide. I won't ever forget what those men were or what they did.

The girl and her brother woke me before dawn by dribbling sand on my face. I sat up, spitting grit out of my mouth. The kids laughed until they couldn't stand.

I grinned and threw a handful of sand in their direction. To tell the truth, I appreciated the wake-up call. With a long hike ahead of me, I sure didn't want to miss my ride back to Motobu.

I stood and slung the carbine over my shoulder. A split second later, I dropped to the beach at the sound of machine gun fire.

Beneath the repeated burst, I heard the screams of terrified people. The village lay a good quarter of a mile up the steep and slippery trail.

The kids ran for the cliff. They scrambled on the path in a flailing panic.

I sprung to my feet and passed them, running flat out, pumping my arms, lungs near to bursting. I fell twice on the loose dirt and jumped back up each time, determined to make the roadside before the girl and her brother. This could be the work of renegade Japanese soldiers, and they were as like to kill those kids as look at them.

"No insignia," I told George, wresting my mind back from that blood-drenched morning. "Like Mick Cassidy."

George sat silent. Bile rose in my throat as I recounted the damning details.

Eight of them, eight Americans came out of the tree line after torching the village, casual as could be, checking their weapons and lighting up cigarettes. I crouched on the trail below the road with the kids pressed vicelike at my sides.

The men radioed in their position. "SR eighteen strike team Cape Hedo, targets eliminated, ready for extraction." Eighteen, not eighty-one—of course, I had looked at the tattoo upside down and backwards.

The transmitter crackled, and a voice radioed back with coordinates. I held my breath and did not let it out again until they had marched off toward the eastern side of the island, in the opposite direction of the Marine encampment.

George laid a comforting hand on my shoulder and shook his head with a perplexed frown. "Why would they kill a bunch of unarmed civilians?"

"The only thing I can figure is those downed Japanese planes. The P-38s spotted us, all of us, watching from the clearing." My stomach churned with a deep sense of guilt. "I even waved to them. And those officers from the environmental survey radioed in our location."

"None of this makes any sense."

I didn't know what to tell him. All I knew, no one had made a peep about those downed planes. For sure, the P-38 crews saw the attack. Maybe other military vessels witnessed the incident too. No talk, no whispered rumors, struck me as strange. Soldiers gossip; secrets get out.

"We'll go to the CO," he insisted. "When I get back tomorrow, we'll talk to Captain Reed."

I hesitated, wary of going to the CO, but I didn't have a better idea. If it had been Captain Griswold, maybe. Still, I relied on George's judgment. Good ole Lancelot, his assured response gave me a little relief from my tortured self-recriminations.

In his own way, George knew how to work the system. The brass liked him and had already marked him as leadership material. He told me about his plans to finish college and re-up as an officer after graduation.

They would listen to him, I told myself. I needed to be patient until he got back, and we'd go together.

I didn't say anything to Frank about the village massacre. I could never figure which way he would blow. Until I knew what to expect, I couldn't risk telling him.

The next day, I waited for George to return. I couldn't write. There was no satisfaction in putting pen to paper anyway.

I kept churning over every second of that terrible morning, each one resounding in my brain like rifle fire. I couldn't focus on anything else for long. Got my hands on a new book, but even that didn't help.

I usually worked to exhaustion and dropped like a rock at night, but not today. Not only did George's crew fly out on assignment, but all the rest of the squadron as well. Chief let us go after routine chores and cleanup. First time I ever regretted getting off the line.

Hanging out in the tent only made me nervous, so I went for a walk. The rocky cliff known as Bolo Point stuck out over the ocean with a hundred-and-fifty-foot drop to the water below. I paced back and forth along the jagged verge and peered up into the sky.

The squadron had flown out on transports into Japan. We started moving troops and equipment into that defeated country a few days before. Rumors were we'd soon be headed there ourselves.

My heart longed for home, but I didn't have the points to head stateside. The occupation looked to be mostly on us, and it was anyone's guess how much longer we'd be stuck here.

I willed James Deacon's C-46 into view. Spots danced before my eyes, but no plane appeared. It might be hours before they returned.

I walked toward the encampment, but changed my mind and headed over to the radio room. The small plank-wood shack housed all communications for the squadron and bustled with purposeful activity at every hour of the day. But since the surrender, discipline had fallen largely by the wayside, and the radio room was no exception.

Five men, including the operator on duty, huddled over a noisy card game. I didn't like to gamble. The whole scene, the whoops of victory and groaning defeat, turned me off.

None of the guys were friends of mine, and they barely glanced my way when I walked in. I'd heard food poisoning had struck down the usual communications crew. Another, more accurate, rumor diagnosed their illness as severe hangover.

I picked up a ragged edition of *Yank* magazine and leafed through the dirty pages. Each time the radio crackled and popped, the operator got up and did his minimal best to guide unit operations. The guys at the game stopped playing and watched him like impatient vultures until he returned. Their loud and aggressive voices intimidated me, and I stayed to one side and tried to ignore them.

The next time the radio sounded, I sucked it up and approached the operator. "Have you heard from Deacon?"

He logged an entry and didn't look up. "Don't know, man. They unloaded their payload, shouldn't be much longer now."

"Think you could raise them? See where they are?"

He glanced at me with the kind of blank expression that passed for cool-guy irritation. "Listen, man—"

His expression changed to one of alarm. He grabbed my wrist and gaped at my watch.

"Fuck," he spewed and pointed at the clock on the wall. "Which one of you fuckers changed the time?"

Their silent giggles turned into loud guffaws as they fell all over themselves with laughter. He spit out a few more profanities before beginning his now-late routine contact with each crew.

I stood next to him as he went through the list. A feeling of dread radiated out from the pit of my stomach. My mind drifted back to Miami Beach and the day the CO told me about my brother. The meeting ran like a play through my mind.

I entered his office stage right and saluted. Against a black backdrop, I stood young and dapper in my uniform khakis. One stark overhead light illuminated his desk. The CO gestured for me to sit. I couldn't hear what he said, but his words scrolled across the bottom of the frame like the subtitles of a silent movie.

"I'm sorry to inform you, son . . ."

Premonition wasn't my strong suit. I had been wrong countless times before.

With my stomach in knots, I unfolded a chair and pulled up next to the radio. We all listened to the operator try to raise Deacon.

By the fifth call, I dropped my head in my hands. The group of laughing hyenas had stilled and sat in grim silence.

**

The whole squadron mourned. We had lost men before, but the blow fell harder now the war had ended. George and Jimmy, that whole crew, had been with us since the beginning.

Near as anyone can figure, they got fogged in and ran into a mountainside. The army dispatched troops from Fussa Airfield to retrieve the bodies. Captain Reed said they would bring them back here to be buried at one of the Marine cemeteries.

I finished writing a letter to Josefina. I stuck another, shorter letter to Rosa and George Jr. into the envelope with it. I hoped they'd read it one day when they were old enough to understand.

Captain Reed said he would send my letters with the special

delivery pouch. Maybe Josefina would get them with the telegram. I hoped so. I wished I could be there in person. I knew George would've tried to do the same for me and mine.

I sealed the envelope and sat back on my cot. What to do about the village massacre still haunted me. Those murderers could not walk away scot-free. Didn't matter it was our boys did the killing.

George had agreed. Now with him gone, I doubted my resolve. I didn't know what to do or who to talk to.

I tried to blank my mind with work. Our move to Japan proceeded in an unorganized rush that had our unit spread out over three islands. The Rear Echelon hung back in Dulag, waiting to join us here, while our Advance Echelon set up camp in Japan. This meant we worked on a tight schedule again.

I hardly noticed. Nothing seemed real. I moved through the days like a sleepwalker stuck in a slow-motion nightmare.

Frank had put distance between us, though it was probably as much my fault as his. He avoided conversation, preferring grunts and one-syllable words, nothing like his camaraderie, prickly though it was, of times past.

I found out from someone else Frank had received word of his German relatives. None of them survived the war. All of them gone. Them, with millions of others—it boggled the mind.

I couldn't tell Frank now, not in his present state. He would blow up and go off on the brass. March right into Headquarters demanding information on the secret commando unit, reminding everyone in sight killing civilians amounted to nothing less than a war crime.

Yep, that's what Frank would do. He was definitely the better man.

When this all began, I dreamed of being a good soldier, maybe even a hero. Turns out, I'm neither.

Chapter Thirty

Liberty means responsibility.
—G.B. Shaw

Alberta's brief, exciting text awakened Meliz in the middle of the night. *I found Frank Hoffman.*

Sleep fell away in an instant. She typed back in a rush of emotion. *My God—Where? Is he alive?*

Meliz could see Alberta's satisfied expression in her response. *Alive and well. He changed his name after the war to his mother's maiden name, Einhorn. The Nazis killed her entire family in the Holocaust. He moved to Israel in 1950 and has lived there ever since.*

Meliz punched the keypad in rapid reply. *Have you spoken with him? Will he talk to me?*

She tapped an impatient finger against her phone until Alberta answered. *I received an e-mail from him today. He was at some retreat somewhere and had only recently learned of JD's death. When I told him we'd been looking for him and why, he didn't seem surprised. He sent me his contact info and asked you to call him.*

Meliz could not believe her luck. *I'll contact him before we leave.* She added, *I talked to Mom and Dad. Everything is good.*

I know. Gwen called. I said you had it together. She thought so too.

Thanks <3.

She tossed and turned, finally giving up on sleep in the early morning hours and descending to the lobby. Her eagerness to speak with Frank overwhelmed her. With Israel lagging several hours behind the Philippines, Meliz checked her impatience.

She paced and drank coffee and finally gave in, messaging him even though it was still only three a.m. in Tel Aviv. A brusque reply told her to let him sleep and call once she touched down in Manila. She cursed the time difference and settled on reading a long e-mail from Alberta.

Her friend had dug up a few intriguing facts about Frank Einhorn, nee Hoffman. He was ninety-six years old and had never married. He worked as a systems-information engineer for thirty-eight years in Tel Aviv before retiring in 1990. In that time, he had traveled throughout Europe, South America, and Asia, but as far as Alberta could discover, he never returned to the United States.

Meliz reported all this to her friends over breakfast. Even before Brigitte opened her mouth, Meliz knew exactly what word would come out.

"Mossad," Brigitte declared.

Meliz and Hikaru laughed, though Hikaru was inclined to agree with her. "What's a systems-information engineer anyway? Sounds fishy . . . and all that travel?"

"Oh yeah, nothing like a government agency dedicated to historical investigation and research," Meliz teased.

He acknowledged the dig with a comical expression and clasped her hand, giving it a warm squeeze. Brigitte winked at her. Nothing seemed to please her friend more than people having sex, unless, of course, it was people involved in covert operations.

Meliz kept it together until the seatbelt sign blinked off in Manila. She jumped from her seat, the first off the plane, and waved to her friends as she ran up the jetway in search of a quiet place to sit.

Located fifty miles outside of Manila, Clark International Airport was in the midst of extensive renovations. Quiet eluded Meliz until she stumbled across a row of four interconnected seats next to a water fountain and an out-of-service women's restroom. She plopped down onto one of the chairs and pulled out her computer.

A butterfly battle raged in her stomach, and a shot of adrenaline jolted her sleep-deprived brain into action. She was about to meet "good ole Grumpy."

She rested the laptop on her crossed legs and flipped it open. The impersonal bustle of the airport grew distant as she put on her headphones. Meliz interlaced her fingers and cracked her knuckles before typing in his number.

How fitting to call from this airport. Once known as Clark Air Base, it had been a stronghold of combined Filipino and American forces during the war. JD, with George and Frank, had flown into Clark on his one visit to Manila.

Meliz listened to the bobble sound and chewed on a fingernail, waiting for the call to connect. The man who materialized on her screen struck her at once as both unfamiliar and entirely recognizable. Sharp brown eyes peered back at her through thick reading glasses. A large nose hovered above a brittle and knowing smile. His scalp showed through thin, close-cropped white hair.

Unexpected tears welled up in her eyes. "Mr. Einhorn, thank you for speaking with me." Meliz sniffed and dabbed at her eyes with her shirtsleeve. Embarrassed, she made a feeble attempt to explain her emotional state. "Sorry. I miss my grandfather."

Meliz caught a glint of dampness at the corners of his eyes. Frank's emotions also threatened to overtake him.

"Not at all," he said with a courtly bow of his head. "Time grows short for us old veterans. I wish I had kept in better touch."

"When did you see him last?"

"Nineteen forty-eight, at his wedding."

"You were at JD's wedding?"

One photograph existed of her grandparent's wedding day. In black-and-white, it pictured JD wearing a suit and her grandmother in an elegant day dress with an elaborate headband in her dark hair. They stood together in the living room of her great-grandparents' house next to a table with a wedding cake upon it. They posed, eyes locked and smiling at each other.

"Yes. They were married in December of that year at the Harper's house in Pearland. I was there. As was George Castle's widow. Although I think she had remarried by that time."

"Josefina was there?"

His laugh was curt, like a bark. "Are you going to repeat everything I say?"

"Sorry. I'm excited. I've only read these names in JD's journal. He never spoke of the war. It's strange to me now, because I can tell from his writing that you . . . that everyone mattered to him a lot."

Frank cocked his head to one side. "JD and June had your mother late, and you don't look so old yourself. The years pass, and maybe that time and those people aren't so important anymore."

"Do you believe that?"

He met her eyes, his made even more owlish by the thick lenses. "No."

"You never spoke to him again after the wedding?"

"Oh yes, I spoke with him. The wedding was the last time I *saw* him. I called a few days before immigrating to Israel."

"That was in 1950, correct?"

"Yes, May of 1950. I gave him my address where he could reach me in Tel Aviv."

"You corresponded?"

He sighed and sadness pulled down the corners of his mouth. "Our communication was one-sided for the most part. I traveled a lot and tried to settle into my new life. I guess I didn't want to be bothered with the past . . . my past, at least. I dropped him a note here and there. He stopped writing after a few years, but he always sent me signed first editions of his books. I have them all."

"What do you remember of Okinawa?"

"We were both dealt a blow there: JD with George's death and me with news of my family back in Germany."

"They were all killed . . ." Meliz prodded gently.

"Murdered . . . all of them: two uncles, two aunts, seven cousins, and my grandfather."

"I'm sorry."

He accepted her condolences with a terse nod. "I've spent my life seeking justice for them and others."

"I believe JD was seeking justice too," Meliz replied, her expression intent.

"What do you know?" Frank asked, his voice clipped and focused.

"Bits and pieces from his journal. I know he had suspicions about those soldiers who left the ship at New Guinea."

"He went on about that for days," Frank remembered. "But after Mick Cassidy, I figured he was right to be suspicious."

"Who?"

"A mean SOB from our unit; he was one of the men who left the *General Hersey* that night. His dead body showed up months later on Biak with no insignia, no ID, nothing. He had a tattoo on his wrist, a couple of numbers, letters, eighty-one-something or other. Never did figure out how he got there."

Meliz jumped in her seat. "SR18," she exclaimed. "A tattoo would make sense if they couldn't wear any identification."

"What?"

"A journalist friend of Alberta's discovered an unidentified military code when he investigated for us: SR18. That same code was used as a tag on the service cards of about forty soldiers deployed to the Pacific. Alberta's friend suggested they were some sort of covert unit. Also, we spoke with Tala Santos, a surviving Filipino resistance fighter, and she confirmed a group like that existed."

He raised his eyebrows, but said nothing.

"From the request JD put into the Historical Investigation and Research Agency," Meliz continued, "we think he may have witnessed something, possibly having to do with the Japanese surrender planes, the Green Cross flights—planes that should have arrived on Iejima Island on August 17, but didn't until the nineteenth.

"Also, Dr. Rivera, a military scholar in Manila, connected the plot of one of JD's books to the whole thing. He thinks JD wrote the story alluding to an incident—"

"What sort of incident?"

"Maybe the planes, maybe something else connected to them, we're not sure. The book describes a massacre of Cherokee families at a place called the Green Crossing, and the only one left alive was a little girl. A woman in Okinawa wrote JD and referred to the book as well, saying he had saved her and her younger brother's lives when she was little. We're on our way to meet her now."

He mulled over what she had just said. "From bits and pieces, that's a whole lot of speculation. I'll tell you what I know. I know George's death devastated JD, and I know something ate away at him that had nothing to do with George. The brass called him in once we got to Japan. After that, he wouldn't tell me anything. No matter how much I badgered him."

"Was the meeting related to his journal?"

The old man blinked in surprise. "How did you know? I just remembered myself."

"I found a journal page he tore out describing his meeting with a mysterious lieutenant. He must have put it away and tried to forget about the whole thing once he got home."

Frank leaned back in his chair, and the room behind him came into view. Two high windows framed large leafy branches in a garden beyond. Photographs and certificates covered the walls. Medals dangled from decorative hooks. Meliz imagined a lifetime of stories hanging in that room.

"A couple of weeks after his meeting with the brass, or that lieutenant as you say, he told me he ran into Captain . . . I mean Major Griswold. No details—made it sound casual."

"Griswold? He was the original CO of your squadron, right?"

"Yeah, your grandfather admired the man. He was a good officer, I have to admit. After that, JD seemed more at peace, or less tortured. We both stayed in Japan for several months and shipped home right after Christmas. Not much else to tell."

He sat silent and pursed his lips with an angry shake of his head. "That's not true."

Meliz leaned in close to the computer. "What is it, Mr. Einhorn?

"I obsessed over Mick Cassidy. And I didn't drop the matter after the war either, but I came up empty-handed. I've never heard of this SR18, and I never discovered what Cassidy or those other men were up to. But I do know covert operations took place throughout the different theaters, the Pacific included. Many of the units, programs, whatever you want to call them, were the beginnings of our modern intelligence agencies—for good . . . and bad."

"What are you saying?"

"Just because the incident occurred over seventy years ago doesn't mean it can come out now. What JD saw, or thought he saw, could be as explosive today as it was then."

**

"I knew he was Mossad," Brigitte crowed. "I knew it."

"Well, he's something. That's for sure." Meliz gave a tired shake of her head.

They flew over the Pacific on their way to Okinawa. The sky shone bright, and sunlight reflected off the window. Meliz sipped at her plastic cup of ginger ale. The carbonated bubbles tickled her nose. Relaxed and strangely comforted by the monotonous drone of the jet engines, she let her mind wander.

She and Brigitte sat together near the front of the plane with Hikaru several rows behind them. Her arrival at the gate was a squeaker with no time to fill her friends in before boarding. She gave Brigitte a brief overview.

"You think he was a Nazi hunter?" Brigitte asked.

"Yeah, I think so."

Brigitte sat in the window seat and gazed out on the unending stretch of blue ocean. "I hope he caught the bastards."

"He's a funny guy," Meliz mused. "He loved JD, I could tell. He laughed when I told him how he had died, slumped over his keyboard. He said, 'JD would've appreciated that. Hell, he would've written the scene himself.' You know what? He's right. JD would've wanted to go that way, writing to the end."

"What else did he say?"

Meliz looked past Brigitte out the window. "That he should have told JD, whatever happened, it wasn't his fault."

Chapter Thirty-One

A faithful friend is the medicine of life.
—Ecclesiastics VI: 16

2 Sept., 1945, Bolo Point, Okinawa—George is dead. I write these words, and I cannot believe it's true. I knew him for maybe two years. Two short years, but it seemed like we'd been friends for longer.

His dying was stupid cruel. Like Boone's.

Don't know if Josefina and the kids got my letters. What do you tell children who will never know their father? I told them how much he loved their mother. How he looked forward to being a dad. Tried to tell them what he meant to me, what he meant to all of us: "Your father was a good man, a good friend."

The words were cliché . . . rote phrases. I could do better.

I should tell them their father wasn't much more than a kid himself, barely a man at all. Like the rest of us, still tied to the safety and comfort of home. But he took on the responsibilities of a man without shirking. He stepped up like every other guy out here, but in his own special way and with his own unique qualities.

I'd be honest and tell them we didn't get along at first. I'd pegged Castle as a rich snob, but he didn't let that first impression define him. That was why George Castle's story was such a good one—the hero's journey of a flawed man. The spoiled rich kid who became much more than he believed he could be, or even had to be.

I would tell them how he gained confidence in himself away from his family's money and influence. How all of us relied on his judgment and clear-headed assessments. How I admired him as a man, a friend, and a fellow soldier.

We nicknamed him Lancelot because he was tall and handsome and did well with the ladies. He earned that name because he was kind, upright, courageous, and good.

**

Fussa Army Airfield, Japan, late September 1945

I'd left off writing in my journal. I didn't have the heart for it since George died. And after Lieutenant Creepy Face cut out my pages and warned me to keep my trap shut, I didn't figure it was safe anymore. The only writing I had done was tucked up under the sweatband of my Aussie bush hat.

Frank was at me to tell him what happened. I made something up. Told him they took the pages where I criticized the officers on the survey team. I railed against the brass with a defiant rant to make the lie sound real.

"You wouldn't believe those lazy SOBs. Just like the brass, right? I did all the work. They took all the credit. Left me to check out the villages and find the water sources. I was lucky if they even got out of the jeep."

Frank agreed with enthusiasm, interjecting once in a while with his own low opinion of officers, but he was a sharp one. After a bit, he caught himself up and glared at me. Frank knew I used his biases against him.

Much as I wanted to, I couldn't tell him. Hell. Who knew what Lieutenant Squeaky Voice planned to do next? I didn't want Frank in his crosshairs too. Best just to keep everything to myself, sleep with one eye open, and hope we get orders for home soon.

I'd forget my problems for long stretches at a time. We worked harder than we had since the war ended. The occupation required everyone's full attention, and our planes flew on a strict rotation. I worked the line more often than not and subbed in on crews flying missions over Japan and to the other islands.

The Japanese were starving, and much of our cargo consisted of food. The bombing raids left many of their cities in ruins, fields destroyed, and harvests left to rot for lack of labor. I'd seen this before, of course, in the Philippines and Okinawa, though the scale of the disaster here surpassed those by miles, so many more people.

Widespread shock and depression descended on the country. Rumors were a lot of the Japanese leaders had committed suicide. Until the emperor broadcasted the surrender, folks here were certain of their inevitable victory.

That broadcast signaled the first time most Japanese had ever heard his voice. I couldn't imagine; President Roosevelt's voice had been as recognizable to me as my own father's.

I didn't feel bad for the Japanese brass. Course, none of us liked watching women and children suffer.

The rest of September passed in a blurred flurry of activity, and I believed I'd put the whole mess behind me. Released American POWs came through the airfield on the regular. I flew a couple of transports ferrying them to the Philippines. Most of the guys were in good spirits, but there were some bad cases.

I readied a group of about twenty-five ex-POWs for transfer to a C-47 when Chief told me to report to Administration. All of a sudden, my fears consumed me and the idea of bolting crossed my mind.

The airfield sprawled out over several acres, but the administration building backed right up to our hangar. That left me little time to formulate a plan.

Making a mad dash into the wilds of Japan with half the country starving didn't appeal to me much. Of course, I'd be better prepared if I knew what I was walking into.

I stood before the assistant's desk. "Corporal Hawkins reporting."

"Yeah, Hawkins, you're to wait in there." He jerked his head in the general direction of an open door. With my heart beating an uneven staccato, I walked into an unoccupied office.

A set of windows overlooked the street. Jeeps and trucks parked alongside the curb. "In" and "Out" baskets with neat piles of papers sat atop a metal military-issue desk, behind which stood a large blackboard. A sofa occupied the opposing wall with a view of the street. Just your regular run-of-the-mill office; it sure didn't look like a place of summary execution.

Not taking any chances, I scoped out two different avenues of escape. I waited, as ready for Lieutenant Dead Eyes as possible.

My heart slowed with profound relief when a familiar face greeted me and closed the door. I stood at attention and saluted.

"At ease, Corporal." Major Griswold gestured to one of the chairs facing the sofa. "Sit."

He sat on the sofa opposite. I had not seen the major since his promotion.

"First, I'd like to tell you how sorry I am to learn of Corporal Castle's death. I know you were close. Best man at his wedding, am I right?"

Emotion welled up in my throat. I knew Major Griswold had come about the journal pages, but he always took care of his men first.

"Yes, sir."

"I am no longer your commanding officer, and the duty of writing to his widow fell to Captain Reed. But I'd like you to convey my admiration of her husband and condolences for her loss when you speak with Mrs. Castle."

"Yes, sir. I will, sir."

He looked me in the eyes. "There's no easy way to talk about what you witnessed, so I'm going to plunge right in. Those downed Bettys were carrying a peace delegation to meet with General MacArthur. They had planned to arrive on Iejima on August 17 and be transported via our military aircraft to Manila."

I stared back at him, stunned: the truth, at last.

"The situation here, before the surrender, was unstable, explosive even." He leaned back into the sofa. "There were conflicting factions, those who were unwilling to accept the Potsdam Declaration on the one hand and the emperor and his loyal supporters on the other. Emperor Hirohito made the decision to surrender. The hard-liner nationalists didn't make that easy. They attempted a coup."

"These hard-liners, the nationalists . . ." I struggled to understand. "They shot down the planes to stop the treaty, but the surrender still happened?"

"Yes. We believe the people who shot down those planes were renegades, and the attack a last-ditch effort to take over and stop Japan from surrendering. It could have worked. Japan teetered on the edge, a tinderbox. Negotiations were fragile. Anything could have set off hostilities again. We scrambled, as did the emperor, to cover up the attack and put together another delegation."

I scoffed and disguised it with an unconvincing cough. "Well, sir, don't you think the Japanese folk are gonna wonder about the men who died in those planes? They must have been important people to meet with General MacArthur."

"I can't stress enough the chaos that consumed the Japanese leadership a few short weeks ago. I'm not sure how they dealt with the loss of their delegation. Many top officials, both in and out of the military, committed suicide. That could have been one explanation."

The major pursed his lips, an intent expression on his face. "Listen, Corporal, we had to hold the peace talks together. That meant making like the attack never happened—to give nothing away to the renegades. Nothing could destabilize the surrender. Two days later, I don't know how, the emperor and his supporters had another delegation in the air."

Our conversation bordered on the surreal. I sat there as if I'd been hit with a baseball bat. A bunch of rebel Japanese almost sabotaged the peace treaty. The whole thing sounded nuts.

"You need to understand, Hawkins. We couldn't let Japan slip into the hands of the hardliners. The war had to end. Countless lives depended on it."

I could have let it go at that, but I had at last reached the limits of my own cowardice. I no longer cared if the scary-ass lieutenant knew I had seen what really went down. "The village, those people—they weren't killed by renegade Japanese soldiers." He glared at me, lips compressed, and I forced myself to continue. "I saw them. Those soldiers were Americans, killers without insignia or ID." My voice dripped with scorn. "They murdered those people. What about *their* lives?"

Major Griswold dropped his gaze. "As far as we know, they were the only civilians to witness the incident. A handful of military personnel saw the attack on the delegation. We could manage our own men. We weren't sure about the civilians."

"They didn't have to die." My face burned with suppressed fury, and guilt at having pinpointed the village consumed me. "They didn't know what they saw. Hell. I didn't even know until later."

"There were other options on the table. The attack on the village wasn't supposed to happen." Major Griswold clenched his jaw. "The ball got rolling and things got out of hand fast. We lost the chain of command and, well . . . things got out of hand," he ended on that pathetic note.

My blood boiled, and my respect for Major Griswold faltered. "That's not good enough. That lieutenant who took my journal, was he responsible? What's his name? What unit is he with?"

"Dial it back, Corporal," he rebuked me with a stern wave of his hand.

I snapped my mouth shut, but I couldn't keep the rage out of my eyes.

"You don't need to know his name. He and his men have been dealt with."

"They're a secret commando unit, aren't they?" Now I had opened up, I couldn't stop talking. "Like Cassidy."

"What do you know about Cassidy," he barked, sitting up ramrod straight.

I glared back at him. He let out a strangled laugh and slumped into the sofa. "You and Hoffman, I should have known."

"We checked out his body when they brought him in. Whoever killed him used a sort of dagger to the back of the head. He had a tattoo on his wrist, SR18. The same tattoo on a woman I met in Manila. I heard those men radio in with that exact designation after the . . . the massacre."

He held up his hand with weary resignation. "JD." He used my given name for the first time. "They read me into this matter two days ago with the expressed purpose of making sure you understand your duty."

He paused and I sat silent, unmoving.

"Do you?" he prompted.

"We heard the Nazis and Japanese will stand trial for war crimes."

"Yes, that's true."

"What happened to those people in Okinawa was a war crime."

"Again, true."

I walked over to the window and gazed out on the quiet street of parked trucks and jeeps. "My duty is to stay quiet, not talk about what happened, not try to find out what those soldiers were doing and on whose orders. Is that correct, sir?"

He joined me at the window. "If you talk, if you pursue any inquiry, the military will disavow you and everything you say, maybe even a court-martial. It's your decision, Corporal. Only you know if you can live with it."

"Can you?"

"Yes," he answered without hesitation.

Chapter Thirty-Two

Be sure you are right, then go ahead.
—Davy Crockett

Brigitte slept. Meliz pulled out her computer. She owed everyone an update. She logged onto the Wi-Fi, uploaded the video interview of Tala Santos onto her website, and wrote:

This video features a remarkable woman who led Filipino resistance fighters on Leyte during WWII. I interviewed her as part of my search. I am also uploading footage of the MacArthur Memorial Park and Red Beach near Tacloban and a clip of Dr. Garrett Rivera. He describes the Battle of Manila and gives an overall picture of Asian-led struggles against the Japanese.

Her mind churned over the events of the last few days. She rubbed her temples and let out an exhausted sigh. The missing pieces of JD's mystery gnawed at the edges of her brain, leaving her drained and depleted.

As they made their approach into Okinawa, Meliz cruised on the last airy filaments of her energy. She laughed. Her mother must have felt this way on that endless car trip across Texas, the one JD made famous in his collection of short stories.

Her ten-year-old mother sat in the back seat of an old Ford station wagon, hot, sticky, and bored. As was his habit, JD refused to stop between fill-ups. He conducted any long-distance car trip like a forced march. No amount of crying or complaining from Gwen, no cajoling on the part of June could persuade him otherwise.

His obstinacy backfired when the fuel gauge registered empty, and the expected gas station did not appear. The car sputtered and barely topped a hill. JD let off the brakes, hoping to pick up speed and gain a few more feet to whatever lay before them.

At that moment, the day turned to dusk, and the car sped down the hill, sending much needed cool air into the back seat. The breeze revived Gwen. The boughs of willow trees danced in the wind and stars emerged from the darkness.

Everyone in the car leaned toward the windows, hair blown back from faces now dry of sweat. As luck would have it, a Mobil station stood at the bottom of the hill. Her grandfather pulled up next to a pump, the station wagon propelled forward on the last feeble cough of gas fumes.

Coming out of the rental car parking lot, Meliz lounged, exhausted yet revived, in the back seat of a comfortable SUV, much different from her grandparents' old Ford station wagon. Gusts of humid tropical air washed over her from the open windows.

Brigitte drove with Hikaru riding shotgun as navigator. They took a detour to view what had once been Bolo Point Airfield and drove straight to Cape Zanpa and a lighthouse that stood sentinel over the dramatic cliffs. The three friends strolled to the lookout and admired the view of roiling turquoise waves beating up against the towering cliffs.

The sun glowed in the sky over the East China Sea as clouds scuttled in to diminish its brilliance. By the time they had piled back into the car, large raindrops pounded the windshield.

The rain lasted the rest of the trip north. They drove past Nago and continued west to Motobu, where Brigitte had booked a condominium on the beach. Not yet dinnertime when they arrived, Meliz barely registered her surroundings. She stumbled into the nearest bedroom and passed out on the tropical print duvet of a large four-poster bed.

Meliz awoke at dawn to find herself alone under the covers. The gray light of early morning revealed a peaceful room with pale green walls and wooden floors.

Curtains drawn back from a sliding glass door opened to a broad expanse of beach. Salted sea air wafted down from the circulating blades of a ceiling fan. She walked out onto the white sand.

Water stretched away from the shore in graduating shades of darker blue. Gentle exfoliating sand brushed her bare feet. The rhythmic sound of waves soothed her. She drew in a deep breath. It smelled like home.

Meliz scanned the empty beach and spotted Hikaru. He sat facing the ocean, staring off in the general direction of Iejima Island.

He turned at her approach. "Hey, you."

"Hey." She sat down next to him. "Did you sleep out here?"

He laughed at her leading question and interlaced his fingers with hers. "No. Brigitte grabbed the other bedroom. I slept on the couch. I think our relationship is just a little too new to crawl into bed without asking. And you kind of conked out."

She dug her toes into the sand and rested her head on his shoulder. "Everything caught up with me. I think I slept ten hours straight."

He smiled. "You definitely slept at least ten hours straight."

She contemplated the vast ocean spread out before them. "My grandfather was here."

"I know."

Meliz pushed up into a squat and placed her hands on his knees. "What are we going to find out?"

He grasped her arms and pulled her toward him until their foreheads touched. "Whatever it is, you can handle it."

The sound of a car caught their attention, and they glanced back at the condo. A van pulled in next to their rental car at the same moment Brigitte stepped out onto the porch.

She carried a pot of hot coffee and poised in midstride, frowning over at the van. Her body stiffened.

They recognized who sat within and raced back to her. Jack Prescott Walker Sr. emerged from the electronic lift.

A burly chauffeur wheeled him over the sandy walkway. They all met on the porch, Meliz and Hikaru with hearts pounding and Brigitte clutching the coffee pot like a weapon.

The wizened old man's skin shone with a thin coat of sweat, his face a ghastly shade of gray. In the space of a few days, his spry and forceful personality had transformed into one of near emotional collapse.

He waved the chauffeur back to the van and asked in a raspy whisper, "Can one of you wheel me inside?"

They exchanged an intense, indecisive look. Jack barked a mirthless laugh. "I'm unarmed. I swear. You can search me, if you like."

Hikaru pushed the wheelchair over the doorstop and into the small combination living and dining room. A conflicting mixture of relief and disappointment at Prescott's absence roiled Meliz. Her mind had engaged in elaborate revenge fantasies to such a degree she doubted her ability not to assault him on sight.

"Where's Prescott?" she demanded, eager to hold the old man accountable for his grandson's actions. "I know he engineered my attack. He drove the car."

Jack Walker shook his head with weary self-reproach. "My fault, I'm afraid. I should never have told him. I only wanted to find out what you knew, but he wouldn't listen. When I saw you together at the restaurant, when I found out he'd used others—the grandson of an old friend even—to break into your room, to do his dirty work, I lost my temper. I knew he was up to something. I just didn't know what. He wanted to protect me, the family . . ." His voice trailed off.

"It wasn't your idea?" Meliz demanded. "Why else would he try to scare me off?"

"Because of what I told your grandfather and what I'm about to tell you. Prescott didn't want me telling anyone. 'Giving the story legitimacy' is the way he put it." The old man licked his dry lips. "Can I have some of that coffee?"

Brigitte still stood with the pot in her hand. "Of course. Do you want some?" she asked Meliz and Hikaru. They declined and waited while Brigitte poured Jack a cup.

"You spoke with JD?" Meliz frowned at yet another of her grandfather's secrets.

He nodded over the rim of the ceramic mug. "We talked a lot in the months before he died."

The three of them stood facing the old man in his wheelchair. After another sip of the hot liquid, he gestured to the sofa. "You might want to get comfortable."

Resentment welled up in Meliz. Here was Jack drinking coffee and inviting them to sit as if the condominium were his own home. She had imagined confronting him and his grandson in a courtroom, preferably with them handcuffed and carted off to jail.

Meliz never considered Prescott had acted alone. She assumed him to be an agent of his grandfather's bidding.

The old man held out his right hand, palm side up. A faded tattoo lay inked across his inner wrist. "SR stands for Surgical Response. The number eighteen is code for covert, or rather special, operations. They recruited thirty-nine men and five women from enlistment, me included. We trained as a group in . . . well, in tactics, close-quarter combat and stealth, dispatching the enemy quickly and quietly."

"The women too?" Brigitte asked.

"No, they didn't train with us. The unit deployed them in a different capacity. More spy stuff."

"Who sanctioned SR18?" Hikaru asked, ever the historian.

"Who knows? Even after the war, when I held an intelligence position, the origins of the unit were obscure. Whoever it was must have been high up in the OSS." Jack handed Brigitte the empty coffee mug, and she set it on the table. "A few weeks before our unit deployed, they planted us in with regular troops, to cover our tracks—make where we came from harder to pinpoint."

He straightened and lifted his chin in a gesture of defiance. "I won't pretend our actions were noble, but they were necessary—until Okinawa." Jack retreated into his wheelchair.

"After the war, they recruited me again. This time by the intelligence organization that grew out of our war efforts."

"The CIA," Brigitte pronounced with tremendous satisfaction.

He neither confirmed nor denied her statement. "I was tasked with building our intelligence network in the Pacific. I received funds to establish a business and make connections."

"Your whole business is CIA funded?" Hikaru jumped to his feet and rushed to the French doors. His intense, focused gaze swept the beach. Families with small children now strolled across the sand as the other households woke up around them.

Jack raised his eyebrows, amused. "This isn't a trap. I am not going to kill you. If that's what you're looking for."

"Why are you telling us this? Even an ex-agent can't go around divulging secrets." Hikaru stood tense and observant.

His apprehension rubbed off on Meliz and Brigitte. They exchanged a worried glance.

"You may have noticed I'm old. I don't want to die with this burdening my soul."

"Yeah, sure." Hikaru nodded, but did not move from his watchful position next to the glass doors.

Jack shrugged and continued with his story, "Unfortunately, my new assignment stuck me with the former head of the SR18, a lieutenant by the name of Owen Henry."

"Was he—?" Meliz began.

"The one who interrogated your grandfather?" Jack's mouth puckered in distaste. "Yep. Henry was a sociopath. I hated him from day one. I'd never known anyone like him. The man had no affect . . . no emotions." He waved both hands around in the air. "He called for the strike on the village. He'd scanned reports from nearby aircraft and deployed us to eliminate the enemy. None of us knew until we got there our targets were unarmed civilians."

The old man's chest heaved. Agitation racked his frail bones. "Me and a couple other boys balked, but the rest . . ." He covered his eyes with one gnarled hand. "They mowed them down. Children . . . everyone . . ."

His voice trembled. "They torched the place and we left."

"Why were you told to kill those people?" Meliz's voice sounded thin and stretched to her ears, as if she stood on the summit of Mount Everest. The revelation of such a horror sucked the oxygen from her lungs.

He looked at her, eyes clouded with pain. "We didn't know, just followed orders. I never got the full story until I contacted your grandfather."

"You were the one," Hikaru declared. "You placed the intelligence alert decades ago."

"Honest to God, never thought anything would come of it. I still have contacts at the . . . well, place I used to work. People I trained.

When your call came through, since the case wasn't active, they passed the information on to me."

"You spoke with JD? He saw the whole thing? The village?" Meliz's voice trembled with disbelief, unable to comprehend her grandfather keeping such a secret for all these years.

"He got to the road as we finished. He and the kids hid in the underbrush. No doubt in my mind, we'd have shot 'em on sight." Jack stared down at his hands clasped so tight his knuckles had turned white. "I bared my soul, told him everything I knew. After years of hearing their screams . . . the children in my nightmares, I . . ." He sighed. "Well, it was a weight off me."

"Why were they killed?" Brigitte cut to the heart of the matter.

"Let me guess." Hikaru walked back to the sofa. "They witnessed the Japanese delegation shot from the sky and were killed in the cover-up to preserve the surrender."

"In a nutshell, that's what JD told me."

"Did they even know what they saw?" Meliz exclaimed, her mouth dry with suppressed nausea. "Who would have believed them anyway? For Christ's sake, they were poor villagers seventy years ago. It's not like they recorded it with their cell phones."

Jack Walker answered her with a bitter laugh. "That's just it. Henry was a man without feelings, without emotion, a monster." He held up a shaking hand and pointed his finger skyward for emphasis. "Listen, none of us were choirboys, for sure. All of us were ruthless—even remorseless—but nothing like him. He crunched numbers—made cold calculations. He calculated those people threatened the surrender. No matter how small the risk, they had to die to protect the treaty. The brass reined him in, but too late for the villagers."

"Reined him in?" Brigitte scoffed. "He worked for the CIA after the war."

"A fact that infuriated JD. Major Griswold swore the army had punished those involved in the massacre. He kept his mouth shut out of duty, but JD always believed we'd been punished."

Meliz sat frozen, appalled at the terrible convergence of events, the staggering amount of chance that had landed the fate of innocents in the hands of an evil man. She walked to the doors and looked blindly out at the beach. "What happened to Lieutenant Henry?"

"Governments always need his kind, you know. They lie and tell you creatures like him are under their control. Then he slips the leash and, well . . . Henry worked as an analyst and even managed field operations. He died in 1989. I went to the funeral so I could spit on his grave.

"I didn't know anyone had escaped the slaughter. Your grandfather told me about the letter, the girl and her brother. We were going to explain, together . . . me, to confess." His mouth worked. "See if she could forgive me. Then JD died, and I didn't have the courage to face her alone." He threw his hands up in a gesture of helplessness. "There's nothing I can do for her now anyway."

Meliz's sight came into focus, the distant cliffs etched in stark relief against a cloudless sky. The early morning sun sprinkled the waves with light.

She hadn't lost him. For a brief time, Meliz feared the man she had known and loved all her life might be a lie. The final, stubborn knots in her stomach unwound. Hot tears leaked from her eyes and trailed down her cheeks.

She knew what JD had tried to do. It was just like him. With retribution beyond his grasp, he would settle for resolution. She could too.

Meliz turned. "I know what you can do for her."

Chapter Thirty-Three

Every man thinks meanly of himself for not having been a soldier.
—Samuel Johnson

September 25, 1945
Dear JD,

Your letters came with the telegram. I was glad of them. Glad to have words from someone else who loved George.

I cannot write my grief in a letter. I do not have your gift. I will only tell you to come home safe. George would want you to come home safe.

Regards,
Fina

V-MAIL

**

Fussa Army Airfield, late September 1945

I trudged back to the hangar in a daze. Maybe Griswold could live with what those men had done, but he hadn't heard the screams.

He didn't see the homes, shacks made from whatever they could find, burnt to the ground. He hadn't seen the bodies, grotesque and smoldering, or gagged on the sickening smell of blood mixed with scorched flesh. He did not see the horror reflected back at him in the faces of those kids.

Maybe Griswold could live with this crime on his conscience, but I wasn't so sure I could. I had awoken countless times in a cold sweat, retching from the phantom stench stuck in my nostrils. I dreamed over and over in slow motion.

Run up the trail. Grab the kids. Hold them down. Stifle their screams.

I heard again the mumbled English and the chatter of soldiers checking their weapons and radioing for instructions. Disgust filled my heart at knowing these were my people, American soldiers.

I didn't tell Major Griswold about the girl and her brother. Nobody knew except me they had survived. The Marines just figured I'd found yet two more of the scores of war orphans wandering the countryside.

After leaving the smoking village, the kids never spoke again. Their eyes glazed over, dull and glassy. Did they wish they were dead with their parents and everybody else in the world who gave a shit about them?

The girl's hand slipped from mine, listless, as the Marines led them away. Neither of them looked back.

Those asshole lieutenants had taken off earlier that morning, leaving me to hitch a ride as best I could back to Motobu. The only break in my clouded thinking came when I told George everything. For a brief twenty-four hours, I believed we could do right by those kids.

Now, Griswold—sent to make sure I knew my duty. Fucking hell, I knew my duty. I should shout it out for everyone to hear. I should write the incident up and publish it in a newspaper.

Fuck Griswold. Fuck all those bastards who made me complicit in their crime. Mostly, fuck that blue-eyed creep. I knew in my gut he did it. I wanted him court-martialed and facing a firing squad, maybe drawn and quartered. Even that was too good for him.

"Hawkins, saddle up," Chief called out as I entered the hangar. "We're gonna need more hands on this flight to the Philippines. A lot of these guys are sick, and we've only one medic for the whole group."

I blew out a steady stream of air; better to be busy than alone with my thoughts or fending off Frank's questions. The medic handed me blankets and pillows. I'd run this drill before and got busy putting one of each on the makeshift bunks.

Many of the guys would need to make the flight lying down. We'd heard a ton about the cruelty the POWs endured. Starved, worked to death, executed at whim, every horror of war you could imagine.

I finished the chore and headed over to the food table. The mess hall guys had set out a spread of donuts, cookies, and the like for the released American prisoners. I hoped to snag a few treats before takeoff.

"JD?"

My name floated over to me on little more than a whisper of air. The voice struck a chord of memory and stopped me midstride. Campouts by the river, bonfires of old leaves, football practices on freezing winter mornings: camaraderie and friendship flashed through my mind like a slideshow.

I turned. A man, emaciated and weak, sat on one of the folding chairs. The army-issue duds he wore hung from his gaunt frame. He held a donut wrapped in a paper napkin in one hand and a cup of orange juice in the other. The bright red hair and freckled faces of the Duncan clan were unmistakable even if the one lay lank and dull and the other weathered almost beyond recognition.

"Kit?" I asked, more than a little afraid I mistook him. "Kit Duncan?"

"The one and only." He grinned with forced bravado.

His teeth flashed huge in his sunken face. I pulled a chair up next to him. "My God, Kit, your folks, they're gonna be that glad to see you."

He put his food and drink down on the floor next to him. "We're told the lists of prisoners are updated every day. Maybe they already know I made it."

I laid a hand on his forearm. The sharpness of bone pressed against my palm through the heavy material. "Your momma, she never gave up hope. The army sent her one of those gold stars, but she wouldn't put it up. No siree, she never gave up believing you'd come home."

His hands trembled, and he worked to control his emotions. He stifled a sob and drew in a deep breath.

"What about Joe?" He sat up straighter, bracing for bad news. "Did he sign up?"

"Yeah, but he's good. He and Leo ended up in Italy together. I haven't heard anything since May. They might even be home by now."

Kit wrapped his arms tight around his middle. He leaned forward. His thin frame shook with sobs. I put an arm around his shoulders and murmured words of comfort. Not much more than flesh and bone, blood still coursed through his veins. The warmth of life still burned, radiating out through the stiff canvas of his jacket.

He gritted his teeth and straightened, swallowing his tears. He had survived.

Is that how God worked? He'd trade me one Kit Duncan for one George Castle.

Or maybe all this death and destruction was some sort of random cosmic reckoning—nothing personal—some come back and others don't. God doesn't discriminate.

I once believed I'd missed out on the real story, the glory of war.

But there was no glory, only winning and losing. And no matter the outcome, every man who came home was a win; didn't matter on which side he fought.

In the history books, they'll add up the casualties. The number will be a big one: one huge waste of life.

Now, the war was over—over and done. If it were up to me, not one more life would be lost to conflict.

Kit was headed home. He would be alright.

I thought of George. I would never forget him. If anything good came from war, any glory at all, it was from the bonds forged in its fire.

Chapter Thirty-Four

Leave not a stain on thine honor.
—Ecclesiastics XXXIII: 22

Convincing Jack took some doing. He balked at making a recorded confession.

"Are you crazy?" he rasped. "Everything I've worked for ruined."

"Everything the CIA gave you," Brigitte countered.

"I built those businesses," he snapped.

"Then you can die with this on your soul." Meliz seethed. Her fury spilled out in an unyielding succession of harsh truths. "Telling us absolves you of nothing. If you're too cowardly to face her, this is the only way. You're the only one with the whole story."

The old man scowled at her. She swallowed her rage and changed tactics. "You owe this to JD. You're the only one who spoke with him about this before he died. He wanted the story to come out. You are responsible for his soul too."

Her argument hit home. Warring expressions flashed across Jack's face. He and her grandfather had bonded over their shared secret. Whatever feelings he had toward her, he hated to let JD down.

"Can you tell the story without bringing in the, ah, origin of my businesses?" he finally asked.

"I'll damn well try. Any mention of the CIA would only make trouble for me anyway."

The interview lasted less than twenty minutes. If Jack hoped for redemption or release in the telling, it didn't show in his aged frame. When it was over, he looked worse than when he first arrived.

**

"We received our orders at 0230hrs on August 18, 1945."

Meliz had filmed in high definition, and every wrinkle on the old man's face stood out in stark relief. A generic painting of a ship hung on the condominium wall over his shoulder.

"There were eight of us stationed at Motobu Airfield. When the war ended, we were spread out in smaller groups throughout the Pacific, assigned to general mop-up."

"What do you mean by 'mop-up'?" Meliz asked from off camera.

He shifted in his wheelchair and cleared his throat. "Killing people," he answered with blunt honesty. "Informers, resistance fighters who knew our faces, operations, etcetera."

"What were your orders on August 18, 1945?"

"We received orders from our CO, Lieutenant Owen Henry. He gave us coordinates, the location of a, ah, group of Japanese. He called them Japanese. I guess technically he was right, but they were Okinawan."

"Your orders?" Meliz prompted

He licked his lips. "To kill all the individuals at that location."

A collective intake of breath resounded in the small room. Meliz looked at the people around her, their attention riveted on the recorded image of Jack Walker Sr.

They gathered in a modest and airy living room in a quiet neighborhood of Nago. Kiko Tamaki sat in a place of honor, directly in front of the computer. Her grandson, Ren, sat beside her, translating as best he could for those present.

Meliz had called Ren the night before to arrange a meeting with his grandmother for the next day. When they showed up, an unexpected crowd met them at the door.

Ushered in among the curious and friendly faces of the Tamaki family, Meliz's chest tightened. These people were the lone descendants of the families who had banded together after the war, all that survived of the small and makeshift village where they had tried to begin again.

"The video won't be easy to watch," she had warned Ren over the phone.

Her words proved true. Kiko grasped Ren's hand in a tight grip. Tears flowed unheeded down her cheeks as she listened to Jack Prescott Walker Sr. recount the murder of her parents and neighbors.

"Why were you ordered to kill them?" Meliz's disembodied voice floated out over the group.

"I found out later from JD Hawkins. He told me they had witnessed a peace delegation shot down by a rebel faction of the Japanese Army."

An explosive babble of voices followed Ren's translation. Meliz paused the recording. The Japanese flowed fast and furious and didn't slow until Hikaru interjected with a long explanation.

"What was that all about?" Meliz asked after he had finished.

"I described the Green Cross flights and the complexities of the surrender. None of them had heard the story before."

Meliz plumbed the depths of the tragedy in that simple statement. Even now, over seventy years later, few people knew of the betrayal and desperate negotiations that had played out around the Japanese surrender.

Jack Walker laid the blame for the massacre at the feet of Owen Henry, a man who had loomed large over her investigation from the beginning. The mysterious and menacing interrogator described by her grandfather in his final attempt to document his heart-wrenching dilemma. Both JD and Jack painted him as a monster.

If so, he proved a remarkably useful one. The lack of punishment and his long career with the CIA clearly hinted at his value to those in power. Meliz suspected Lieutenant Henry might just be the tip of the iceberg. Maybe he had the goods on someone else, someone more important. From the final pages of *Everything Touches the Sky*, JD must have shared her suspicions.

Meliz restarted the video. The group squeezed in tight around the computer, eyes intent. A general air of tension prevailed, but only Kiko's face reflected profound grief. To her family, these were the events of long ago. An atrocity inflicted upon people they had never met. A tragedy, until now, they had known nothing about.

Meliz leaned back in her chair and closed her eyes. She recoiled from watching Kiko's face as Jack described the scene that ensued when they arrived at Cape Hedo.

"Me and two of my buddies refused to carry out the order, but the others didn't have a problem with it."

"How did the villagers react when they saw you?"

"More puzzled than anything else. They weren't alarmed. We were Americans after all. I stood by as my unit carried out the attack. They finished in a matter of minutes."

Meliz opened her eyes. She glanced over at Brigitte who stood stiff and grim at the back of the group.

"After the village was wiped out, we radioed in." Jack's strained, haunted face filled the computer screen. "We were told not to return to Motobu. A launch would pick us up twenty klicks around the point on the eastern side of the island."

His lips trembled. "I want to say I'm sorry. I didn't do any killing, but I didn't stop them, either—didn't even try. I hope you can forgive me."

The video ended, and a stunned silence followed. Kiko grasped her grandson's hand in both of hers and mumbled words indistinguishable from her sobs.

"What is she saying?" Meliz reached out, distressed by her reaction.

Ren lifted his own tearstained face. "She says she'll never forgive him. She'll never forgive him."

Chapter Thirty-Five

Excerpt from *Everything Touches the Sky*

I never enjoyed being in one place for long. Being laid up suited me even less, no matter the rare pleasure of having womenfolk fuss over me.

Abigail walked with a graceful stride and managed to be both capable and restful. Her two daughters were a fair way to being as fine as their mother. Not many could hold a candle to Abigail and her girls.

After Bruce died, the army let Abigail stay in a small frame house on the fort. The army didn't do this out of the goodness of its heart. Nope. They needed those women to run the infirmary.

I wasn't housed at the infirmary. Abigail insisted I would recuperate quicker with them.

For what seemed like ages, my life comprised a series of trays: breakfast trays, dinner trays, supper trays. The doctor ordered me bedridden, and by God, those women followed his words to the letter. They met my grumbles with kind smiles and patient words.

Had to admit, just walking a straight line took all my strength, though I tried to hide it. The headaches blinded me. If I closed my eyes and gritted my teeth, they usually passed. After a couple of weeks, the women let me out once a day to sit a spell on the porch.

The house, situated up under a big oak, sat off the gate with a view of the parade grounds. I settled myself in a comfortable chair and watched the general activity. My mind mulled over events of the last weeks.

The new commanding officer, Colonel Eakins, soon joined me. He did this often. I suspected the elder—and unmarried—Miss Lang drew him to my vicinity in hopes she'd show up. He usually kept up a pleasant line of chat, so I didn't mind the company.

As it turned out, he came bearing news. "Colonel Jordan won't be court-martialed after all."

A feeling of relief surprised me. There weren't many men as vain and stupid as Jordan. Even so, the slaughter didn't fall to him. He just turned out too dumb to see what others did in his name and under his command.

"He'll be stripped of rank and discharged as a private."

"Sounds about right," I grumbled. "How he got past that rank in the first place is a mystery."

Too polite to laugh, Eakins coughed into his hand. "The others, the junior officers who conspired with the rebel Comanche, will face serious charges."

I looked off into the distance. My silence did not deter the colonel. He sat down on the top stair of the porch to wait.

"Don't you have something to do?" I asked.

"Nope. I'll hang here a spell—"

He stopped talking at the sight of Miss Emily Lang turning the corner, her arms wrapped around a linen basket. He jumped to his feet and hustled over to help her.

Colonel Eakins was a man not yet forty. He had been widowed as a young officer, barely married a year. Strong and well made, if not precisely handsome, I had heard the Lang women describe him as "pleasant looking."

They climbed up the porch, Eakins now carrying the basket. Miss Emily pressed a cool hand to my forehead.

"How are those headaches, Marshal?" she asked in a low, brisk voice.

"What headaches?" I laughed, hoping she hadn't noticed me wince.

She cocked her head to one side, unconvinced. "I'll bring you a glass of iced lemonade." She headed to the door, Colonel Eakins trailing her with the basket of linens.

They went in, and I heard her tell him where to put his burden. Eakins, for his part, did what men do to keep the object of their interest talking and asked Emily about her day. Their words jumbled together, and my sight grew vague. I turned over in my mind all that had happened and, for the life of me, didn't know what my future held.

As well as being an imperfect man, I was now an injured and enfeebled one. I retrained my eyes on the wood grain of the porch.

Whatever my faults, I put my faith in justice. I guess me being a lawman, that shouldn't surprise anybody.

But like men, justice could be an imperfect thing. We brought most of the conspirators to light. Hell. Everybody believed we'd rooted out the whole lot of 'em.

Not me. I had a sneaky suspicion this thing went a damn sight higher on both the army and Indian side than anybody knew.

I'd never be able to prove it.

That little girl, though . . . well, I just hoped she'd be okay.

Chapter Thirty-Six

Remember this—that very little is needed to make a happy life.
—Marcus Aurelius

The American Cemetery, Manila, the Philippines

I stood at the center of the American Cemetery in Manila. Its graceful arching rows of white crosses spread out from me in ever-widening circles. I held close a bouquet of native flowers and stared with unfocused eyes at the battle maps adorning the walls of the open-air chapel.

This cemetery, one of twenty-four outside the United States, held the graves of American soldiers fallen on foreign soil. Seventeen thousand World War II dead lay beneath the marble markers, most of them killed in New Guinea and here in the Philippines.

The soldier I visited today had died over Japan. The military moved his body more than seventy years ago from its resting place in Okinawa to this manicured and peaceful lawn. His widow chose to bury him here rather than in California. A decision, her daughter later confided in me, that set Josefina at odds with George Castle's family.

"Mom knew he would want to be buried with his fellow soldiers," Rosa explained during one of our first interviews.

In the six months since that day in Nago, we had worked to confirm our discoveries and begin to tell this story. In those busy weeks, I carved out some quiet time to grieve for my grandfather and try to make sense of all that had happened.

The trauma of my kidnapping and assault still haunted me, but I could not claim to be the most injured party in this whole affair. That dubious honor fell, by far, to Kiko Tamaki.

"They're coming," Hikaru announced. He stood a few feet away from me, alternately checking his phone and panning the camera over the gravesites.

A petite woman and a tall man approached us from across the lawn. Rosa Gonzales, nee Castle, and George Castle Jr. were the children of George and Josefina.

"Where's everybody?" I had expected the whole Castle-Gonzales clan that included spouses, children, grandchildren, as well as the two younger siblings from Josefina's second marriage.

"We thought it best to come by ourselves first," Rosa replied in a breathy, nervous voice.

She trembled, and I laid a comforting hand on her forearm. "Are you alright?"

Rosa barely came up to my shoulder and, from the many family photos I had seen, resembled greatly her mother. Now in her mid-seventies, Rosa still had the melting brown eyes and smooth skin of a Spanish señorita.

"Of course. I'm being silly . . . it's . . . I can't believe we've never come."

George Jr. cleared his throat. "Mom kept his memory alive as best she could. Even after she married Dad . . . you know, her second husband. But time passes, I guess, and people move on."

If Rosa looked like her mother, George was his father made over. A friendly, handsome man, he was eleven months younger than his older sister. He put an arm around her shoulders. We waited while Hikaru gathered the camera gear.

Brigitte had come up with the idea of filming this last bit at the cemetery. She made the suggestion and then deserted me for two weeks to help Sean run charters around the Eastern Visayas. In her usual haphazard way, she snagged my bikini on her way out.

"I don't have one. You don't mind?"

I didn't. Brigitte buzzed in and out of my life with casual abandon.

Technology connected us. We held virtual coffee dates to talk about the documentary and everything else happening in our lives. Travel brought us together mostly in Asia. She visited New York City once, staying in our tiny apartment. An experience Wendy dubbed "Exhausting, yet exhilarating."

Like George to JD, Brigitte's friendship struck me with the force of a lightning bolt, powerful and unexpected. Incompatible though our characters seemed, the intensity of our shared experiences served to highlight our similarities. I trusted her as I trusted few people.

"Should we go?" Hikaru held his camera at the ready.

Rosa and George nodded in unison. I led the way with Hikaru following us, recording from a respectful distance. Butterflies fluttered in the pit of my stomach.

Once, mistakenly, I had thought to have no personal connection to this cemetery. Now, my steps drew me toward the grave of a man whose death affected me as if he were family. I cast a nervous look back at Hikaru. He flashed me an encouraging grin.

Officially my boyfriend, our relationship was several degrees more conventional than the one I had with Brigitte. He met my parents and Alberta and even braved a reunion with my cousins at the ranch. We traipsed back and forth between New York City and DC, both of us immersed in completing the film.

I updated our progress on my blog and posted clips, a couple of which snagged some serious attention. Jack Walker's confession exploded on social media.

The internet sleuths were all over it. They dug up some flimsy evidence of Jack's CIA connections. The "proof," though hardly conclusive, set off attempts by the Filipino government to nationalize all companies in his name.

I had the immense satisfaction of reading Walker Industries teetered on the verge of bankruptcy, and their chief counsel, Jack Prescott Walker the Third, practically lived at court fending off their creditors. It could not have happened to a more deserving guy. He would never be punished for what he did to me, but I found some compensation in his pending loss of wealth and status.

The CIA ignored all the hoopla (thank God), but Jack's confession exposed me to the unwanted attention of the FBI. Their request for an interview caused my anxiety level to spike. Fortunately, I had a secret weapon.

Alberta stepped in and arranged experienced legal representation when they came knocking. I answered all their questions and gave them a full transcript of our meeting with Jack. I haven't heard anything more and still don't know why they were so interested.

Jack Walker himself wasn't available. He died a couple of months after our meeting in Okinawa and only days after Kiko found it in her heart to forgive the unforgivable.

The internet sleuths kept digging and found contemporary references to the downed Green Cross planes in old personal letters. Veterans had posted them on obscure World War II sites without anyone noticing their significance before.

This prompted a White House petition to send divers in search of the wreckage. Can't imagine they'll have much luck—if they ever actually try.

The Okinawan authorities were in talks with Kiko about

exhuming the massacre site. Courage had never been my strong suit, but I was determined to be there to support her if they did.

As for the documentary team, we plugged away at uncovering what evidence remained to be found. Frank and Garrett searched archives and consulted their contacts and other experts. Once word spread of our project, we even received letters and documents from old veterans.

Even so, much remained unproven. SR18 was a black hole, and we couldn't track down surviving members. If any still lived, none contacted us.

Seventy-five years stretched far in the past, memories were imperfect, and evidence was in short supply. In the end, evidence didn't matter all that much to me anyway. Beyond the details of the village massacre, I wasn't out to *prove* anything. What consumed me were the commonalities between JD's story and those of other veterans.

A shared thread of ambivalence wove through the tapestry of their experiences. I heard the echo of his regret in the voices of the veterans who reached out to us. Many had, decades ago, abandoned the righteousness of their cause to feel only loss: the loss of friends, boyhoods, and innocence.

Marshal Clyde Jameson often scoffed at "mere innocence." He strove for virtue. According to the marshal, to be virtuous, one must recognize and resist evil. "Innocence and purity of mind are for the weak." He repeated this mantra throughout the series.

But I could not ignore the terrible cost of virtue. My heart ached for those old men who longed for a time when childhood seemed endless and evil remote. My heart ached for JD and the burden of his perceived weakness and needless shame.

So, we chipped away at decades of romanticizing the war, peeled back the heroic veneer to reveal something deeper, universal. In the aftermath of violence and brutality, everyone struggles to get on with their lives, whether moving on from war, the death of a friend, or the senseless slaughter of innocents.

Our little group finally stopped in front of a white cross, identical to all the others. Tourists trod with soft steps on the grassy verge in between the gravestones. Their voices murmured low.

These respectful strangers comforted me. We might be alone with our personal grief, but we stood together in communal mourning.

Though I had prepared myself for this moment, my chest still tightened and my eyes stung as George Jr. bent on one knee and bowed his head. Rosa placed her hand on his shoulder, her sobs muffled by the humid air.

They stilled in a picture of profound grief and regret. Hikaru and I exchanged a look of mutual understanding, and he turned off the camera.

Rosa once told me that by reading JD's journal, she and her brother had gained a deeper understanding of who their father had been. I believed her.

Sadly, JD shared more of George Castle's short life than did Josefina. Yet his children mourned at his graveside, their knowledge of him gained only through the recollections of others, bound by their mother's love of a man they had never truly known.

The strands of memory pull at our hearts and connect us to the past. They are woven into stories both unexpected and inexplicable. I found JD's desperate entry and his journal with missing pages. Kiko Tamaki heard the whisper of her own tragedy retold as an American western. Jack Walker's decades-old intelligence alert offered him one last chance at redemption. As I pulled together these disparate threads, it fell to me to continue the story.

Once, following in my grandfather's footsteps felt like cheating. But few of us start from scratch, and I was tired of fighting my own desires and ambitions. I must stake my claim, face down the naysayers, and use my good luck wisely.

Not long ago, I started reading the Marshal Jameson books in the vague hope of finding other hidden mysteries. Instead, I found my grandfather.

JD lived on in the pages of his stories. His humor, his imperfections, his humanity—all that made him who he was.

I read a few chapters every day. I even have a favorite catchphrase: "I belong to them who claim me, and make the world my home."

Despite the fact that Marshal Clyde Jameson rode off into the sunset years before I was born, I like to think JD wrote that one with me in mind.

About the Author

Diana Lee lives and writes (mostly) in California.